Santa, Snowflakes, & Strychnine

Mary Seifert

Books by Mary Seifert

Maverick, Movies, & Murder
Rescue, Rogues, & Renegade
Tinsel, Trials, & Traitors
Santa, Snowflakes, & Strychnine

Halloween, Hound, & Housesitting
(a short story published in
Secret Staircase Holiday Mysteries)

Visit Mary's website and get a free recipe collection!
Scan the QR code

Santa, Snowflakes, & Strychnine

Katie & Maverick Cozy Mysteries, Book 4

Mary Seifert

Secret Staircase Books

Santa, Snowflakes, & Strychnine
Published by Secret Staircase Books, an imprint of
Columbine Publishing Group, LLC
PO Box 416, Angel Fire, NM 87710

Book layout and design by Secret Staircase Books
Cover images © Deeboldrick, Pablo Caridad, Marcel Pelz, Romolo
Tavani, Brita Seifert
First trade paperback edition: October, 2022

First e-book edition: October, 2022

* * *

Publisher's Cataloging-in-Publication Data
Seifert, Mary
Santa, Snowflakes, & Strychnine / by Mary Seifert.
p. cm.
ISBN 978-1649141088 (paperback)
ISBN 978-1649141095 (e-book)

1. Katie Wilk (Fictitious character). 2. Minnesota—Fiction. 3.
Amateur sleuths—Fiction. 4. Women sleuths—Fiction. 5. Dogs in
fiction. 6. Christmas fiction. I. Title

Katie & Maverick Cozy Mystery Series : Book 4.
Siefert, Mary, Katie & Maverick cozy mysteries.

BISAC : FICTION / Mystery & Detective.
813/.54

ACKNOWLEDGMENTS

I am lucky to have found a home for the stories of Katie and Maverick and want to extend my unending gratitude to Stephanie Dewey and Lee Ellison for their help making this extraordinary experience a reality, and the marvelous Beta readers—Marcia Koopmann and Isobel Tamney—who check the words and make them shine.

After an exciting whirlwind of good cheer, I have a moment to extend my appreciation to those who have read or listened to my stories, let me muddle through, and laughed with me. My list of names keeps growing, and if I miss someone, please accept my apologies.

Thank you to those dear to my heart who have provided encouragement, answers, shoulders to cry on, unfailing support, and advice along the way: my friends, readers, and cheerleaders—Colleen Okland; Jenifer Leitch, Evy Hatjistilianos, and Ruth Neely; my book buddies—Sandra Unger, Dr. Joan Christianson, Dr. Amy Ellingson, Eve Blomquist, and Maria Hughes; and tech support from Thomas Seifert.

A huge hug to my siblings and their spouses who've known me longest and never gave up on me—Margaret and Pat Sullivan, Michael and Patricia Gehlen, and Michele and Steve Germscheid. I hope you all see part of yourselves. My love of reading mysteries came from our mother, Jean, our grandfather, Harry, and our dad, John, who loved telling grand stories.

My biggest thank you goes to my family—a lifetime of appreciation to my husband John (you always let me dream), my children: Kindra, Danica, Charles, and Thomas, sons-in-law Adam and Mitch (you all maintained I could do it), and my grandchildren (your smiles warm my heart). I couldn't have done it without you.

A huge thank you to all who have taken time to read. If you like what you read, please leave a review on your bookseller's webpage or on your favorite media site.

Comparison is the thief of joy.

—Teddy Roosevelt

CHAPTER ONE

I sat at the beautifully appointed table among wonderful companions in a spectacular venue, eating delicious food, wishing I was home with my dog.

Ida Clemashevski, our town's self-appointed ambassador and my landlady, had reserved a table at the black-tie event. She took it upon herself to introduce new residents to Columbia, Minnesota, and insisted my dad and his wife attend. At the last minute, my stepmother Elizabeth reneged on the invitation, unable to make the two-hour trip because of a work commitment, or so she said. Ida roped me into using the ticket.

Dad shot me a wicked wink across our table. I didn't think anyone could've detected his slight hesitation or deliberate movements. The giant strides he'd made after his traumatic brain injury were nothing short of a miracle. We were sharing our living space until the demands of Elizabeth's job declined. Afterall, he'd taken a bullet meant for me.

I sipped the smooth white chocolate martini but nearly dropped my glass, startled by the smack of the gavel on a wood block.

"Sold for three hundred fifty dollars."

The words boomed from the sound system in a room built to replicate the First-Class Dining Saloon of the *Titanic,* complete with White Star china place settings, glitzy crystal glassware, and over-the-top holiday decorations. The room, originally used as part of the sound stage for Robert Bruckner's film, *Titanic: One Story*, was a welcome addition to the Midwest Minnesota History Center. The luxury and immensity made it a desirable venue for large gatherings.

The fundraising gala provided an opportunity to play dress up. My friend Jane Mackey had lent me a gorgeous amethyst gown. When she'd worn it to the screening of the history center's cornerstone film at Columbia's Convention Center, it brushed the floor. On me it hit mid-calf and looked decidedly different.

I adjusted the strap on my dress and snuck another glance at the head table. My success in the romance department bordered on the non-existent, and the view I had of the guests seated there solidified my resolve to swear off men.

Pete Erickson caught me looking, and my face warmed.

He raised his glass, and I tipped mine in response. I met Pete, the doctor on duty during my first trip to the ER, when I needed stitches. He was charming and smart, and he'd shown interest. I'd been careful, reserved, and thoughtful, taking baby steps, still coming to terms with the murder of my husband eighteen months before.

When I'd finally decided to give our relationship a shot, I'd missed my chance. He and his faithful nurse had been accepted into an elite fellowship program in telemedicine designed to benefit small outstate communities like ours.

We were still friends, but they were engaged.

My next heartthrob discovered a daughter he never knew existed and channeled all his energy into building a strong relationship with her. I couldn't have been happier for them, but I understood learning how to be a dad took time and effort.

The fact the last man who'd put a twinkle in my eye currently awaited trial on murder charges strengthened my determination to guard my heart.

I felt a light pat on the back of my hand. "Katherine Jean Wilk, tell her." Whenever Ida demanded I pay attention, she used my first, middle, and last names for emphasis. Ida's eyes landed on my friend, Jane. "Tell her she paid too much for the wreath. It's made entirely of costume jewelry."

My bubbly friend dragged her moony brown eyes away from her tall blond beau, Drew Kidd. "But I love Christmas and decorations and lights, and it will hang nicely on my front door." She sighed and gazed back again. The lights of the room glinted off her flaxen curls, the kind that didn't come from a bottle. Her fiery red dress hugged her petite frame as if she'd been sewn into her gown, sequin by sequin. Her chin dropped into her palm, and the blood-red nail of her forefinger rhythmically tapped her jaw.

Drew laughed. "You'd better appreciate every bid you've won. I don't know anyone else who would have paid so much for that box contraption."

"It's called an antique shadowbox. When I switch out the keepsakes, I'll have a beautiful display."

Drew bent his head so his words wouldn't stray beyond our table. "And I wish you'd be more circumspect. You're acting like you could have a lot of money."

Jane frowned. She *did* have a lot of money. We all kidded her about flaunting more than just her physical assets.

"It would be criminal if someone used the information about your dad owning Sapphire Skyway to get something from you." Drew would know. As an agent for the Bureau of Criminal Apprehension, he'd seen his fair share of the seedy side of life.

Jane waved off his concern.

A tuxedo-clad man filled the empty spot on the stand with the next offering, and Drew leaned forward to get a better look at the colorful placard. It advertised an all-inclusive three-day, two-night weekend sports trip to the Twin Cities for two. The winner claimed tickets to a Twins baseball game, a United soccer match, and a round of golf at Interlachen with accommodations arranged at a luxury hotel and vouchers for dinner from an impressive list of four-star restaurants.

"Now, here's something you should bid on," Drew hinted, forgetting his words of caution a minute earlier.

Before gearing up again, the emcee enlivened the crowd with an animated rendition of "The Auctioneer," her trademark song, and we clapped along until she hooted and curtsied.

She wiped her brow. "Now we're rolling."

As bidder cards flew up around me, more items fell to the hammer. I sipped my drink and purposely kept my eyes off a certain table at the front.

"Excuse me," said a server as he reached around and set a beautiful Pavlova in front of Dad and another in front of Ida. They clinked forks and contemplated how to attack the *dulce de leche* dripping down the sides of the baked meringue piled high with creamy whipped topping and studded with ruby-red strawberries. Ida plucked the blackberry topper, popped it into her mouth, and licked her lips.

The server, a student belonging to my science club, set a dessert the size of an iceberg in front of me, laughed, and said, "See you Monday, Ms. Wilk, that is, if you'll be able to move after ..." He looked up and scowled. I followed his gaze. A short, round female, tottering on her high heels, sidled near an easel. She pulled aside the fabric covering one of the auction items, trying to sneak a peek. "Ma'am." He stepped in front of the easel and pressed the fabric back into place. "I don't think you're supposed to be doing that."

"I don't know what all the fuss is about," she said with a huff.

The server graciously escorted her to her table, and she plopped into the seat next to the guest of honor, Grace Loehr.

Miss Grace hadn't attended the fundraiser before. To make up for lost time, she promised to match the funds raised during the live pledge proceedings—a very big deal. You'd never have known by her frugal lifestyle, but Miss

Grace came from three generations of poultry producers. With no desire to live on a farm, she'd sold her shares at market value to cousins and successfully invested in the tech industry decades earlier. *Who knew?*

Grace Loehr and Ida Clemashevski lived across the street from one another for forty years and hadn't spoken for much of that time. They recently donned the mantle of friendship and smoothed out some of the rough spots in order to provide a stable home for two high school girls in need of assistance.

"Remember our plan," Ida said in a stage whisper.

She'd given each of us a task. With her eye on the prize, she'd plotted a bidding war to raise the stakes and make the evening more enjoyable for observers and participants alike. I scooted my chair to face front and couldn't wait for them to reveal the art on the easel covered by the gold-sequined drape.

"Next on the docket is an original piece by a local artist." The auctioneer scanned a note card. "Encaustics, or hot wax painting, is one of the oldest art forms in the world. Pieces have survived for centuries on mummy sarcophagi, Italian masterpieces, and age-old painted panels. The artist, Phillip McCall, has blended artifacts donated by the estate of the late Robert Bruckner, founder of the *New Titanic Exhibit*, which you are all welcome to visit during regular business hours.

"The work is bathed in colors that simulate roiling water carved into the wax and evokes feelings of desperation and perhaps salvation in a collage for enthusiasts of the doomed ship. The work is valued at five hundred dollars."

She hurled the sparkly fabric over the top and unveiled a totally blank square. The crowd gasped. The little, plump woman who'd tried to sneak a peek snorted.

At the table next to us, a stout man with a scraggly beard and a poor comb-over hoisted himself erect. His chair crashed to the floor behind him. He stabilized his wobbly stance by planting his knuckles on the table and leaning forward, peering at the blank canvas. He shoved tortoiseshell glasses higher up on his nose.

"Mr. McCall," the auctioneer said, surprised. "The artist." A few guests applauded.

The young, black-haired woman seated next to him righted the fallen chair. He leaned over to her, and they traded serious words.

She cleared her throat. "Mr. McCall's pieces generate fierce emotion ... as you can see." Titters rose from the crowd. "He begins with a blank canvas like this, and I ... will ... retrieve a sample of what he can produce. If you'll excuse me for a minute." She scurried from the room, her stilettos clattering in the silence.

McCall sank into his seat, grumbling.

The audience waited.

The woman returned, dragging another square to the front. "Mr. McCall would like to create a personal work of art for the winner, but this is what an encaustic can look like." She threw off a white covering. The exposed work gave the illusion of frenetic movement in brackish waters, like dark ink circling a drain, sucking bits of everything into a dark hole and prompted murmurs of admiration. "Or the winner may choose this piece." The spectators applauded. She beamed. McCall relaxed.

"Let's get out those wallets and pocketbooks and remember the funds we raise tonight will help purchase equipment badly needed in the nephrology department of the children's wing at Columbia Memorial," the auctioneer said. "Who'll bid three hundred dollars?"

At first, the auctioneer's rapid-fire rhythmic chant elicited few responses, but she knew the names, careers, and family histories of many of the evening's attendees. She described where the piece might hang in a home or office, or to whom the gift could be given. She played one bidder against another for a few paltry dollars until Ida waved her card.

"Six hundred."

"Mrs. Clemashevski, Ida," said the auctioneer. "What makes this piece special to you?"

Ida had put the auctioneer up to this, a part of her strategy. "Phillip is a terrific artist. He was a student of mine, of course." The crowd laughed. "Learned everything at the knee of a master. Creating this hot wax painting required hours of concentration and attention to detail, shaping and reshaping the surface for the three-dimensional effect. I'm a great admirer and hope this artistic endeavor puts McCall on the map."

The auctioneer restarted her spiel. "Six fifty? Anyone bid six fifty. I'll let you know when the bid gets too high." The auctioneer pointed her gavel and nodded her curly strawberry blond head. "I'll take that bid of six fifty."

Jane giggled and lowered her card.

"Seven hundred. Who'll bid seven hundred? Six fifty, once. Six fifty, twice."

Dad said, "Seven hundred." Ida's eyes twinkled.

"Seven hundred. Do I hear eight?" She accepted another bid from someone in the front. "Do I have nine?"

Ida's brow wrinkled and she said, "Nine hundred." She knew the value of the art and set one thousand dollars as her bid cap.

"Nine fifty."

Ida recognized the voice at the front and relaxed into her chair. "One thousand dollars," she said, triumphantly.

"Fifteen hundred," came the voice from the front table.

"Grace knows how much I want that piece," Ida whispered as her eyebrows came together. "Two thousand dollars," she shouted.

"Two thousand five hundred," said Miss Grace above the murmuring crowd.

"Three thousand."

The fierce look in Ida's eyes indicated the mantle of friendship had slipped. I sat on the edge of my chair.

"Three thousand going once, going twice."

"Five thousand dollars."

The auctioneer searched Ida's face. She shook her head. "Sold to Miss Grace Loehr for five thousand dollars for a magnificent cause. Would you like the original or a new piece?"

Not waiting to hear the answer, Ida stood, slammed her chair against the table, and stormed away. The stillness in the room caught every footfall.

Ida broke stride as she passed McCall's table. I could've sworn he said, "Cheapskate."

Dad gave me the nod.

I followed Ida.

CHAPTER TWO

I found Ida sagged over the sink in the restroom, dabbing at her puffy kelly-green eyes with a lace handkerchief, cleaning up the lines of mascara. She inhaled and exhaled slowly, letting the counter support her weight. She rummaged through her purse, digging out a tube of lipstick.

"Well." She studied the mirror, turning her face from side to side, and tried refreshing the magenta color with shaky hands. She ran her fingers through her freshly dyed red hair. "That didn't go as planned, but I don't know why I'm so torn up over it." She sighed. "I thought Grace and I were on the same page. But I couldn't have been more mistaken. After all this time, I shouldn't be surprised."

When she took a breath, I said. "It's for a good cause."

"Of course, you're right—the children," she said,

bringing her full four-foot-eleven-inch frame upright and forcing a grin.

We turned when the door creaked. The rhythmic tap of a cane followed by measured steps preceded Miss Grace. Ida's features fell.

"What was that all about?" asked Miss Grace. "Are we throwing a tantrum?"

Ida shook her head. Her nostrils flared. "Why did you buy my piece?

"Your piece? If you wanted it, you should have bid higher."

"I told you my plan and what I was willing to bid," Ida said through clenched teeth. "You know how much it meant to me."

"Scrooge."

"Battle-axe."

"Skinflint."

"Thief."

"You have more than enough money."

"That's not the point."

No one spoke. *What was the point?*

"Phillip was a student of mine as well. Your reminder merely gave me added incentive. Do you think you should always be able to get everything you want, Ida Clemashevski?" Miss Grace straightened her back. "Remember the car?"

Ida's eyes clouded.

"You bought it out from under my nose," Miss Grace said, waving her right hand. "And you still drive it, even offering me a ride."

"My Plymouth? You don't drive and you never said anything. I never knew," Ida stammered.

The door opened a crack and a face peered in, read the

tension in the room, and retreated.

"My piano students were every bit as good as yours."

"That contest was a long time ago, Grace."

"They were disqualified on a technicality."

"That wasn't—"

"Although, without a doubt, I am the better performer."

"As you are fond of telling me, repeatedly. You beat me every time, Grace. You have every trophy."

"Except one."

Ida's eyes narrowed and she took a step back. The air grew thick. I didn't see it coming.

Miss Grace raised her chin. "You know, Casimer only asked you to marry him after I told him no." With that pronouncement she pivoted and departed.

Ida staggered as if she'd been punched.

I managed to get her out of the claustrophobic restroom with soothing words and settled her into an overstuffed upholstered chair in the hall. Her usually gigantic personality had withered. I left her gazing at the wall.

"She didn't mean it," I said when I returned and handed her a glass of red wine.

Ida nodded and inhaled deeply. "I know." She took a big swig. "There has to be something else going on."

We turned to the sound of snuffles coming from around the corner. Ida scooted to the front of her chair.

"You wait here. I'll go." My hand grazed her shoulder.

Grace Loehr leaned over her cane. She jerked when I touched her back. She sniffed and squared her shoulders, but when she looked at me, her face crumpled, and tears coursed down her cheeks.

"I don't know what came over me. I've been practicing my vitriol for forty years and it came back full tilt. Tell Ida—"

A throat cleared and we turned. Ida stood at the end of the hallway.

"Oh, Ida. I'm so sorry. I didn't mean …"

Ida walked forward and Miss Grace stepped into her arms.

"Phillip asked me to make sure I won the bid."

Ida held Miss Grace at arm's length and furrowed her brow. "You?"

"Please believe me. I didn't realize you weren't in on it."

"That wasn't very sporting," I said.

Both women glared at me, and I put up my hands in surrender.

I had a thought, maybe a good one. "What if you accept the original and commission Mr. McCall to create a complementary piece on that blank canvas for another donation of five thousand dollars?"

Ida shook her head. "We can't expect Phillip to make another piece for free."

"I'll pay him five hundred dollars, the stipulated value of the original piece," offered Miss Grace. "Word has it I'm loaded." A small smile worked its way into her rheumy blue eyes. "Unveiling the two pieces together would certainly boost his exposure."

"That way everyone wins," I said, forcing a smile.

Ida grabbed Miss Grace's hand.

"Let's do it," said Ida. They shook.

Miss Grace entered the dining room through the cut glass doors at the bottom of the Grand Staircase, befitting a first-class passenger. Ida and I crept into the dining saloon from what might have been a door to the ship's deck.

As I approached our table, the gavel struck again, and I jumped.

"Sold to the handsome mature gentleman at table

fifteen for three hundred fifty-five dollars."

Dad stood and bowed, but his smile drooped and his eyebrows climbed when he saw me. He skirted the perimeter of the room and headed toward the checkout at the exit to remit his generous donation and make his escape.

"What are you doing, Dad?" I said when I caught up to him.

"Well, darlin', I had a little cash stashed away and I thought Elizabeth might like a new bauble." He pocketed his wallet.

He carefully set the smooth long box in my hand. I opened the lid and looked into his twinkling eyes.

"It's stunning, Dad." The glint of a diamond perched on the inside edge of a gold oval pendant, hanging from a serpentine chain. "She'll love it." And if she doesn't, she'd better not say anything. Dad's emotions lingered just below the surface, ready to ambush him at the slightest provocation. Dad, Charles, and I had been out on the bike trail in my hometown, riding in celebration after a particularly splendid cooperative effort when my dad had been downed by a bullet. The effects haunted him yet. The second shot killed Charles, my husband of seventeen days. And we still didn't know who'd pulled the trigger.

I blinked backed the painful memories and glanced up as Miss Grace approached the auctioneer and whispered in her ear. The crowd quieted.

"We have a unique and unprecedented proposition from the Grande Dame of Columbia, and I hope we," her arm encompassed the room, "can persuade Mr. McCall to go along." She pointed the gavel at McCall's table and flicked the end twice. Mr. McCall hauled his solid frame out of the chair again. "For five hundred dollars and another five-thousand-dollar donation ..." She paused. "Would you accept a commission to create a complementary *Titanic* encaustic?"

The spotlight found Mr. McCall. He sputtered, and for a moment I thought I saw a bit of anxiety. His eyebrows met in the middle. A hand patted his sleeve. Words were exchanged. Then his thin lips formed a crooked smile. His head bobbed up and down and he raised his hand to speak.

"I'd be honored to create coordinating pieces."

The attendees murmured.

"However, if I truly am to create a harmonizing pair, I'd need to take the original back to my studio to match colors and textures more closely. If you can meet me tomorrow, I'll be prepared to begin the new image."

From her queen's perch, Miss Grace nodded once.

Phillip McCall took his seat as an ear-piercing scream reverberated around the hall.

The second-story door opened with a crash and all eyes lasered in on Mr. McCall's black-headed tablemate, pale and gripping the rail. Then she crumpled onto the makeshift deck.

Pete's long legs propelled him to the top of the stairs before anyone else moved. He helped her stand upright, and supported her elbows, talking to her. Phillip McCall scrunched up his napkin and tossed it onto the table. His chair screeched when he rose, and he plowed up the steps to join them. She quivered and vehemently shook her head, but after a few more words, they disappeared through the door.

The volume in the room swelled and speculation ran amok—a mouse, a ghost, an attack. Nothing prepared us for the reality.

CHAPTER THREE

When McCall held up that drenched mannequin, I thought I'd scream too. I could barely hear him yelling 'false alarm' over the din," said Ida. "Poor Anita. The pool, with its near-freezing temps and sloshing sound effects, exists for ambience, and in the dim light of the ocean-mimicking room, the dummy looked real. It was a nasty prank. The history center director was nearly apoplectic."

"Yes, but before the benefactors could escape into the night, the auctioneer commenced the pledge event," said Dad with a little chortle. "In their panic to get out of there, guests didn't hold back, and she raised so much money in those few short minutes that by the time the director bid us a good night, the incident was almost forgotten."

"In total, they raised two hundred ten thousand dollars," said Ida, glancing at the new smart watch on her wrist for the umpteenth time. "That's the highest total they've ever had. Grace's generous matching funds put it over the top and inspired like-minded donors."

"Your eight-person dinner raised quite a sum too. Do you know who won it?" Dad licked his lips. "I'll suffer through taste testing."

Ida smiled. "The winner is to call, and we'll work out the date." She wriggled her hand in the air and reread the watch face. "I just got three exercise steps." Her throaty laughter filled the car. "I've never won anything," she said with a gleam in her eye. When the foundation director drew her name for the raffle, her hand had flown to her face. She'd raced to the stage and hadn't stopped moving since, as recorded by her smart watch.

We bumped the rest of the way down the street through mounds of snow, hitting frozen ruts and chunks of ice. We viewed houses studded with colorful blinking lights, heralding the weeks until Christmas. We crawled passed a car parked at the end of our driveway.

Limp paper license tags hung in the window of a brand new metallic-blue BMW, and I took a wider turn to avoid contact.

"Who's here?" Dad asked.

"Who's here?" Ida parroted; eyes glued to the shiny wheels.

I dropped Ida and Dad at the end of the walkway and drove Ida's car into the garage behind the house. As I approached the front yard, a slender figure wrapped in a sleek camel hair coat emerged from the car.

"Elizabeth," my dad sang, true happiness lilting in his rich baritone. He stepped toward her, both arms outstretched. She bussed his cheek and took the elbow offered. He patted her hand as they strolled toward the front door.

"Ida," he called. "My wife, Elizabeth Hennes. Elizabeth, this is Katie's landlady, Ida Clemashevski." Ida threw out both hands for a hug at the same time Elizabeth pivoted toward her car and pressed her key fob. After it chirped, she waited long enough for Ida to retract her hands and bury them deep in her coat pockets.

Ida made her way to the front door and fumbled with her key. When the lock finally gave way, she shoved the door with her foot and flipped the light switch, illuminating the entryway. A five and a half foot animated Santa broke into a belly laugh and danced a robotic jig followed by a mechanical version of "Jolly Old Saint Nicholas." Ida's cheeks flamed and she rooted around its base for the off button.

"Sorry about that," she blustered.

"Can I get you anything, hon?" Dad asked Elizabeth.

"Harry. We need to talk." Elizabeth gave me the same look she'd given when she wanted me out of the room, for my own good of course, when I was a kid.

"Ida. Can you give me a hand?" Ida looked befuddled. "In my kitchen?" I could see the dominoes lining up in her eyes. She didn't want to listen in on their conversation any more than I did.

"Give me a moment." She hustled up her stairs and returned wearing jeans and a sweatshirt with Frosty the Snowman cross-stitched on the front. "I think it's time to make some lefse."

I searched my wrist for the timepiece I hadn't worn because Jane said it would detract from my look, but I knew we left the history center at half past nine. There must be a cooking cut off time. Of course, for me, it was always too late to cook. I followed her into her kitchen. She handed me a weighty lidded bowl. I held on tight as she stacked flour, cinnamon, and sugar on top. Then I carried it into my kitchen through our adjoining doorway. We had to be making lefse for the entire Norwegian army.

She staggered a bit and dropped a rectangular plastic tote on the floor. My black Lab, Maverick, sauntered over to investigate, looking for a treat. The lid belched when Ida unsnapped it and pulled out a fabric covered rolling pin, a large circular board, a tool that looked like a supersized garlic press, and a long flat wooden stick. She plugged a circular griddle into the wall. She blew fine flour particles off a recipe card with crinkled corners. Bright red and green fabric puddled in the bottom of the box. She grabbed a handful, shook them into aprons, and handed one to me.

"You looked fine but go change."

In my room, I carefully removed the dress and draped the gauzy fabric over its hanger. I slid it into the dress bag with a rueful smile, wishing someone else besides my landlady had noticed. I pulled on sweatpants and a t-shirt and followed my nose to the kitchen, which already smelled warm and enticing.

"When the going gets tough, the tough get cooking." Ida squeezed the boiled potatoes through the large sieve. "This is a ricer. It makes the potatoes ultra-smooth. It belonged to my grandmother." She held it out to me and, when I balked at handling the vintage heirloom, thrust it into my hands.

She squashed the skinny strands of potatoes together with a few simple ingredients, and then smashed a walnut sized lump into a feather-light circle, sprinkling more flour from a measuring cup when the mixture didn't react the way she wanted. She transferred the flattened dough to the griddle, and, in seconds, she flipped it.

"Get a plate," she ordered. "And butter."

The butter melted on the warm Norwegian delicacy. She shook sugar from the dispenser, topped it with cinnamon, and rolled it into a narrow tube.

"Bread knife." She held out her hand as if awaiting a surgical tool. She cut the tube into three diagonal spirals and handed me the neatest piece.

I closed my eyes and savored the morsel.

"I know. Right?" she said, smacking her lips. "The first bite of lefse for the season is the best. This recipe belonged to my grandmother too."

While I read the directions—potatoes, salt, butter, cream, sugar, and flour—and searched for amounts, the third piece of lefse disappeared in a spray of slobber.

"Maverick!" I couldn't really correct him. It was my fault. I knew Maverick could reach every corner of the counter and if I wanted to protect any foodstuff, I had to be vigilant.

He smacked his lips too.

The stack of rounds grew to an inch in no time.

"If you can't do anything else," she said with a twinkle in her eye, "why don't you get us both a glass of wine."

I poured a refreshing New Zealand Sauvignon Blanc into two glasses.

"Put in three ice cubes," Ida ordered. "I need to keep my wits about me." She nodded at the growing stack of lefse, and I complied.

"What instructions do you want to give Mr. McCall

for the complementary piece?" I asked. As a retired art instructor, she knew all the ins and outs of the encaustic process, the time needed to add the colors, texture, and cure the hot wax work.

"I have a few tokens I'd like him to think about incorporating, including some fabric from a quilt. It didn't cross the Atlantic on the *Titanic,* but it was made by Sinead," she said, sipping her wine while waiting to flip the round. "Six months pregnant, when Sinead boarded the *Caronia* in Liverpool on March 30, 1912, it was the last time she saw her husband. Padraig Ceallacháin followed her on the ill-fated ship and almost made it but was murdered for his impeccable identity just after he boarded the *Carpathia.* When you discovered that journal and my ancestor's ring, we unearthed the story kept secret for over a hundred years."

I yawned and Ida said, "How long do you think that old witch will be? She's up to no good, that one." She nodded her head in the direction of her apartment.

Before I could answer, the kitchen door flew open. Dad walked in as if in a daze. I strained to hear his words.

"She's moving to California."

CHAPTER FOUR

Ida pulled the plug on the griddle and snapped the plastic lid over the dough. "What's in California?"

Dad didn't answer.

She dug around in the cupboard and drew out cling wrap she used to cover the cooled rounds. Then she struggled to reach the pull on the door above the refrigerator until my senses returned and I figured out what she was after.

My long arm went over her head and nabbed the bottle of Midleton Ida hid in my cupboard to use for special occasions. She filled three Waterford crystal glasses with ice and poured the amber liquid. I recorked the rare Barry Crockett. She raised her glass. Dad and I did the same.

"To Harry," she said. We delicately clinked Dad's glass. He didn't move. I put my hand on his forearm, and he shook himself.

"Elizabeth said I seemed happier here. I tried to argue with her, told her I was putting on a courageous front, but she said she loves her work and isn't looking to stop anytime soon. She was offered a great promotion and she took it. She'll be working out of Los Angeles for six months."

Ida stuck her head out the doorway and checked left and right. It looked like Elizabeth had left the building. Good, the old witch.

That wasn't true. She'd been there for me and my stepsiblings, helping us to come into our own with whatever we needed to get there, but I never considered her my mother, just a female personality in Dad's life who, until now, had made him happy.

Ida and I swished ice cubes in empty glasses. Dad still hadn't sipped his drink. We each took an arm and dragged him to the table.

"Harry," Ida said. "I know this is difficult, but we're here for you."

He chugged his drink, shuddering as it made its warm way down his throat. "Where am I going to live?"

A laugh erupted from Ida. "Is that all you're worried about? Katie has plenty of room. Don't you, Katie?" I nodded, afraid of what I might be agreeing to. "I love your company and so does Katie. Don't you, Katie?"

I kept nodding. I loved my dad, but I'd have to shift gears to make this temporary arrangement work long term.

"I love having someone to join me for lunch. I can try new recipes." She sounded sincere. "And Harry, you said you've been too busy to attend more than a handful of dance classes, but there's a bit of accountability if we keep each other motivated." She turned to me. "He's really quite a good dancer."

"My dad?"

"I don't need much space," Dad said quietly. "My Murphy bed is comfortable. I don't like stairs anyway, so you'd have your private bedroom, bathroom, and office to spread out in on the second floor." He brightened. "Temporarily. I can start looking for my own place."

We shared cooking space and the living room. I taught all day and worked with my extra-curricular activities after school and on some weekends. My mind tossed and turned, and I began to perspire. And then I thought about how lucky I was that he was here with me.

Dad looked concerned.

"No, you won't look for anything else," I said. I folded him in a hug.

Ida put her arms around both of us and hummed, "Family." When she stumbled and then laughed, I realized Maverick stood on his hind legs and had joined our embrace with one paw on Dad and one on Ida. "Family," she repeated.

Back to business, Ida said, "What's next?"

Dad held out his empty glass. Ida put in two fingers. He held out for more. She shook her head. This could work.

Dad sipped and said, "Elizabeth is ten years younger than I am and still has things she wants to do. I like to exercise but I have no desire to accompany her scuba diving, hiking, hang-gliding, or ziplining." He took a bigger sip. "Project management is her forte and this promotion came with exceptional perks, but also more responsibility and she was afraid she couldn't be there when I needed her. She was surprised by how well I'm doing. When I came here, I thought if I wasn't such a bother, she'd get her rest, and when she was ready, we could get back together but that plan backfired. She's doing well without me and I'm doing well without her. It's time she had her own space for a while."

"I'm sorry, Dad. I know how much she means to you."

"You mean a ton too, kiddo." He reached into his pocket and extracted the gift box. "Anyone need a diamond necklace?" he said with a devilish glint in his eye.

Ida and I looked at each other and giggled.

"How about a car?" He raised his right hand. A set of keys hung from his forefinger. "It's parked down the street so we'll have to move it tonight, but we should have room in the garage since you totaled the van." The knowing look he gave me would have stopped a freight train.

My Jetta met its demise in October when it collided with a royal buck. I replaced it with an unpretentious twenty-year-old van, purchased from a police impound lot in North Dakota. After an attempt on my life, it disappeared only to be found with the seats sliced open, the radio removed, the wires and hoses cut, and sugar in the gas tank. My insurance company considered it a total loss, but the assigned value wouldn't have replaced a bicycle tire.

"Elizabeth had it towed here with some of my belongings stowed in the back. There isn't much of mine left at home … at her home, and she's going to ship the rest of it over the next few weeks. She didn't want the car." His eyes misted. "It's yours, Katie."

His pride and joy.

"I couldn't." *Could I?*

His left eyebrow rose. Ida crossed her hands over her tummy and arched her back, a wait-and-see stance.

"Could I?"

"The doctors don't want me driving …" He paused. "…
much. And you can't expect Ida to do all the chauffeuring
around this metropolis."

"Thanks, Dad."

"Elizabeth held on a lot longer than I expected. I'm
lucky. I have a great daughter, a super landlady, and my wife
doesn't have to worry about me and can finally spread her
wings in the corporate world." He choked up. "I'll have to
try harder with Austin and Sandra. She said they want to
keep me in their lives. And who knows. She's not giving up.
Maybe this will make things right for us."

Austin was twenty-nine, one year older than me, and
I marveled at his transformation from a pudgy, quiet,
introverted youth into a brilliant academic with an advanced
tech degree. He lived near Elizabeth and helped her get
her job in cryogenics. Elizabeth repeatedly informed
me that he specialized in marketing small companies,
crafting websites, organizing digital media, and performing
algorithmic calisthenics on indecipherable metrics to
assess the performance of companies' business practices
or something like that. Since the write-up about his firm
in the *Our Business Weekly* regional journal, clients flocked
to his office.

We spoiled our youngest sibling, and, as I remembered
the times I had to bail Sandra out, or provide phony excuses,
the muscles in my neck seized. Her dreadful choices
included drugs, alcohol, and sex. She'd had a child when
she was sixteen and had given her up for adoption. I never
questioned Sandra's intelligence, but I always questioned
her motivation. When she left her teenage years behind,
she grew out of her selfish ways. With her bright smile
and outgoing personality, I envied the effect she had on

everyone who met her. When Sandra and I got together now, which wasn't often enough, I found her engaging, funny, and dynamic. She made everyone feel important.

Dad's voice sliced through my reminiscing. "Elizabeth had much of it already figured out." His head drooped and his shoulders sagged. Reality stomped on his heart, and he sank into the chair. He set one elbow, then the other on the table and dropped his head into his hands, his slender fingers threaded through his more-salt-than-pepper hair.

"I think I'll just stay here for a while. You two should get some sleep." He peered at us. "I mean it. I need time to process … alone."

Ida touched Dad's shoulder before leaving and when her door clicked, I realized I needed time too. I grabbed a puffy jacket, a hat, gloves, and Maverick's leash, but for the first time in a long time, Maverick seemed less than ecstatic about a walk. We both looked back as we ventured out into the crisp star-filled evening.

Fifteen minutes passed in a snap. When we returned, the rinsed glasses drained in the sink, and I found Ida's coveted bottle returned to its secure spot out of Ida's reach. Dad's door was closed. Maverick circled his mat twice and curled into a ball. Sleep beckoned, but before I mounted the stairs, I picked up the blue velvet jewelry box and checked the contents. The delicate gold necklace joyously winked from its velvet bed. The lid snapped closed, and I stowed it on the top shelf of the pantry for whenever Dad decided he needed it again.

CHAPTER FIVE

A low, grinding noise, like gravel in a cement mixer, dragged me from a pleasant slumber. I crept down the dark stairway, tiptoeing off to the right next to the railing where the squeak was quieter. I clasped my robe to ward off the morning chill and stepped into the kitchen then rubbed my eyes and squinted into the bright light.

Dad and Ida stood shoulder to shoulder at the kitchen counter.

"What are you doing?"

"Oh, Katie." Ida's hand flew to her heart. "I thought we'd bring Phillip a jug of fresh squeezed juice and warm blueberry muffins—" The oven dinged, and Ida transferred the tin from the counter to the oven. "Which will be ready in eighteen minutes. He's an early riser and I want to deliver them while they're still warm."

She passed Dad another orange half. "It's been rough since his wife left. Paula fancied herself a horticulturist and planned to grow and sell exotic plants, so Phillip built a greenhouse addition for her, but when his art business took off, he appropriated the studio space. She'd only grown weeds, but she complained to anyone who would listen. Paula figured she'd suffered enough, packed up, and drove to Minneapolis into the arms of her ex. I'd say back into his arms, but, personally, I don't think she ever gave him up. She inferred that she'd put her career on hold to support Phillip while he honed his talent. But I had her as a student and she couldn't even make a mess."

"You're not biased at all, are you?" I said, with just a smidgeon of sarcasm.

Ida lowered her head. "She never knew how good she had it."

Dad let his attention shift and his hand slipped. The orange peel churned out of control and splattered on Ida's face. He sucked in a breath. I waited for her reaction, and when the smile edged across her lips, I knew we'd be all right.

"Get going, Katie," said Ida, wiping the pulp from her chin. "Or we'll be late."

"We?" I whined and stifled a yawn. "It's only seven twenty-five. That can't be a proper time to go calling."

"Phillip's been a proponent of the early morning success for years now, rising every day at four thirty, taking care of emails, orders, packaging items sold, and prepping his work. I'd be surprised if he hasn't already applied the base coat to the substrate for my piece. Maybe even a second layer."

If Ida intended for me to feel like a slug, she couldn't

have been more wrong. My day began before sunrise only
by necessity, but I hauled myself upstairs anyway.

* * *

The scent of blueberries burst from the lunchbox
swinging from my right arm like a pendulum and I could
feel the weight shift as the juice sloshed in the thermos.
Maverick towed me as if he were a sled dog anxious to
strike out at a much quicker pace. Ida clutched a clanking,
tin box, holding it like a football carried the last two yards
before winning the Super Bowl. Any tighter and she'd have
impressions where her fingers contacted the scratched,
dented metal.

"What do you have in there?" I asked.

Hustling beside me, taking three steps to my two, she
panted. "There are a few vintage buttons and a comb,
copies of some dated newspaper headlines, that piece of
fabric I told you about, sheet music from 1912, and a copy
of a *Titanic* boarding pass. If Phillip can blend any of these
pieces with the movement he created on Grace's piece, I'll
be ecstatic."

Maverick dedicated his singlemindedness to getting
wherever we needed to be as fast as we could get there,
and Ida dashed along beside me.

"Isn't this a pretty street?" she said.

I grunted, taking in the aging homes, strapping
monstrosities that might have potential with a lot of tender
loving care and heaps of money, but the artist in Ida always
saw beyond the reality.

"It's the third house on the next block," she said,
panting. "Number—"

Before she finished the address, Maverick yanked me in front of her. He plopped down at the intersection holding us in place as a car gunned its engine and squealed through a red light.

Phillip nearly had toast for breakfast.

"That was close," I said, trying to catch my breath.

Ida's right hand gripped her throat, puffing until it sounded almost normal. "Thank you, Maverick."

We waited for another round of lights before looking all directions and venturing off the curb, across the street, and down the block.

Phillip's artistic arsenal did not include snow removal. We trudged through the fluffy white over what might have been the sidewalk and Ida used the railing to haul herself up Phillip's steps. She rang the bell, a gong that could have belonged on a church spire. She rang again. Then she rapped on the door.

"He knew we were coming," she said. "I sent a text."

"Did he respond?" Ida didn't answer. "Maybe he expected us at a more reasonable hour," I said, hopefully.

She shook her head.

"Or he's not here."

She turned and took one icy step at a time to the bottom. When she reached us, Maverick spun in a circle. The lunchbox flew from my fingers, and I held on for dear life as he dragged me to the side of the house, weaving and bobbing in front of the side entry, like a high school wrestler at the beginning of a tough match. I cringed at the screech he created when he trailed his nails down the steel trim on the service door to a solarium.

"Maverick, heel."

Instead, he stood up on his hind legs and leaned on the

metal frame. The door swung open under his weight.

"Heel, Maverick," I said, more forcefully. The leash went taut. Ida had followed, skirted around me, and stepped inside. *Ida heel,* I thought.

Maverick whimpered, but I held the leash and leaned back with all my weight. He wrapped around me, and I struggled not to go down. The leash slipped from my frozen fingers, and he chased after Ida while I sailed to the ground. *We need practice,* I thought as I dusted snow from my backside.

"Katie," Ida said. "Katie," she called louder.

Ida stood in the middle of the room surrounded by canvases in varying states of completion, presenting every color of the rainbow, faintly illuminated by the daylight just waking up. She hugged her box with both arms, transfixed by a swirling study of blues and greens studded with three-dimensional yellow and pink bubbles. It was a nice beginning, and I could see the appeal. If he could incorporate some of her keepsakes, Ida would be happy. The bottom half of the canvas lay in wait of inspiration.

Another easel displayed the piece Miss Grace had won at the auction. Teal, umber, yellow, and white bubbles boiled to the surface through the variegated blue-green swirls in the top third. But wax dripped from the bottom two-thirds of the opus, mixing to brown and mounding on the floor under the easel, leaving behind a shiny translucent nothingness where a page from a diary and Brucker's artifacts had been embedded in the three-dimensional maelstrom. Angry jagged points of medium remained as if the items had been peeled from the melted wax of the encaustic.

Had McCall not taken Miss Grace's to use as the

inspiration for Ida's complementary piece, it might still be intact. All that remained was a wide strip of color at the top of the canvas. Someone had destroyed it.

Or had they?

Sometimes it could be difficult to tell.

Maybe this was another piece altogether.

I stepped in to take a closer look, but Maverick pulled me past the easel and barked.

I sucked in a breath, pulled out my phone, and punched in the numbers.

"We've got an emergency."

CHAPTER SIX

Wisps of dark hair jutted out from his head in every direction. A bowtie rested on the pleated bib and framed the dark curly hair that peeked out from the four open buttons of his rumpled tuxedo shirt. A to-go cup tipped from his hand and light-brown dregs dripped onto the cement floor. Oversized glasses sat crookedly on Phillip's face, magnifying eyes that would never see again.

I checked for a pulse. Then looked at Ida and shook my head.

Her vibrant green eyes faded; she pulled her stocking cap from her head and her mussed hair didn't match her usual impeccable appearance, creating a masterpiece of misery. I gripped Maverick's leash and cradled Ida's elbow as I led her from the studio, closing the door behind us.

Two police cars tore into the drive, and we waited outside while the investigating officers entered the premises. Temporary Police Chief Ronnie Christianson's car roared up minutes later, and when he exited, I marched in front of him. "Please send us someplace warm. It's freezing."

Maybe I overstepped but Ida's teeth chattered behind blue lips. She quaked and I feared she might be going into shock.

He raised his chin and leaned away. "You'll be free to leave as soon as I take your statements, but first I need to check out the scene." He turned and stomped away.

I thought for a moment before I opened the door of his squad car and guided Ida to the back seat. She hadn't said a word, but she continued to clutch the tin box, guarding her precious tokens. I closed the door.

My hair swirled in the frigid wind, catching on my lashes and lips and I brushed it away while recalling what we'd seen. I wondered why McCall had dismantled his artwork, or *if* he was the one who destroyed it. I shuddered.

Officials strode in and out of the front door to the home and the entrance to the studio like bees around a hive. A pair of officers unrolled the black-and-yellow caution tape and wrapped it around the perimeter. A silent ambulance followed the coroner's van and rolled to a stop in front of the house.

Pete Erickson climbed out of the van. He shrugged against the cold as the wind tossed a few tendrils of his dark hair. He motioned to the EMTs who hauled a gurney into the studio. He searched the crowd and his dark eyes stopped on me. One corner of my mouth lifted, and I raised my forefinger. He closed his eyes, lowered his head, and trudged toward us through the snow.

"What happened, Katie?"

"Ida wanted to bring Mr. McCall breakfast and talk to him about a piece she commissioned. When we got here, Maverick shoved through the unlocked door and we found him sitting in his chair, dead."

"This is getting to be a habit with you." He shook his head.

Pete caught sight of Ida and opened the squad car door. He leaned in. "Ida? How are you doing?" He took note of her sluggish reaction time. "Let me see if I can get you out of here." He closed the door.

"I need to get Ida someplace warm."

He nodded, slogged up to the house, and disappeared.

The streets awoke as neighbors, looky-loos, and the press joined the crowd taking photos of the spectacle from behind the official barriers. A buzz drifted through the crowd and those taking pictures aimed their cameras at the squad car with Ida inside, the beginning of a rampant gossip chain.

"She got in a big fight over one of Phillip's pieces," called a haughty woman on the sidelines. Her Ugg slippers peeked out from under a long down coat worn over sweats. "It was an old lover's feud." She fluttered her eyes at the amateur filmmakers.

Maverick and I moved to block their view. If the videos and photos went viral, Ida would be the center of attention, but not in a good way.

Ronnie emerged and glanced at the gawkers. He scowled when his eyes met mine. I'm not sure he appreciated where he found Ida. With an attempt at looking official, he tucked the right side of his jacket behind his right arm and his hand rested on his firearm. He trooped down the drive. He stopped in front of me, glowered, and yanked at the handle.

Hanging over the open car door, he said, "Why did you open the studio, Ida?"

She stared at him. Maverick glared at him.

I cleared my throat and said, "Maverick stood on his hind legs and dragged the handle down and the door fell open. And if we hadn't gone inside no one would have discovered his body and the ruined artwork."

Ida closed her eyes and took in a deep breath. She centered herself and opened them.

"We walked in and found what I think is the abstract piece he completed for the gala. If it is the one Grace paid for, it's been destroyed. I can't imagine Phillip would ruin his own work. It looks as if he'd begun work on our second piece as well. Phillip was sitting in his chair just like he is now. It doesn't make sense. He was so young." She sniffed. "What do you think happened?" She shivered and couldn't stop.

"We'll find out. You may leave but I'll expect you to be home when I call on you later this afternoon to take an official statement."

"Ronnie," Ida spoke through gritted teeth. "Philip's always up early. I texted him at five thirty about the arrangement we made. He responded. He said he had some ideas. Maybe if we'd come a little sooner, we could've helped him." Pools of tears glistened in her eyes.

Ida hauled her stout frame out of the car. She slammed the door with a wallop, and in her most imperious voice, she tried to sound pulled together. "He was a gifted artist and a good friend. He'll be missed by so many."

Maverick nudged her hand.

Ronnie hit a fob on his key ring. The locks clicked. "We'll know more after Pete's report," he said with little empathy.

As if on cue, the studio door opened, and Pete followed the gurney. He acknowledged us with a two-fingered salute then slid behind the steering wheel.

As the van disappeared, Ida's shoulders sagged and she said, "What can I do?"

"Go home." Ronnie yanked at the two sides of the front of his jacket, tugging at the zipper. He gave up and trekked back to McCall's house.

"Let's go, Katie. At least I know I can do something at home."

Ida shuffled down the sidewalk and slowed at the corner when Maverick halted. I reached my arm out to hold Ida back so we wouldn't have to pick up what little would be left if she were run down by the next car racing through the intersection.

I loved the little lady walking with me. And I think she loved me too. We had quickly become family and I would do anything for her.

Her hand went to her forehead. I thought maybe she'd been hurt, but she said, "What are we going to tell Grace?"

"Let's wait to hear what Ronnie has to say before we break the news."

Dad met us at the door. He could tell something had happened. His face asked questions but he wisely kept his own counsel.

Before she removed her coat, she said, "Let's make some lefse." She took the ingredients from my fridge and set everything on the counter but then grabbed a scarf and wrapped it around her neck. Dad followed her outside and I returned the ingredients to the fridge. I watched her clear snow from the top step then she stood the shovel next to the door. She looked up for a long while and stepped back inside. Dad finished clearing the steps.

She unfurled her scarf and dropped it on the floor in front of Maverick.

"Ida? Maybe you should rest," I said. She nodded absently. I trailed her into her apartment. She dropped onto the couch and closed her eyes.

When I checked on her an hour later, the plastic bottle she used to water her Christmas tree was overflowing in the sink. I turned off the tap and watered the tree. I picked up the day's mail piled on the floor in front of the mail slot and stacked it on the coffee table in front of her. The weather turned dark, foreshadowing more snowfall.

After I finished my lesson plans for the week and recorded grades, I let my head fall onto my forearms at my desk. The next thing I knew, my phone chimed. I couldn't identify the frosty voice on the other end of the call and almost hung up.

"Don't you dare hang up on me, Katherine Jean Wilk." The voice demanded attention. "What happened? What did you see?"

"Who is this?" I asked, rubbing my face to get the feeling back.

"Grace Loehr, as if you didn't know," she said.

"Miss Grace, I'm sorry. I guess I fell asleep—"

"How could you fall asleep? It's all over the news. Is it true Ida is a person of interest in Phillip's murder?"

"Murder?"

CHAPTER SEVEN

My back went rigid. "I'll call you back."

I disconnected the call and googled the breaking-news section of our online paper. The headline read, FORMER ART TEACHER PERSON OF INTEREST IN SUSPICIOUS DEATH. The photo beneath the headline of Ida sitting in the rear seat of Ronnie's car guarded by a ferocious dog and his merciless handler made her look guilty. I hadn't done her any favors.

The journalist provided a short paragraph about finding the body of Phillip McCall and continued with a full-blown article retelling the first murder case that involved Ida.

As a new teacher in Columbia—I commiserated immediately—Ida Clemashevski (nee Donovan) had become the object of a maniac's obsession. A local waitress accused Ida of stealing her boyfriend. She followed Ida, called her at all hours, and slashed her tires. But when she followed Ida into her classroom, into her sanctuary, Ida, fearing for the safety of her students, petitioned and obtained a restraining order. The following day, the waitress's roommate found the body of the twenty-two-year-old stalker clinging to Ida's school ID, and law enforcement arrested Ida. Before the trial, a local attorney—an adjunct professor of law—and his girlfriend—a professional musician and composer—pointed out that the flimsy evidence could, in fact, point to several suspects.

With the help of a hardworking first-year patrolman, the trio discovered the identity of the real killer. The ex-boyfriend had purchased a one-way ticket to Brazil, and in an undercover sting at the airport bar, employing some powerful acting and masterful manipulations, the pianist and the attorney caught the perpetrator boasting about getting away with murder. They'd been wired for sound and recorded the confession. The patrolman went on to become a detective. The attorney had a successful law practice. The pianist performed her own compositions around the globe, topping it off at Carnegie Hall.

The patrolman was Lance Erickson, Pete's dad.

The attorney's name was Casimer Clemashevski, Ida's husband.

The pianist was Grace Loehr.

I collapsed into my chair. Why hadn't Ida told me any of this? *Why would she?*

I needed to take a walk as fast and furiously as my legs could carry me away from the house, where a soap opera had played out on the Columbia stage forty years earlier. I threw on a jacket, cap, and gloves and snatched Maverick's leash from the hook by the door.

We trudged through the drifts to the wildlife protection area until guilt settled on my shoulders. Ida needed me and here I was, running away. I knew she couldn't kill anybody. Since I'd moved to Columbia, she'd saved my life both literally and figuratively and she needed me now. I wouldn't let Ida get railroaded for the death of Phillip McCall. I just didn't know how yet. Maverick and I turned around.

Our house stood gloomy and bleak, a stark contrast to every other house on Maple Street festooned with sparkling Christmas lights. Every evening since Thanksgiving weekend, Ida flipped the switch on her favorite holiday. Not tonight.

I knocked on our adjoining door. She didn't answer. Maverick's paw brushed the edging. Although I didn't want him to mar the finish, I figured he'd get an answer before I did. And he did, but not from Ida.

Harry Wilk opened Ida's door with a frown on his face, one I'd witnessed many times in my life. Like the time I refused to accept an invitation to our senior homecoming dance by a neighbor whose well-meaning mother felt sorry for me and bribed him. I didn't want his pity, even if he was adorable, and, subsequently, he didn't get the use of her cherished Jaguar for the car parade.

Or the time I stood on stage, suspecting yet another loss to our eighth-grade chess queen. My dad snaked his way to the front of the crowd when the homemade crown fell from its intended head and rolled off the stage onto the auditorium floor, indicating it was meant for someone clumsier—me. His glare came when I jumped from the stage, grabbed the crown, and caught Sister Hildegard's skirt when I came up from under her chair brandishing the truly unexpected trophy. I'll admit I probably looked a little too eager.

I said the same thing every time.

"Sorry."

Dad backed up to let us enter. Maverick yanked the leash out of my hand, raced into the living room, and jumped onto the couch next to Ida, nestling into the fat cushions. His eyes blinked in rhythm to the involuntary strokes that ran from his nose midway down his back.

With the dark circles around her eyes, Ida reminded me of a raccoon. The gray-green of her face clashed with her messy red hair. She wore a faded paisley house dress and fuzzy pink slippers I'd never seen before.

I knelt at her feet. "Ida, do they know what happened?"

She inhaled, and her phone trilled, rumbling as it vibrated on the table in front of us. After three rings, I picked it up.

Dad said, "Please, don't answer."

"I usually like being the news," Ida said. She closed her eyes and leaned back, still petting Maverick. "Now I hate it. I've had calls from people I thought were friends, asking for intimate details of my love triangle and the ongoing feud." Her hand halted until Maverick nudged her. "Your dad has fielded calls from news outlets all over the state. When we stopped answering, two uniformed law enforcement officers parked on the street, marched up the walk, and pounded on the door to make sure everything was all right."

I cradled her free hand in mine. "We're here for you, Ida."

"I was just telling your dad about Grace and Casimer."

He cleared his throat and waited. Ida nodded. Dad said, "They both grew up in Columbia. Grace lived in her childhood home, and we live in Casimer's. They were high school sweethearts. Grace was salutatorian of her class and a brilliant pianist. She received scholarship offers from all over. Casimer, on the other hand, did as little as necessary to get by but loved sports. He played football for St. John's University in Collegeville. They would see each other, when possible, but Casimer worked two jobs to afford school and Grace practiced all the time. When she finished undergrad, Grace returned to Minnesota for a master's degree in performance with dreams of being on the world's biggest stages.

"Casimer thrived in college and graduated summa cum laude. He took a year off before deciding what he wanted to do. And during that year, he and Grace lived in Minneapolis and saw each other whenever schedules permitted."

Ida joined in the storytelling. She smiled, remembering. "Casimer was surprised by his acceptance letter from Georgetown, but what a coup. They got engaged. He headed east. Grace finished her master's degree and started a PhD in perform—"

"She's *Dr.* Loehr?"

Ida shook her head. "She never finished.

The phone trilled again. Dad looked at the caller ID. "It's Ronnie."

Ida gestured for Dad to hand her the phone.

"Hello, Ronnie." She sounded resigned. "Yes, I can be there."

She hung up. "I need a walk, Katie. Care to join me?"

A few seconds later, I received a similar call. Ronnie needed formal statements, but Ida needed to clear her head so she, Maverick, and I made a big loop around the neighborhood, and then the cold drove us indoors.

The afternoon's activities at the station blurred. The worst parts were knowing we didn't do anything and signing our names to the affidavit. When we were finally allowed to leave, Ronnie escorted us out the back door to an awaiting vehicle. Ida's eyes grew wide when we rounded the corner of the building and saw the size of the crowd that apparently waited for us.

Officer Rodgers took a strategic left, instead of the right which would have been the most direct path home, to keep us safe.

Dad had started supper. Ida warmed a loaf of Italian bread which we used to sop up a sauce of olive oil, balsamic vinegar, and a sprinkle of *herbs de Provence*. I tore open a bag of greens and carried bottles of dressing to the table. We doctored the mushy pasta and burnt marinara with lots of parmesan cheese. For a change, Maverick made no attempt to scrounge for crumbs.

When Ida excused herself, I cleaned up and Dad finished Ida's story. "Casimer interned one summer with a big firm that handled, let's say, flamboyant wealthy clients, and before one of the cases went to trial, a victim's wife broke into the offices and verbally assaulted the client as he sat in the conference room. Casimer was a big guy, ex-football player, and figured he could handle the little woman, but she was in panic mode and pulled out a knife, stabbing Casimer multiple times.

"He missed the beginning of the term, which threw off their three-year plan. The law firm paid for his hospitalization and rehabilitation, but he had a long recovery ahead of him. Grace was in the middle of her program, and they decided she should stay in Minnesota to finish. But the week before her doctoral recital and subsequent defense of her dissertation, sepsis set in, and she raced out to take care of Casimer. She never completed her degree."

"Casimer graduated and joined a law practice in New York. Grace gave piano lessons and performed wherever she could, including Paris, London, Los Angeles, and Houston. And their careers kept them busy until they moved back to Columbia."

"And they never married?"

"That's all I know. You'll have to ask Ida."

I didn't need enlightenment that badly.

CHAPTER EIGHT

After Sunday Mass, Ida retreated to bake more cookies. I dragged Dad to a round of caroling at Sterling Manor, one of the local nursing homes where some of my students worked on weekends. The kids and Dad and I serenaded a grateful audience in the dining room during their lunch and when we broke into four parts, *a cappella*, I knew we had talent among us. The room boomed when residents joined us singing the final song, "We Wish You a Merry Christmas," and we were treated to gigantic sugar cookies and hot apple cider.

"Where to next?" Lorelei Calder asked. She tossed her blond hair and grinned.

"The children's wing at the hospital," said Brock. "I heard all about it at the shindig Friday while I was serving."

Over the grumbling sarcasm and snide remarks about his not knowing how to work, he said. "Ain't that right, Mr. Wilk?"

"Quite right, Mr. Isaacson. And a mighty fine job you did too. Next stop, Columbia Memorial."

I stiffened. I hated hospitals. I hated everything about them. Dad gripped my hand but looked straight ahead. He knew what I'd been thinking. I'd almost lost him in the surgical suite, and he was still fighting his way back.

The horrific memory flashed across my mind. We'd been riding bicycles at a leisurely pace on the trail when Dad yelled, "Gun," and sped ahead of us. He went down, Charles crashed into me, knocking us into a shallow ditch. His body covered mine. It jerked when the bullets struck. I fumbled with my phone. I watched the light leave his precious blue eyes and felt his fingers grow cold as they rested in my blood-slicked hand. Somehow the ambulance found us but arrived too late. Even though I promised him I'd live a good life, at times I struggled. I pressed the palm of my mitten against my right eye, stopping the tears that had begun to form.

Dad patted my arm when the hospital came into view. I knew I'd be safe. I trusted him and pasted on a smile.

The doors whooshed in front of us. Our parade stopped at the admissions desk to get permission to visit and directions to the ward. Halfway to our destination, a tall, stout, grumpy nurse with a pinched face and short steel-gray tufts of hair met us and marched alongside as if she herded sheep to their doom. Her nametag read, "Rachel."

I strained to hear what she whispered to the front of our flock. She had them quiet and tiptoeing through the atrium. If only I knew those magic words for my classroom.

It took two elevator trips, packed to capacity, to accommodate our group. On my ascent, I could almost hear the grinding gears over the pounding of my heart. I *really* hated hospitals. We stepped into a receiving area and before our chaperone swiped the lock on the final door. She glared at us and ordered, "They're just kids. Smile and sing happy." With that, her plastic card snicked through the reader and the door whisked open.

We entered a commons area surrounded by expectant children and their parents parked in small groups. There were so many. Some were tethered to IV poles, and some wore huge colorful casts. Some had bandages, and some looked ready to go home. Set apart from the group sat a scowling boy in a wheelchair. He pulled a stocking cap over his ears and hunched his shoulders.

At first my students were silent. Life could be so unfair.

Then a single bell began to jingle. The tinkling sound is never wrong during December. Although Patricia was deaf, she could read a room, and her friends joined her rhythmic ringing in a boisterous "Frosty the Snowman" followed by "Rudolph the Red-Nosed Reindeer." When the corners of Rachel's mouth bowed up, I knew we'd made it. The kids and parents sang and clapped along, and the time flew.

We were in the middle of singing the verse about eleven pipers piping and the voices of our audience dropped off. They stared at us or, rather, through us. We never finished the final verse as one by one, members of our group found it necessary to discover what struck such awe. I feared we'd goofed up the song or one of us had something disgusting hanging on our face, but I followed the eyes behind me and spotted an elf.

Clad in a short green velvet dress with white fur around the collar, cuffs, and hem, she tugged a green-and-white hat over her long chestnut tresses. Catching her reflection in the glass divider, she smacked her lips, and straightened her wide, black, patent-leather belt. She lifted a matching satchel and slung it over her shoulder. The tips of her green-and-white felt booties curled over her toes, and the seamed black hose looked like they'd be more at home on the legs of Jennifer Lopez. Jealousy skulked in quietly and I clenched my teeth before taking a deep breath.

Dr. Pete Erickson's nurse, muse, right-hand woman, and new fiancée flashed her too white teeth and shimmied her behind through my carolers to the front of our group. She sang the last line as loudly and off-key as I'd ever heard and flapped her arms to encourage singers to join her. I had nothing against Susie Kelton. Not much, at any rate. In fact, a few times I wanted to be her, a very few, but that wasn't going to happen.

The children were agape. The stylish elf doled out thick red-and-white striped candy canes. She inspired glee in all but one patient. He sat in his wheelchair, scrutinizing the hands he held in his lap, moving one finger at a time. I'd have to give her credit. She got down on one knee so she could peer into his face, but gave up when he backed away, his chin quivering. She handed the treat to the woman standing behind his chair. She looked familiar, but I couldn't quite place her.

Then Rachel whispered to nearby families. The murmur mushroomed as they shared the message. The words floated to the ends of the room. Susie sashayed to the elevator and pushed the button.

The doors hissed and out stepped jolly old Saint

Nicholas himself. Lorelei intoned a starting pitch and our group joined her singing the song of the same name. Parents clapped. The children pointed. Rachel's true self peeked through and she beamed.

The chubby man in red knelt in front of each child and drew a beautifully gift-wrapped present from his sack. Some kids ripped the paper from their package; some peeled back tape and folded the paper to reuse; some looked at the box as if it were unreal, something too strange to deal with. The little boy in the wheelchair continued to look down at his hands but turned to the woman next to him when Santa set a box in his lap. The woman smiled. I thought I knew her eyes.

With a grimace, the boy shredded the poinsettias decorating the wrapping paper, made a ball, and threw it at Santa who caught it in his left hand. The boy grabbed one cardboard flap and bent it back against the side. Then he stopped. He gazed up again and the woman nodded, tears shining in her dark eyes.

He bent over the box and reached in with both hands. His dull eyes took on a glow and his lips softened. The tension left his little body. When he lifted a writhing light-brown bundle from the box, the other children set down whatever was in their hands and tumbled toward him, wished him a Merry Christmas, and asked what its name would be. The woman huddled next to Rachel whose arm held her tight. Their heads touched, and their joy brought tears to my eyes.

I almost smacked my forehead when I recognized the woman who'd found the mannequin at the gala.

Lorelei cued us, and we sang a snappy, "We Wish You a Merry Christmas" as we circled the room, shaking hands and taking hugs from the crowd. I stopped in front of the wheelchair and the little boy said, "Did you see my dog?" His brown eyes sparkled.

The little scamp crawled up the boy's neck and nabbed the stocking cop. It fell to the floor, and I knelt to pick it up. "May I pet him?"

"Oh, yes."

I rubbed the velvety ears and sighed. "I have a dog too. His name is Maverick."

"This is Tucker." He giggled under the tongue lashing given him by the squirming bundle and put out his hand. "I'm Ricky."

"Katie." I shook it.

"Come back any time, Katie." Ricky flashed a smile and smashed the cap over his bald head. "Maybe bring Maverick."

Santa sidled up next to me while I waited my turn at the elevator. "Nice singing. Rachel had this Santa visit set up to coincide with the first group that came caroling on the ward. She does this every Christmas. She keeps a stash of candy canes and has the parents pick out something Santa can deliver for each of her charges. She loves her kids, and you made them all very happy. Thanks for being here."

"How did you get the puppy in?"

"Why do you think *she* marched you to the ward?" His eyes blazed with delight. I turned to look at Nurse Rachel through a new lens.

"She has gift cards for your students as a token thank you." He handed me an envelope.

"My students don't need anything, Pete." I tried to return it. "They, rather, *we're* having too much fun."

"Rachel knows, but she's hoping for a return engagement."

I glanced at Rachel, who now looked like a pussycat, and I acknowledged her nod with a salute. Then I nudged Santa. "Nice duds, and good job, Pete."

Pete's brown eyes twinkled. "When did you know it was me?"

My eyebrows almost rose to my hairline. I'd always known.

He forced a hearty, "Ho, ho, ho," and turned back toward the kids. "I've got a few more stops to make so I have to get going, but remember, you better watch out."

The kids stopped what they were doing and gawked, wide-eyed. Most of the kids yelled, "Thank you, Santa," or "I'll be good."

Ricky beamed and cuddled his puppy, ignoring the man in the red suit.

The elevator swallowed the first wave of my students as Santa's elf flounced toward me with a Cheshire cat grin on her face.

"Great job," I said. If Susie and Pete were happy, I'd be happy for them.

"Thanks," said Susie.

I think she had more to say, but Rachel tapped her shoulder and said, "A word?" Susie followed her to the nurse's station.

The elevator doors opened again. Dad, Pete, and I entered, and the remaining students squeezed in, forcing me to mash against the cushion around Pete's middle. I hugged my arms and tried to make myself as small as possible. To keep my thoughts from wandering, I locked eyes on the control panel and read the capacity, then added the possible weight of each of us to make sure we wouldn't crash to the bottom of the shaft. It would be a long four-floor descent.

"Hey, Doc," Dad said.

"Hi, Harry."

"Where do I get a getup like that? Do you need any helpers?" Dad was in good form and had saved the day—again.

CHAPTER NINE

To accommodate my students' work schedules and other extracurricular commitments, our science club met before school on Monday mornings.

"I think I can get permission to hide a geocache in the history center," said Brock. "When I called yesterday, the director said it would be best if the puzzle taught something."

He brushed back the flap of curly black hair that fell over his face, and he hovered over his girlfriend. Lorelei punched her glasses up on her nose. She had the geocaching website open on her laptop. She bit her lip in concentration, twirling a blond tendril. "GPS units may be unreliable, inaccurate, or inconsistent indoors, so many of the hides are mystery multicaches that begin somewhere outside. What's a mystery cache?"

"To find the geocache, the searcher needs to solve a puzzle," I said.

"We could design one of those. We have some pretty high-powered brains in our group." Brock waggled his brows at Lorelei, and she rolled her periwinkle eyes, but he was right. She continued tapping the keyboard. In order to secure my teaching job, I agreed to supervise the science club. No one else wanted to do it. But my kids were brainy, resolute, and fun.

The door of the math area banged, and three students joined us.

"What are we doing?" asked Carlee. She hurled her backpack onto the table.

"History," Brock answered. He winced at the disbelieving looks he got. "We are," he whined.

"For a geocache," Lorelei said. "We need to teach something, to be able to hide a cache in the history center." Her fingers stopped dancing over the keys. "Ideas?"

The legs of a chair screeched and Galen grinned, knowing the sound would make Carlee cringe.

Lorelei ignored them. "There are so many facts about the *Titanic*, and the new exhibit makes up a huge part of the museum, so we should be able to come up with something related. We just have to cull through a century of data."

The students buried their noses online in search of a unique nugget of information to share. I pulled out a short stack of books. The mock trial team I worked with had wanted to research the ship's musicians for our *Titanic* trial, a fictional lawsuit brought by the fiancée of one of the bandsmen who perished, and it had paid off in their most recent competition. Defying all odds, they won. Perhaps it would pay off again.

The books thumped onto the table.

Carlee skimmed through the top one. She lit up, sat straighter, then sagged and said, "False alarm."

Brock read from his phone, "Depending on your sources, three of twelve dogs which originally boarded the ship were rescued." No one looked up. "No, huh? Did you hear about the guy that died last weekend?" He stared intently at his phone. "I waited on him at the gala. What a grouch." Before I could change the subject, he managed to say, "I bet his assistant did it." He glanced up. "How about the fact there were twenty thousand bottles of beer?"

Four pairs of eyes drew imaginary laser beams on him until he resumed tapping his phone. "Eight thousand cigars?" he read.

"No," came at him from four directions.

"The kitchen stored forty thousand fresh eggs. That's seventeen eggs per person to be consumed on their journey in breads, desserts, egg dishes, specialty cocktails, and other delicacies." Lorelei read from her screen. "There were also fourteen thousand gallons of drinking water consumed every twenty-four hours, which means every person on board could have been offered ..." She scribbled on a piece of paper. "... one hundred cups a day."

Disbelieving pencils and pens scribbled on notebooks and fingers tapped on keyboards to verify her calculations.

"And listen to this," said Lorelei. Everyone stopped what they were doing. "Of over fifteen hundred victims of the catastrophe, only three hundred thirty-four bodies were recovered."

The sobering statistic replaced some of the giddiness and brought us back to the task at hand.

Galen rubbed his chin. "That could be it."

"We've been to the exhibit a few times now and we've studied different aspects of the doomed ship, but I don't know if we've ever come across that statistic," I said. "Brock, you got this ball rolling so I think it's up to you to choose—wisely. And communicate with the director to make certain this is an endgame she can support. Meanwhile, what do we want the cache to look like?"

"The final segment of the cache could be a captain's log. Our answer could be found inside the cover," said Lorelei.

Brock set his phone on the tabletop. "I think a mystery cache with multiple parts would work. The GPS units would get the finder to the history center and an outside clue would tell you where to go first. We could use the historical placards to generate directions to get to the next segment and eventually they could sign and date the log and take away the answer."

"Everything will be easier to put together when we know we'll have a place to put it," said Galen.

I rummaged in the closet for my plastic tub of possible containers. I lugged it to the center of the math commons and pulled off the top. Inside were magnets, bison tubes, large and small empty plastic bottles, metal storage containers, camouflage duct tape, a popcorn tin, and an ammo canister. I included small pencils, pocket-sized notebooks, journals, and a smattering of loot—a plastic bag of tchotchkes wrapped in a jacket I threw in for use in inclement weather. We just needed to choose the best hiding place and an appropriate receptacle.

"That's a great idea. Brock can you …"

His phone flew to his ear and the amiable look on his

face made me smile. He stepped into an empty classroom. Thirty seconds later he strode out, talking into his phone, "We can meet Wednesday, at four o'clock and give you a run down." We all gave him a thumbs up. "Great."

Brock disconnected the call, and an impish glint in his steely gray eyes reflected his intensity.

"Let's bring it to the director as complete as we can. She said she'd love anything that would increase traffic and expand their profile. Geocaches could bring in a few new faces."

Galen emptied the storage bin, organizing the contents from smallest to largest, and the students circled the table, examining each piece for possible use.

Lorelei grabbed a journal. "I think I can embellish this to look like a captain's log. I have an old piece of leather." She turned to Brock. "Do you still have your grandfather's leather-burning set?"

"I'm never getting rid of that. He willed it to me."

"Perfect. Can we get together tonight?"

With a swagger Brad Pitt would envy, he replied, "Anytime, babe."

She rolled her eyes and pretended to punch his arm. He rubbed it in mock pain.

Carlee pulled out a fountain pen. "What about this?" She received head nods and grunts of appreciation.

Kindra stood straight and stretched. Her blue eyes gleamed. "They sell a replica of the necklace Rose tossed off the back of the *Titanic* in the gift shop. You know the one." She winked. "What if we can rig the necklace to display our fact? To get credit for the find they'd have to email the answer to our question."

Carlee's dark eyes glittered. "We could start the hunt

and direct the searchers into the history center and the log could lead them to the locket we would plant at the rear of the ship."

"Let's meet tomorrow with whatever we can scrounge up. Can you all go Wednesday?" Brock asked.

Kindra said, "I'll be here tomorrow but I work Wednesday."

"Tomorrow," I said, barely finishing my word before the students vanished, leaving me to clean up. I looked up when I heard a strong rap on the doorframe. "Hey, girlfriend."

"I got a call that freaked me out," Jane said.

CHAPTER TEN

I arrived at her apartment as soon as I could. Streetlights winked on above Jane as she paced on the sidewalk. Her golden curls blended with her furry hood creating an enormous fluffy border around her face. Her red nose blinked at the center.

I exited the car and gently closed the door of Dad's beloved wheels. "You could have gone inside,"

"I thought I'd wait for my best friend." The keys twirled around the fingers of her gloved hand. "By the way, did you ever find out who those bikers were?"

"No. Thank heavens. I haven't seen any more renegade cyclists." While walking, Maverick and I had been accosted a few times by some kids hurling epithets and telling me to forget what I'd seen. I couldn't identify them; they'd always covered their faces. And I didn't know what they wanted me to forget. But I hadn't had anyone bother me since the last snowfall. It was difficult to bike in eight inches of snow.

Jane took a deep breath. "The voice I heard sounded like it went through a long tunnel, and I couldn't tell if it was female or male." She shook her head from side to side.

"Did you tell Drew?"

"Are you kidding?" She stared at me. "He'd get all bent out of shape."

I felt a little out of shape myself. "Some creepy voice said that if you didn't give *it* back, you'd pay, and you didn't tell Drew. When he finds out, he won't be happy."

"He won't find out, will he." She stated a fact. "Even if I knew what they were referring to, and I don't, I wouldn't give it to an anonymous, nebulous voice from beyond." She rolled her hand away from her face to somewhere out there.

I looked down at my boots. When I looked up, I caught the blaze in her eyes. "Okay. Let's unravel this mystery. This is the first time you've heard from, shall we say, Mr. X?"

She nodded.

"What's new in your life?"

"Drew." Her eyes softened and lost a bit of focus or, more likely, focused more intently on her heart.

"Concentrate." I willed her some strength and a little common sense, but not too much. "He said give 'it' up not him."

She stopped. Her hands clenched the keys in front of her. She fixed her gaze somewhere beyond and forced a smile. "I did some retail therapy last Thursday and bought a new dress to wear to the fundraiser, but, seriously, who'd want things in my size?"

She raised her hand above her head and measured short. I thought size zero but neither description worked for many takers.

She shifted her eyes to me. "I did win Ida's wreath, and it's a Christmas treasure but seriously?"

"What about that memory box you bought?"

"Why would anybody want that?"

"Someone destroyed the encaustic piece Miss Grace won at the auction."

"That's terrible. Can McCall fix it?"

I tried to formulate a profound answer, but the words which left my lips were anything but. "McCall is dead."

She scrutinized my face. "I've been watching holiday movies and haven't listened to anything but Christmas carols. What happened?"

"Ida and I found Mr. McCall in his studio."

"Not again. You have to stop doing that."

I huffed out a long breath. "On Saturday, the media called Ida a person of interest but nothing since. No news is good news, right? I can't believe anyone would believe she could have anything to do with hurting someone."

We took slow, careful steps up her slippery walk. "How are we going to help Ida?"

"I don't really know, but if Ronnie sets his sights on her, and it really was murder, we'll have to think of something."

"We're not going to let anything happen." She raised one eyebrow and turned to face the front door. She set her jaw and I did the same.

"Let's go," she said, and she marched up the steps. She stood as tall as she could and inserted the key.

She prodded the door with her foot and flicked the

light switch. Nothing happened. My heart raced. She stomped into her living room and groaned. I followed. Glass shards and fragments of earthenware crunched beneath my footfalls. The frames on the walls hung at odd angles. Even in the muted shadows, nothing looked right. I punched in Drew's number.

He picked up. "Hey, Katie."

"Someone broke into Jane's and—"

He ended the call.

"Jane," I called and tripped on an umbrella stand. I straightened it, then lifted a vintage coat rack weighed down with about a million pounds of Minnesota outer wear. "Jane?" I said, stepping gingerly behind the light beam from my phone.

Faint rays filtered through the windows, catching the silhouette of my petite friend, rooted in the middle of the living room in front of her fireplace. Her hands rested on her hips. Then she stooped and picked something off the floor and moaned.

My eyes became more accustomed to the light, or lack thereof, and I watched Jane. Her head swiveled as she measured the chaos. The couch cushions spewed fluffy white stuffing. Books and papers covered the floor in front of the empty bookcase. The window blinds swung at odd angles. The ends of the carpet folded back to reveal a wood floor spotted with dried glue. Her television lay face down in front of the stand. She picked up a broken leg from the overturned coffee table and smacked it against her palm.

"What I wouldn't do if—"

Her back door slammed. She took one look at me and raced through the dim hallway. Reluctantly I followed her. She yanked open the back door and peered into the yard.

I pointed my phone light at the ground. Before she could obliterate the evidence, I grabbed her and pointed two feet to our left. We made a second trail next to big boot prints we followed through the snow in the yard to the alley where they vanished into the tire ruts of a vehicle. Red brake lights appeared at the end of her alley and headlights came on.

"Jane!" I grabbed her arm and hauled her toward the apartment. "Let them go!"

Her mukluks slid on the snow, or I wouldn't have been able to drag her anywhere. She strained against me almost as much as Maverick.

We fell into the kitchen, and I shoved all my weight against the door. The braided rag rug bunched at the base and acted like a stopper. The door couldn't latch. I opened the door, toe-tossed the rug, and slammed it again while Jane stared at me with a deep scowl on her face.

"We could've caught them!"

"Thank heavens we didn't. We don't know who *they* are. We don't know what they might have done. A cornered animal is totally unpredictable."

"Katie, they were in my home going through my things." She held up a small figurine. "They broke a wing off of the angel my mother gave me on my seventh birthday." When the words left her lips, she crumpled. A sob escaped. "Oh, Mom." She dropped to the tile floor. "She died so long ago, but I still miss her every day." She shook her fists as she spoke through gritted teeth, "I'm going to throttle someone."

"Do you have any idea what they might have wanted and if they got it?"

She shook her head. Then we heard the thud of a

car door. Jane sniffed and stilled, then she crawled to the window and peered out. She glowered at me. "It's Drew."

"It's about time."

He hobbled fast. The bell chimed, the door opened, and he limped into the room. His eyes studied every corner. He acknowledged me, but hitched his way to Jane and crushed her until she wriggled loose.

"I'm okay," she said.

Drew looked at me for confirmation. I nodded. "What happened?" he asked, his right hand pointing out the room in all its untidy glory.

"We interrupted an intruder," said Jane.

"Interrupted?"

"We think we heard him leave by the back door while were assessing the carnage in the living room." I tried to sound detached, but I could still hear the blood pounding in my ears.

A siren whooped and some car doors clunked. Drew answered the knock and led the officers into the living room.

"I'll see about the lights," Drew said and shuffled on his crutches into the kitchen, down the basement to the breaker box, moving well on his injured leg. On his last assignment, he had sustained injuries to an arm and a leg while trying to follow a lead into the local state park. It didn't pan out, but when Maverick came to his rescue, we solidified our friendship.

Jane started to stand the table up on its three good legs.

"Leave it," said a gruff voice.

After a rush of power from the breaker, something beeped and the lights popped on. One glance at the surroundings and Ronnie Christianson pulled out a pen and a small notebook.

"Ronnie," Jane said.

"That's Chief Christianson."

Jane rolled her eyes. The other officer, Officer Rodger, focused on his nametag.

"Well, little Miss Mackey. What happened here?"

Little Miss Mackey was a feisty thing. "If I knew, I wouldn't need you now, would I, Temporary Chief Christianson," she said sweetly, emphasizing the *temporary*. She must be afraid. She didn't often bait law enforcement.

"We can do this here or down at the station," said Ronnie.

Ronnie whirled when Drew cleared his throat. "I received a call at six fifteen from Katie Wilk. Someone had broken into Jane's apartment. I called you." He turned to look at me. "Katie?"

"Jane and I had been discussing the threatening phone call." I swallowed. "And then we decided—"

"What threatening phone call?" asked Drew.

"I was going to tell you." Jane could really put on an act. "I thought the call was a prank and not important enough to worry about. I forgot all about it … until now." The fire in Jane's eyes would have peeled skin from the fainter of heart. I felt my cheeks to make sure they hadn't melted. "Someone called and told me to 'give it up' or else, but I don't know what *it* is!"

Alarms sounded from a device on Officer Rodgers' belt. He read the screen. "We gotta go, Ron … Chief. Emergency."

"The problem with a small department. You three, get yourselves down to the station and make your statements. Janie, you can't stay here until we've had our crime scene team investigate." Ronnie's big boots crushed the remains of a crystal goblet before he turned and added, "They'll be by later."

The door closed with a soft click.

"He can't really make me leave, can he?"

Drew tipped his head. "I'm afraid so, hon. But you can stay with me."

"Or you can stay with me," I said, although I really didn't think she'd want to sleep on the pull-out couch.

"Can I get a few things?"

"I'll come with you. That way we can make that part of the official record and you'll have a witness." Drew worked with the Minnesota Bureau of Criminal Apprehension and knew how to maintain the integrity of an investigation.

Jane shook her head in disgust and stomped toward the stairs. "C'mon gimpy."

Drew chuckled and said in a very low voice, "This is going to be fun." His crutches clumped up the stairs.

Not thinking, I grabbed for a pile of books but halted before disturbing the disarray. I huffed. I appreciated neat and orderly. It was difficult to keep my hands off, and it wasn't even my stuff.

A floral overnight bag on wheels bumped down the stairs behind Jane. Drew trooped after her.

He didn't complain. His mobility had improved, and I admired his determination. He took one uncomfortable step at a time, balancing, regrouping his body parts, and making another step. But his face telegraphed his dissatisfaction with his new shortcomings.

Jane stopped short and looked around the room. She opened the front closet door and moved the shoes around on the floor.

"My wreath is gone."

CHAPTER ELEVEN

Fat white flakes drifted through the golden hue of the streetlamp outside the police station. It didn't look as cold as it felt when I stepped onto the sidewalk and left the warmth of the car.

When I joined Drew and Jane, he dropped the arm he'd wrapped around her shoulders and held the door for us, clomping the crutches through the entrance.

"What do we tell them?" Jane asked.

"The truth is always a good idea. We don't have any stories to keep straight. We give our statements. Ronnie assigns a crime scene crew to check for evidence and files a report. You get a topnotch security system or …" Drew waggled his eyebrows. "… you move in with me." Rather than jostle him and maybe knock him flat, Jane flicked her fingers in agitation. Drew said, mimicking contrition, "Everything goes back to normal."

We stepped into the vestibule, shook off the snow, and stamped our boots.

Jane bowed her head. "I'm sorry. This is much harder than I thought. I feel so violated. Somebody touched my things, broke my angel, and took my wreath. I'm trembling inside."

Drew pulled her into a hug and kissed the top of her head. "They'll find the perp," he said, holding her away and examining her face. "And you've always got me."

When Drew told the officer at the desk who we were, she whisked us into an interrogation room. She handed each of us a yellow legal pad and pen and instructed us to write out what happened while we waited for Chief Christianson. Although she left the door open, I still felt the walls closing in on me and I wrote out my description as fast as I could.

Another officer dropped off a tray laden with three cups of coffee, creamer shots, sweetener, a plate heaped with donuts, and bottles of water.

"What is it with cops and donuts?" Jane said. He met her smile with a shrug. She cracked open a water bottle.

Drew stacked the three completed tablets on the corner of the table, aligning the edges, and set the pens on top, perpendicular to the lines on the page which is exactly the way I liked.

"We shouldn't have long to wait. Someone will be with us shortly."

We waited.

Drew pulled himself up on the crutches. He arched his back and stretched his neck then rotated his head from side to side. Jane paced. She twisted her hands together and watched the time on her wrist. I glanced at the door, and when Ronnie plodded by on his way to his office, I thought our wishes had come true.

Instead, we waited.

Drew made a bid toward the door and just as quickly back-pedaled when we heard Ronnie shout. "You couldn't support me? You had to pretend you weren't biased so you're supporting the search for a new chief. I've been doing all your work. Don't you think I'm qualified? I've years of training at your magnificent feet." It sounded as if a drawer slammed. "Doesn't that just beat all!"

Drew hung his head, but the same questions seemed to flit by on Jane's face. Who was he talking to? Didn't they believe he would make a good chief of police? Did I? I thought he followed orders well enough, but could he give them? Would a search find the best possible candidate for Columbia's chief of police? What would happen meanwhile?

"You could have recommended me at least. It wouldn't be any skin off your back. Thanks for nothing."

The latch bolt clicked and the door at the end of the hall squawked open.

Not wanting to be caught eavesdropping, though it couldn't be helped, Jane grabbed the top tablet, spilling the pens to the floor. She scooped them up and selected one. She turned the page on the tablet and scribbled a few more notes. Drew leaned against the wall farthest away from the doorway. I bowed my head over my fists and prayed we could go home soon.

But I peeked.

Pete's dad and former Chief of Police Lance Erickson

marched past; his solemn face registered regret. After multiple heart attacks, he'd backed away from the career he loved. It seemed obvious he wanted the very best candidate to fill his shoes, and although he didn't tank Ronnie's chances, I imagined Ronnie felt he hadn't helped either.

Minutes later, Ronnie stormed into our room and seized the tablets off the table.

He waved the pages in front of us. "I have your written statements." Then he pointed the tablets at Jane. "Our team has gone through your apartment and dusted for fingerprints. Have you thought of anything else that might help us find the perpetrator?"

Jane sighed but before she could describe the loss of the wreath, Ronnie continued, "Invest in a security system."

Drew answered, "Already on it."

Jane balked and then the tears she'd held at bay started down her cheeks.

Drew and I waited for Jane to spill the beans.

"I purchased a wreath at the hospital fundraiser. It was created from old jewelry, odds and ends, items no one would want. And it's missing. The artist informed me she only used costume jewelry so, except for its sentimental value, it wasn't worth half of what I paid for it. It's only valuable to someone who appreciated the creation." Jane's knee jerked up and down, anxiety fighting its way out.

"Can you describe it?"

"Gold and silver colored costume jewelry were attached to a Styrofoam wreath, but the pieces had little value individually. The artist laced fake greenery and ribbons among the baubles, then added a bow covered with shiny beads."

"And the artist's name?"

Jane cleared her throat and nibbled on her bottom lip. "Ida."

Ronnie stood up straighter and slapped the tablets against his thigh. "Her again." He nodded and stalked out of the interrogation room.

Drew said, "I don't know about you, but I'm starving. Do you two want to pick up some Chinese and eat at my place? Jane, your apartment will look better in the light of day."

She nodded and let him lead her out of the room. He glanced over his shoulder and said, "Coming, Katie?"

"I've got to get home. Maverick, you know." I had little desire to be a third wheel. "And Dad. He'll likely have something burning, I mean bubbling on the stove." I usually heard from him by now, either with his menu or a reprimand for being late, but he hadn't sent me any messages. I'd just have to take a chance.

CHAPTER TWELVE

The snow swirled gently against a backdrop of vibrant blinking lights on Maple Street. Stiff plastic Rudolphs and enormous inflatable Frostys grinned from their frozen posts. I drove carefully and caught movement through the picture window in the first home. Two of my neighbor kids sat in their front room and waved. They laughed and mimed honking a horn. I complied, piercing the peaceful quiet with a toot.

I passed a battered light-colored Jetta and a flashy dark-colored car. I sighed. I missed my Jetta, but it lost its battle for road king in the collision. Vehicles were not safe with me.

And then I smiled. Happy lights shined from each of Miss Grace's windows, the sign of a festive holiday gathering. The overflow of cars spilled from her driveway and lined both sides of the street. I passed by slowly.

I waved at our neighbor, Adam Farley. His quilted down jacket fit him snugly, and so did his adorable daughter and striking wife. The hulk of a man dragged a long wooden toboggan, following the indentation of a circle in his front yard. Pamela cushioned their three-year-old daughter between her legs and arms, and even with my windows rolled up, I heard Emma's squeal of glee.

I parked the car and headed up the walk. Flakes sifted onto my face, and I sniffed the brisk cold. The temperature leeched warmth from my fingers, toes, and nose and I hurried inside. When I opened the door, Maverick knocked me out of the way as he raced into the yard. He did his business and then trotted back in through the doggie door.

He stood on his hind legs and licked my face. "Happy to see me?" I swallowed hard, remembering when I tried to find him a different home, but he'd saved my life in more ways than one. I squeezed him with love and set him down on four paws.

"Off," I said in my teacher voice. My stomach growled.

Then he gamboled toward the cupboard where I kept his food, bounding back and forth. He pawed at the knob and melted my resolve with the head tilt.

If he could talk, he'd say, *You're late,* and he'd tell me his stomach growled too. He orbited his dish as I poured his kibble and it disappeared before I finished hanging my coat.

"Dad," I called.

I tossed my briefcase onto the circular wrought iron table at the base of the stairs and flipped the living room light switch I passed on my way to Dad's room. I knocked. His door swung open. Maverick pranced into the empty space and jumped onto the bed, circled twice, and laid down.

"Don't bat your baby brown eyes at me, big boy. I don't think Dad would like you making yourself comfortable, but then again, maybe you do this all day long when I'm not here. Any idea where he's off too?" This place screamed in silence.

I wandered through the apartment, tripping on an extension cord in the living room. One end snaked up our small Christmas tree, the other lay feet from the power outlet. I plugged it in then flinched through the full three-minute cacophony from the noisemaking, mechanical-talking, and animated electric-powered ornaments. Almost every evening, the fireplace in the living room boasted red, orange, and yellow flames. Dad loved his fires. When I spread my nightly homework out on the coffee table, he'd sit next to the fire and watch me from his new brown-leather recliner, usually reading the inside of his eyelids. Tonight, I missed the crackle and the smoky wood scent

The cold stove and colder oven didn't bode well for a home-cooked meal either. I'd grown accustomed to Dad's menu of grilled cheese, even when it was black on one side; bacon, though it could often be used as a shingle on a doll's house; and waffles, which, slathered in butter and thick maple syrup tasted mighty fine. He tried new recipes and when he felt confident in the outcome, he'd invite Ida for dinner. Most evenings, however, Dad rewarmed something Ida had dropped off because she made too much, or she'd bring supper saying she required guinea pigs to taste some new concoction. I opened the refrigerator and recoiled. I tossed the wilted bowl of greens, swimming in a brown liquid and rinsed the bowl. I grabbed an apple from the fruit basket and tossed it in the air; it almost hit the linoleum when Maverick let loose a loud bark.

"What is it boy?" I knelt next to him and scratched his chest as I slid the curtain on the living room window to the side. A figure passed by our driveway and slipped around the corner of the house. I rubbed between Maverick's ears. He closed his eyes and leaned closer to get a deeper scratch. "Good boy." I reached onto the counter for his favorite treat and hugged him. He scarfed it down and I almost lost a finger.

When I called Dad's cell, it rang from his room. Elizabeth didn't call him a Luddite for nothing. Her job required computer skills and she embraced it. He eschewed technology. I flopped on the couch and examined my phone screen.

I called Ida's phone. It went to voicemail. Then my mind did a somersault, and I felt the terror again, returning to this house as two EMTs carted Dad out on a gurney with an oxygen mask over his pale face. I hadn't even been able to talk to him. They'd taken him to the hospital by ambulance. It turned out he'd been extremely dehydrated, and they could fix that.

My heart raced. I located a name on my phone but hesitated before pressing the call button. Fear got the better of me.

"Columbia Hospital ER. How may I direct your call?"

"Dr. Pete Erickson."

"May I tell him who's calling?"

"Katie Wilk."

"One moment please."

Maverick's tail thumped as we waited.

"Katie?" My heart gave an embarrassed flutter. "How

are you?" he asked.

"Pete, I can't find Dad and I'm worried. Neither he nor Ida are answering their phones and I wanted to find out if he—"

"I've been on since three and I've seen neither hide nor hair of either one. Let me check admissions." Keys clacked under rapid fingers. "They aren't here."

"Thank you."

"I can't tell you where they are, but I'll keep watch." He became quiet. "How are you?" he asked again.

Asking twice he must have intended me to answer. We could still be friends. He'd answered my question about Dad. The least I could do was answer his. "I'm good. You?"

"Everything's great."

I mustered my courage and added politely, "Susie?"

"She's good. Good," he repeated. "Grace told me she and Ida had words, but don't worry, they'll get over it."

"I think they already have."

"Watch out for them, okay? I've always known them as two obstinate, eccentric, artistic women. When they met at music contests, recitals, or other performance venues they tolerated each other, but I think it started out with a little more—" A beeper sounded. "Sorry, Katie. Gotta go."

No Dad. No Ida.

If Maverick hadn't laid his weighty head on my knee and nudged me, I might have worried more. The fingers of my left hand crawled through his fur and my right hand corrected papers and recorded the scores in my gradebook until the cuckoo clock struck nine. Each peep encroached farther in on my thoughts.

At nine seventeen, Dad and Ida tripped into the living room, giddy.

My ears felt hot, and I'm sure my cheeks glowed pink. "Katie," Ida sang.

Dad read my face and untangled himself from his long, brown knit scarf, an early Christmas present from Ida. He aimed her out the door. "Good night, dear lady."

She shrugged her shoulders and staggered back the way she'd come.

"Where've you been?" It came out much more like an accusation than I'd planned.

"Grace had company. Ida had cookies. I had beer and plenty of it." He stated and hiccupped. His coat buttons were giving him trouble.

"Here, let me help." I relented and reached for the middle button and wrinkled my nose. "That smell of liquor is circling you like dirt around Pig Pen." I filtered the odor and breathed through my sleeve.

"You were worried about me," he said as he fell out of his coat.

"Yes, and I was worried about Ida too. You could have left a message, written a note, something, let me know what's going on."

"Grace invited us over."

My phone rang and I turned to answer. "Hello."

"Did you find them?" he said in a rush.

"Yes. They just walked in."

"Thank heavens," Pete sighed. "They've sent our EMTs out on a call at the site of a five-car pileup and I pictured them getting caught up in the melee. Be safe." He hung up.

"Well, what have you got to say for yourself?"

"The tables have turned. I believe I've asked you the same thing on many occasions. I'm a grown man, perfectly capable of making my own decisions and taking responsibility for my actions. But if you need to know, Grace's great-nephew or something has come for a visit, and we went over to meet him. Grace held a cocktail party, and it was a doozy. Her backyard looked just like ours until she turned on thousands of dazzling white and yellow lights. It's a fairy garden. Now, if I may please be excused."

I tried to hide my tears by wiping my cheeks and the tip of my nose before I snuffled, but he knew me too well.

"I'm sorry if I upset you, darlin'. I should have let you know, but we never planned on staying. I didn't even bring my phone. Ida said she'd never go empty handed during the holidays, so we delivered a bottle of wine and a plate of Christmas cutouts and Grace hauled us inside. Truth be told, I don't think she wanted to be alone with this kid. She'd never met him before. Must be about forty now. Pam and Adam were taking Emma home to bed when we arrived, and CJ and Carlee stopped by but never removed their coats. They said to say hi, by the way."

Dad put his arm around my shoulders.

"I thought something happened to you." Might as well let everything hang out. I pressed the heels of my palms against my eyes.

"Why would you think that?"

I inhaled sharply and faced him, about to remind him of the last time I chased an ambulance headed to the ER with him inside, strapped to a gurney.

"Oh," he said, as the memory dawned on him. "Sorry, darlin'."

I hugged him until he prodded my shoulders to get a little space between us.

"We won't go anywhere else." Dad yawned. "Scratch that. Jordan invited us for supper tomorrow. He's going to grill. Can you make it?"

I shrugged. "Maybe. But my students are trying to place a geocache in the *Titanic* exhibit and we're putting together a presentation for the director."

"I bought you a little something you should use if you continue to walk Maverick when it's not light. It's in the brown paper packaging under the tree." He yawned. "I'm going to get some shut eye and you should too."

His door closed with a firm click and then I remembered Jane's trouble. I'd have to start making notes if I wanted to keep *Dad* apprised and not have my words come back and bite me.

The ribbons and bows on the packages beneath the tree gleamed in the sparkly lights on all but one. The label read, "To My Darlin' and Her Boy." Inside was a two-appendage reflective vest, a four-appendage reflective vest, and a stocking cap with a built-in, multi-function headlamp. We'd be lit up like a Christmas tree.

CHAPTER THIRTEEN

Morning came too quickly.

While I finished my tea, Maverick sat in front of me, his leash in his mouth, drooling.

"Okay, big guy," I said wrapping another of Ida's knitted scarves around my neck and tucking the ends under my collar. "But we've got to be quick about it."

I grabbed the slimy leash and clipped it on. I cinched my heavy boots and pulled mittens over my hands, then we put on the reflective vests. Careful to test each step for traction, we crunched through the crisp frozen layer on the snow.

When I picked up the pace, I skidded on the icy street in the drab morning, towed by my determined black lab. He lunged with every stride and jerked my arms and shoulders in his need to be somewhere. I just prayed I wouldn't fall and end up with disconnected joints, strained muscles, or broken bones. Thoughts of McCall's death broke my concentration. Why would he have been killed? How did he die? How could Chief Christianson possibly believe Ida would kill anyone?

Maverick dragged me to the edge of the waterfowl preservation pond and sat.

"Let's go, Maverick," I said, winded. He wouldn't move. "I have school this morning. I need to see the kids. Heel." I feigned excitement. "Come on, boy. Heel."

The area gave me the willies. Four months earlier, we'd been looking for a geocache in the tall reeds surrounding the pond in the middle of the wildlife preserve and instead of recording a find, Maverick located the body of the man who signed my teaching contract. The murderer would no longer bother anyone, but the location still made me squirm.

I bent at my waist, elbows on knees, concentrating my efforts, but I couldn't get him to budge. "Let's go, Maverick," I said. "C'mon, big boy."

I pulled a smelly salmon treat from the training pouch in my pocket. He looked at me with something akin to pity, stood on all four paws, aimed for the spindly dry grasses, and hauled me behind him. I didn't have to lift one booted foot but skied in his wake with the grace of a hippopotamus.

A pristine blanket of white surrounded me and I couldn't enjoy a bit of it.

The leash tore out of my hands and Maverick flushed a ring-necked pheasant. He raced after it, untethered. I chased him, feeling the loss of each precious minute, and knowing I'd be late if we didn't get home soon. I followed the dog tracks Maverick had superimposed on top of multiple people-prints.

When I finally caught up with him, he sat at attention on a tall bank looking over the frozen water. He snuck a peak at me, and I could almost hear him say, *Do you see it now?* He raised one paw, uncovering a gold ring embedded in the snow. I picked it up. *Pretty,* I thought, and shoved it into my jacket pocket. Maverick took two steps toward the snowy plain and that's when I saw the shining fragments scattered over the ice.

My first call went to voicemail. Jane's box was full. Neither Ida nor Dad answered. I dialed again.

"Columbia Police Department. Is this an emergency?"

"No, I don't think so."

"How can I help you?"

"May I speak to Ronnie, Chief Christianson."

"What's this about?"

"This is Katie Wilk. He investigated a burglary last night and I have new information."

Elevator music played, and I gave Maverick another salmon snack, checking the fleeting time.

"Christianson."

"This is Katie Wilk."

"What do you need now, Katie?" he asked with a bit of sarcasm.

I took a calming breath. "I might have found Jane's wreath. Pieces are scattered over the ice at the waterfowl protection pond." I didn't hear any response. "Chief?" I checked the screen to make sure we were still connected. "Ronnie? Didn't you want me to call?"

"Give me a minute." Drawers slammed and he gave muffled orders to someone in the background. Back on the line, he said, "Where are you?"

I looked around to get my bearings. "We're near the parking lot on Ida's side of the pond."

"Who's with you?"

I started to answer but he said gruffly, "It doesn't matter. Don't go anywhere. Don't touch anything."

Mrs. McEntee, my principal's administrative assistant kindly answered on the first ring.

"I came across a ..." What could I safely and truthfully say? "... curiosity and I need to wait for Chief Christianson. I shouldn't be long." She was one of my favorite people, and she made everything easier.

Mrs. McEntee performed her keyboard magic and said, "You're covered."

The whipping wind burned my cheeks while we waited. When Ronnie marched into the clearing, he stopped fifteen feet from us and examined the ground, the trees, and the reeds. He motioned to the officers who followed his hand signals and gingerly stepped onto the ice, retrieving the shiny bits, and placing them in plastic evidence bags. Ronnie stomped through the snow toward me. He skidded and I caught his elbow but would have landed on top of him if Maverick hadn't yanked the leash in the opposite direction at the same time.

"Good boy," I muttered and dug another treat from my pocket.

I offered Ronnie a hand up. He shook his head, wisely not trusting to pit his weight against mine, and crawled on all fours until he could get solid footing.

"I'll have Jane come down to the station and identify what's left of the wreath," he said. "What were you doing out here?"

"Maverick and I were walking."

"Did you see anybody?"

"Sorry. I didn't see or hear anything. May I go?" I glanced at my wrist. "My first class starts in seven minutes."

He nodded. "They must have been looking for something." He said humorlessly, "Go, but don't leave town." He smirked and walked toward the pond's edge.

Maverick took off for home at a fast clip, dragging me behind him. "I'd appreciate it if you didn't find anything new for a while," I grumbled.

CHAPTER FOURTEEN

Since the idea belonged to Brock, he had a vested interest in the development and placement of the cache and came prepared with a page of notes.

"We need a catchy cache name," said Carlee.

"Rose?" said Kindra, then she shook her head.

"*Titanic* Trouble," said Galen and he winked at Carlee.

Lorelei nibbled on the end of her pen. "*Titanic* Gem."

"Gem of the Ocean?" said Brock. Disbelieving eyes studied him. "Sorry. I don't know what I was thinking."

Laughter bubbled out of Lorelei. "That's a great idea."

"Really?"

Lorelei pinched his cheek. "You're so cute." His eyes opened wide over a lopsided grin.

"I agree," said Kindra. "The gem of the ocean can

refer to the ship or it can refer to a jewel. It's a win-win."

"That's settled." Lorelei pulled an exquisite, sculpted-leather-covered book from her backpack. "Brock and I decorated the journal."

"No one would have ever believed this wasn't done by a professional. It's great," Galen said. "How did you do that?"

Brock lowered his face and the tips of his ears glowed pink. "My grandpa and I have been burning leather since I could hold the pyrography pen—"

"Say what?" asked Galen, looking at his friend in a new light.

"It's a heated pointy thing," said Brock.

"Brock learned at the knee of a master, and he's been doing it for a long time. I think it turned out great," said Lorelei, turning the book over in her hands.

Jane popped her head in the door.

"Hi, guys. What are you doing?"

"Hey, Ms. Mackey. We have permission to place a geocache at the history center. Want to help?" said Carlee.

"Can't today. But can I borrow Ms. Wilk for just a minute?"

We stepped into my classroom, and you'd have thought Jane and I dropped onto another planet. We disappeared from their consciousness immediately.

Jane turned on me. "What were you thinking, Katie?" she hissed. "Now I have to go back and talk to that pompous jackass."

I stammered through my response. "I tried to call you. You reported the wreath stolen so you'd have to tell him sooner or later." Simmering pools threatened to sink her brown eyes. "Jane, what's wrong?"

She sniffed. "I think they also stole my mom's ring. I can't find it anywhere and everything is so messed up."

Cancer claimed her mother when Jane was eleven and the ring tied her to good memories. Until Dad married Elizabeth, he'd been my entire family and done everything he could to make my childhood as normal and as memorable as possible, and although I'd never known my mom, I could sympathize.

"Hold that thought." I stepped into the math office and rummaged through my coat pockets, removing the ring I forgot to give Ronnie.

I held it out in my palm. Jane gasped and tears came to her eyes.

"It wasn't even worth all that much, but it was the first ring she got from my dad. Where did you find it?"

"In the snow near the wreath."

She grabbed a tissue. "I suppose I have to report this as well." She moaned.

She closed her eyes and dropped her head back, squeezing the last of the tears from her eyes. She inhaled and brought her head up. She opened her eyes and threw back her shoulders, stretching out to her full height.

"Wish me luck," she said at the same time we heard a crash from the commons.

Brock and Galen stood nose to nose; Carlee held Galen's fist; Kindra tugged on Brock's upper arm.

"What's happening?" Jane said, and I stepped between the solid titans.

"They're arguing over who has the best chance of going to state this year when we all know it's going to be our mock trial team," Lorelei said, oblivious of or indifferent to their tension, or maybe she just had a way with words.

The four heads swiveled to look at her typing at the keyboard. The boys' shoulders relaxed, and they snorted at the absurdity. Kindra grabbed and missed Brock's hand as it rose and headed toward Galen, and her face flooded with relief when it clamped in a handshake.

"Much better," said Jane. She picked up a chair that had fallen, and as she swept out of the math area, she said, "Katie, expect a call later."

Fight averted, Carlee announced, "We need to go to the history center to get the lay of the land and map out the cache. Then we can present a complete package tomorrow." Everyone nodded.

Kindra said, "I think I have an idea on how to build the cache answer holder, but I need to purchase a locket."

"I'll buy the pendant, Kindra. Mrs. McEntee controls the extracurricular petty cash stash, and there are still funds available for incidentals."

* * *

Out in the middle of the prairie, Robert Bruckner had replicated the ship's bow at half-scale and my mouth dropped open again when the intimidating form materialized in front of me. It served as a magnificent entrance to the exhibit. In addition, he'd re-created a variety of rooms from the *Titanic* and used them as a soundstage to film parts of his movie. He'd attached the new construction to the county building which was in dire need of repair. Now, however, with the funds raised by visitors to the exhibit and the special gift earmarked in the gala pledges, the board, headed by Ida, planned a renovation and a desperately needed update.

I plodded up the boarding plank and met my students

at the entry. Lorelei snapped a series of photos.

We stepped inside and Brock scratched the back of his neck "I forgot about the tickets."

"Got it covered," I said, and stepped to the counter. "Six tickets, please."

"Your money ain't any good here, Ms. Wilk," said the young man behind the counter. He cocked a crooked smile, crossed his arms over his scrawny chest, and then tugged on the gold stud in his right earlobe. The gesture reminded me of the late-night television reruns my dad watched of Carol Burnett and her closing gesture. "The president of the board said if you ever brought students to view the exhibit, you should be given free passes."

Ida. I sighed.

"How ya doin', Galen?"

"Good, Derek. You?"

"Can't complain. Still wrestling?"

Galen gave him a high five. "Hope to and I'll be a force to be reckoned with."

The young man handed me six *Titanic* boarding passes. "It's educational," he said with an exaggerated wink.

I fanned them out. Each student grabbed one, reading the biographical data of the passenger contained on the card which they would compare to the facts listed on the display at the exhibit so we could follow the character's story aboard ship and determine if he or she survived. Deep down, I hoped whoever designed the tickets included more survivors than victims because if they used a distribution comparable to the tragedy, sixty-seven percent of the visitors would choose a boarding pass of a passenger who perished and that would be somewhat depressing.

One hundred percent of my previous boarding

passes identified survivors of the sinking. Mrs. Charlotte Appleton, after burying her sister in England, helped row lifeboat two until the rescue ship *Carpathia* arrived. August Wennerström, a journalist, wrote about the souls either dragged to their Atlantic graves or rescued aboard collapsible lifeboat A. Alfred Percy Pugh lost his brother in the disaster, but corresponded with Walter Lord and later attended the premiere of the film, *A Night to Remember*. And my first boarding pass contained the story of second-class passenger Patrick Callahan whose newly discovered journal necessitated a revision of his personal story.

Not this time.

CHAPTER FIFTEEN

Titanic's chief engineer, Thomas Andrews, is immortalized in every depiction of the final hours aboard the ocean liner as a man ruefully accepting the implausible yet inescapable. He never believed his creation could sink, but when he did the math and realized there was no future for his ship, he gave himself over to the sea. I held a facsimile of his boarding pass.

We walked through the eerie quiet. Composition notebooks in hand, my students scribbled notes whenever we came upon an information notice board and pointed out words, phrases, or numbers we could use to direct our searchers.

"Remember, we want the cache to be challenging but entertaining and fun."

Carlee sketched the map of the route we'd completed and marked the vestibule as our starting point with a big X.

"Brock and I thought the logbook would fit best near the bridge. Let's look there." Lorelei barreled ahead of us.

Thick, plush, red ropes kept us from entering the mock-up of the bridge. A film clip of the dead calm, dark night, and noiseless waters of April 14, 1912, played on the reflective windows. Then, without preamble, an alarm bell pealed and the telephone connecting the crow's nest jangled. A disembodied voice yelled, "Iceberg right ahead."

The solid bass voice of the officer in charge of the wheelhouse gave simple instructions to avoid impact, and the follow-up as he prepared for the inevitable.

The film juddered and so realistically simulated a collision, I grabbed the wall.

Kindra used a phone app to measure the space to the right of the doorway. "My mom has a beat-up, old stand we could set against this wall to hold our logbook. The cache description could provide the instructions for searchers."

Brock knew his way around and strutted as he led our group onto a deck, alive with brilliant stars and almost as cold as our Minnesota winter. The bitter temperature reminded me of the evening I attended the gala. I recalled the discussion McCall had with the black-haired woman, but my musings were interrupted.

"Didn't Rose throw the necklace from the rear of the *Titanic* in the movie?" Galen glanced around the space. "This exhibit has no stern," he said. "Now what?"

Brock took an about face and led us to the bow.

Kindra rushed to the railing and stood in the triangular space, leaning forward, and lifting her arms as if she were a bird. "Someone, take a photo please."

Brock snapped the picture and five phones beeped with an incoming text.

"Thanks. Couldn't we just as easily attach our Gem of the Ocean to the bow as the stern?"

"Then the best combination for the last two legs of the cache would be the logbook that should take us to the bow where they find the pendant and the final answer," Lorelei said, pleased.

"Let's aim for four segments." Lorelei jotted notes again. "Ms. Wilk, what could we use to encode the information?"

"An Ottendorf cipher uses text to direct the searcher by page, paragraph, line, word number, or whatever path you devise, to identify the important characters in a message." We passed by the first-class dining hall and a menu hung in a plexiglass case on the wall. We stopped. "For instance, if we wanted to tell someone to go to the gift shop, we could find the letters to spell out the words and leave a numeric description of their placement."

Lorelei counted down to the fourth line, over to the third word, and pointed out the fourth letter. "G." She started over and counted down eight lines, hovered over the first word, and indicated three letters into the word. "I." "We could use the description of Honour and Glory to spell out 'bridge,' and from there 'bow.' The visitors wouldn't need to use GPS devices indoors."

Brock said, "Our cache description could say the coordinates take you to the front door. Let's get a GPS reading right outside. Once inside, we could list the ordered pairs or triplets from the signage to go anywhere in the exhibit."

His four friends stared at him.

"Wow," Galen teased. "Who knew there was a brain in there?" He wrapped his arm around his friend's neck and rubbed his knuckles on Brock's head. Both laughed.

We entered the gift shop. Galen checked out the T-shirts and sweatshirts. Lorelei ran her fingers over the titles on the bookcase. Brock picked up a *Titanic* model kit. Kindra and Carlee examined the necklaces, puzzling out a way to include the answer to our cache question on the Gem of the Ocean.

"Ms. Wilk, we could stick the answer to the back of the pendant." Kindra held the beautiful blue stone in her hand and picked up a second. Her eyes lit up with an idea.

"Or we could hinge two pendants together, back-to-back, to look like a locket. Then the two sides would hide the solution for a little while."

Carlee and Lorelei nodded so enthusiastically I thought something might fall off.

We paid for our purchases and exited, and the GPS units came out to map our location at the entry. They each cited the latitude and longitude, and Lorelei wrote down their observations.

The wooden rack attached to the wall at the entrance displayed pamphlets dedicated to areas of interest in the exhibit.

"The coordinates will bring the cacher here, and they will see the leaflets. We can identify the pamphlet describing Honour and Glory, using an ordered pair. Seventh column, second row. That would take them to the clock. Let's pretend we're doing the cache now," said Carlee.

Lorelei grabbed the brochure. We reentered the exhibit and Derek waved us through. After locating the clock, we found letters in the signage to spell out 'bridge.' When we stood in the bridge area, we mimed signing the logbook and deciphered the next location.

"I like it," said Lorelei.

"Me, too," said Kindra.

"I'll get a school van tomorrow."

Carlee grabbed my arm and swung me around. She wanted me to pay attention to something.

I held up one finger. "Just one moment. We've almost got the cache together. Kindra, you're going to create the necklace containing the answer and provide a stand. Lorelei, you and Brock finish decorating the logbook which will include the final question and instructions to find the solution. Carlee, if you and Galen would write up the cache, I think we'll have everything ready for tomorrow. We'll meet in my room after school, and I can drive us all to the history center."

I rounded the corner and ran into a black T-shirt covered chest.

"Excuse me," I said. "It's so quiet I didn't know anyone else was visiting." I looked up.

I stared at Pete Erickson's dimple. Susie Kelton had her arm threaded through his. She flipped her chestnut hair over her shoulder. "We're not visiting. We're working."

"Oh, no! What happened?" My mind focused on his job as county coroner.

A huff escaped Susie's perfectly made-up face. "We're looking at wedding venues."

My face got warm. Carlee said in an exasperated voice, "Ms. Wilk, I have to get home now."

"Gotta run when duty calls." I waved and pivoted toward the door. It was only when the chill buffeted my nose and cheeks that I remembered we all drove separately. Dear, sweet Carlee.

CHAPTER SIXTEEN

Dad left a maddening short message on the kitchen table: WENT TO SEE ELIZABETH. BACK SOON.

How? With whom? For how long? Why? I hated not knowing the specifics. I left for school before he got up this morning and I already missed his sometimes irascible, sometimes understanding, sometimes snarky, always unpredictable character. Given enough time, I'd probably miss his cooking. I punched in his number. The phone rang from his room.

He broke promise number one already, I thought.

I knocked on Ida's door. No answer. I punched in Ida's phone number. It went to voicemail.

"Hi, Ida. I hope Dad is with you. His insufficient message has me wondering. Call me, please."

I hadn't heard any more about McCall's murder, but Ida hadn't yet been cleared. Who else would've had it in for him? His assistant? The history director? The lady trying to sneak a peek at the encaustic? His ex?

My stomach growled. I opened a frozen dinner and set the microwave for six minutes. After cooking, it could sit for another few minutes, so I grabbed Maverick's leash and we jogged around the block.

The welcoming Italian aroma made my mouth water. I opened the microwave door and took out my supper but before I could close the door, Maverick lapped up the tasty marinara that had spattered the interior.

"Off, Maverick." I guarded my dinner from his long tongue maneuvers while I retrieved his kibble. Then I sat down next to him with my bowl of pasta.

My charging phone chimed from the counter.

Ida sent an eight-word text: YOUR DAD IS WITH ME. BACK TOMORROW. LOVE. I knew where, with whom, and how. I'd ferret out the why when they returned.

Dad's measured recovery from his traumatic brain injury left a few lingering discrepancies between the dad of my youth and the dad of today. I loved having him here, but I worried about him every day. Elizabeth never cooked but I'd looked forward to holiday meals filled with Dad's juicy grilled meats, roasted veggies, marinated fruits, multi-textured salads, fanciful beverages, and sweets fit for a confectionary, but now he cooked like me.

Dad exercised religiously, swimming and spinning at the Y, attending during daylight hours when he could catch a ride with Ida or me, call for a ride, or walk. He even accompanied Ida to dance. Every day he made progress.

With Dad in Ida's capable hands tonight, my shoulders relaxed, and my mind drifted to calmer waters. I donned a pair of hot-pink flannel pajamas and stretched out on the sofa. Maverick crawled next to me; his head flopped onto my lap. I rubbed his velvety ears and fell asleep.

Maverick's barking compounded by a loud rapping and yelling woke me. The hackles on Maverick's neck stood at attention. I pulled him away from the back door and peered through the frosted window.

A square-jawed man stood on the landing, screaming obscenities, and rattling the handle. "It's freezing out here. Lemme in, you old crone. You got no right to lock me out of the house." He slurred his words.

The knob shook as he jammed a key into the deadbolt. I held the thumb turn with both hands, bowed my head, and prayed.

"Get your hands off the deadbolt." He slowly spoke each word with a low snarl.

My heart leaped to my throat.

He shook the knob again, then stopped. The man swore and I heard him bang down the steps. I grabbed my phone from the countertop and punched 911 before clutching the dead bolt again.

"What's the nature of your emergency?"

"Someone's trying to break in," I whispered.

"Address?"

"Three one four one North Maple Street. Hurry, please."

The wood creaked. My shoulder felt a thud. He'd come back.

Maverick bark louder. I squeezed my eyes shut and gripped the lever as the man scraped his way up to the door. He pounded and kicked at the toe plate. I pulled myself into a ball. It seemed like he sagged against the door and slid down, out of sight. The intermittent pounding continued but it came as if an afterthought.

My mouth dried up, but before the tears fell, a woman's voice ordered, "Get up, Jordan. You're not even at the right house."

"Huh? What? Auntie Grace." A male voice whined contritely. The rest of the words were unintelligible. He thumped against the door and the knob jiggled as he seemed to lift himself. Then I heard nothing.

I waited. I stood, lifted the corner of the blue gingham curtain, and peeked out the window. The underdressed husky man wobbled on the landing, then stumbled down the steps, clasping a lightweight jacket over his chest, and tottered after Miss Grace down the driveway, patting a messy head of hair.

Maverick licked my hand.

"Good boy," I said and then he stood on his hind legs, put his forepaws on my shoulders and launched at my face. I almost toppled and couldn't contain my giggles as his rough tongue lapped my cheeks and ears. "Maverick."

I never fully understood if, when I treated his eventual good behavior landing on all four paws, was I reinforcing his recent bad behavior of standing up on his hind legs? Would he remember both actions? I certainly did. I reached for his treats anyway.

"Thanks for the heads up. Your alarm system is quite ingenious. But as for—"

A siren increased its volume four-fold when it turned onto our driveway and headlights bounced into the backyard. I glanced at the clock. Twelve twenty-five. Then I looked down at my attire and clutched the buttons in front. I snatched a puffy thermal jacket from the hook by the door, threw it over my shoulders, and shoved my arms in before the knock sounded.

I sent Maverick to his kennel and opened the door.

His right hand stopped in midair, clenching a glove. Ronnie Christianson stood, poised to knock again. "Katie, we received a report of a possible break in, but all looks pretty quiet to me." Ronnie took one look at me and rolled his eyes.

Before I could come up with a retort, I noticed the key stuck in the lock.

"A man tried to break in." I pointed to the key. "I held the dead bolt on my side, and he yelled at me to let go. He sounded drunk. But then Miss Grace arrived, and he followed her home. I guess she knows him."

"Who else has a key?"

"My dad and Ida," I said. I leaned forward for a better look at the key in the door. "I don't have a Yale lock."

"How long has this guy been gone?" Ronnie said. He jostled the key and removed it—without gloves. There went any fingerprints. My breath hitched.

Ronnie frowned at my reaction. I dropped my eyes and concentrated on my cold bare toes. "He left right after I called."

Ronnie's voice took on a slight edge. "Our response time holds records, Katie."

"It's only been a few minutes. Anyway, I think he might have been Miss Grace's visiting relative." I looked up, waiting for a reaction.

Ronnie's left eyebrow flew to his sparse hairline. He leaned back and rested his arms over his stomach.

"Ida and Dad met him last night. Just before you arrived, Miss Grace claimed him." Ronnie seemed to think I might be fabricating a story.

"I'd like to talk to Ida and your dad." He scratched his cheek.

"They're not here."

Ronnie sniggered.

"You know it's not like that."

"Where are they?"

I didn't know if Ida had received orders from Ronnie not to leave the area and searched for a truthful answer that wouldn't disclose her absence and get her in trouble when Maverick rattled his kennel. Ronnie's hand fell to his sidearm and he looked toward the sound.

"That's Maverick," I said quickly.

Ronnie exhaled.

"Could you check on Miss Grace, please? She shouldn't have been out in this frigid weather and the guy seemed pretty out of it."

Ronnie regarded me casually. "Right." The way he said it, the word had three syllables. He tossed the key and grabbed it in midair. "I'll just do that."

He tipped his hat. "Goodnight, Katie."

I secured the door behind him and opened the kennel. It was Maverick and me against the world tonight.

My bedroom was a long way up the stairs and Maverick had already curled up on the couch. I joined him, pulled a well-worn quilt over my shoulders, hunkered down, and closed my eyes, but I kept wondering who would want Phillip McCall dead. Brock said he was grumpy. He had words with his assistant. His wife wasn't in the picture. And the stunt he pulled at the gala almost backfired. I tried to keep my ears open for the rest of the night, but I never heard more from Ronnie.

I must have dozed. I missed the sun's first peek at the day.

CHAPTER SEVENTEEN

I fetched the school van keys from Mrs. McEntee and, when I rounded the corner to my classroom, found Kindra, Lorelei, and Brock crowded around a desk, heads bent together, engrossed in the task in front of them.

"What's going on?" I asked.

Kindra jumped. Something dropped and clattered off the desktop onto the floor. She scooped it up and handed it to me, then looked down at her shoes.

Crystal-clear stones glinted around the shimmering blue hearts. She waited patiently as I turned the pendant over in my hand, assessed its heft, tested the chain, and examined it for our answer. A hinge held two identical charms together. When I unfastened the clip on the unhinged side, it opened like a locket, and I found our numeric solution etched in script onto one of the backs.

"This is gorgeous. Where did you learn how to do this?"

Kindra shrugged. "We all have hidden talents, don't we? The box with the stand is in the office." She glanced at the clock. "I've got to get going. I work at four." She hefted her backpack onto her shoulder. "Have fun and let me know how it all turns out." She waved and disappeared around the corner.

Then I oohed over the logbook. Lorelei and Brock finished the cover by burning the outline of small ocean waves, sea birds, a distant ship, and a fin-sporting marine creature. I ran my fingertip along the edge of the pages.

"Gold spray paint," said Lorelei.

"Very effective."

They glowed.

"I think the director is going to be thrilled." I checked the time. "We need to be on the road soon."

The air pressure changed as the door to the math commons opened and closed.

"Here come Carlee and Galen." Lorelei wrapped the logbook in bubble wrap to safeguard in her backpack. Brock placed the pendant in a blue mesh bag, slid it alongside the logbook, and fitted the buckles.

The five of us traipsed through the quiet halls with happy feet, eager to share our new-found hobby.

The boys stopped in the office and hauled Kindra's wooden box out the front doors to the circle drive and the school van. In her haste, Carlee slipped on the top step, tripped, and tumbled over her ankle. She cried out. Galen dropped his half of the carton and rushed up the flight.

Tears spilled down her cheeks. When Galen tried to lift her, she yelped.

He knelt next to her. "What can I do?" He looked as though he might cry with her.

"Lorelei, see if the nurse is still in house. Brock, run down to the athletic office. They always have ice in their freezer. Grab a bag. Galen, call Carlee's dad."

Galen stared at Carlee.

"Galen," I said again.

He pulled out his phone and punched a key. "Dr. Bluestone? Galen." He listened. "Carlee fell at school, and I think she's going to need to have her ankle looked at." He listened again. "I'll have her at the front door."

"Carlee," he said gently. "Your dad's coming. He'll meet us here and take you to get your ankle looked at."

She bit her bottom lip. She'd been known to argue on occasion but accepted what Galen told her without a peep.

With a door bang, Brock rushed out with an ice pack and Velcro strapping. He knelt in front of her.

"Well, Cinderella?" He elicited a tiny smile and Carlee sniffed.

"Be careful," Galen warned.

"I've done this way too often," Brock said, his head bent to the task at hand.

With a gentleness I didn't see coming, he secured the ice with the strap. Brock and I helped her to her feet and Galen swept her into his arms and up to the vestibule. We followed to make sure she made it safely but there was no doubt Galen would make certain Carlee would be well taken care of.

I grabbed a chair and slid it near the door. Galen settled Carlee in it, keeping his eyes peeled on the drive-through. Lorelei glanced at her watch and whispered to Brock. He made a phone call while we waited.

CJ pulled in front of the double doors and jolted to a

stop. He unfolded his long lean frame and bounded from the truck with only a trace of a limp. If I hadn't known him, his fierceness would have frightened me.

CJ married his childhood sweetheart before they finished high school. He found his calling as a Navy SEAL. During his second year of deployment, the love of his life, Danica, died giving birth to his daughter, never having told him she was expecting. If it hadn't been for his homemade engagement gift, a lapis lazuli pendant, he might have gone his whole life not knowing his daughter. CJ and Carlee met two months ago. Now CJ filled his time learning the ropes of parenting and Carlee relished building a life with her father. To my disappointment, he put all other relationships on hold for the time being. Not that *we* had a relationship, but he would make someone a great catch.

In addition to practicing veterinary medicine, CJ trained search-and-rescue dogs and worked greenhorn Maverick's tail off. CJ occupied a throne in my heart and when Ronnie Christianson had accused him of murder, I'd worked my tail off to find the real killer.

I shook my head as he gently lifted Carlee from the plastic chair and whisked her out to his chariot as her father-knight in shining armor.

Galen looked lost.

Brock jostled his friend out of his reverie. "I changed our appointment to four fifteen. Are you coming?"

Galen nodded, dazed.

"Good. Then you can help me carry Kindra's things." He sighted down his pointer finger to Kindra's contribution.

Galen and Brock finished loading the wooden stand and we piled into the school van. As the engine sputtered to life, Jane crashed through the front door, waving her gloved hand. Her quilted white coat flapped behind her like a pair of angel wings. She ripped open the passenger door, panting. "Do you have room for one more?"

"Get in," I said.

Lorelei and Brock jabbered through every mile. They read the description aloud, asked for comments, and penciled in possible answers to questions the director might have. Jane complimented them on their ingenious puzzle and the intricate detail of the log cover, but when Brock showed her the necklace, her squeal nearly had me driving into the ditch.

"I love lockets. Who made this?" Jane asked.

"It's Kindra's masterpiece. Did you find the answer?" asked Galen, a smile edging onto the corner of his mouth as he awakened to her excitement.

It opened under her gentle ministrations, and she cooed. "This is ingenious. What's the question again?"

"How many bodies were recovered from the *Titanic*?" Galen said.

"Over fifteen hundred souls perished, and they only brought back three hundred thirty-four bodies?"

Galen focused on Jane. "No," he said slowly. "They recovered three hundred thirty-four bodies but transported only two hundred nine to Halifax. The other casualties were too badly damaged or decomposed and they ran out of resources, so they were buried at sea. Fifty-nine bodies were claimed and buried somewhere other than Halifax. They think they've identified all but forty and using DNA, they're still checking. First class victims had a better chance of being retrieved and buried on land than second and third class. Inequality lingered even in death."

Jane sighed. As a history major and *Titanic* buff, she probably knew all of that as well as how many jars of strawberry preserves they carted on the inaugural crossing, the scent of the hand soap in first-class, and the paint color of the walls in Captain Smith's private quarters.

"Did you talk to Ronnie?" I asked.

"Tell you later," Jane said through gritted teeth.

We arrived with four minutes to spare, and our van was the only vehicle in the parking lot. The students carried the handheld GPS units, and Jane and I used our smart phones. We entered the coordinates Brock dictated and, fortunately, they all pointed us in the same direction. Then he read what they would post for this geocache.

"So far, so good," Brock said. We stood in front of a wooden pamphlet rack. He stamped the snow from his boots. "Ms. Mackey, your hint is Seven Two."

Jane looked around. There weren't too many choices. She counted seven columns to the right and two rows down in the information rack and grabbed a trifold labeled Honour and Glory. So far, so good.

We tramped up the replicated gangplank, through a mural of waving well-wishers, amid a recording of a bustling crowd, a busy pier, and boat whistles, and landed in front of an unmanned ticket booth. Galen tugged on the door to the exhibit.

"It's locked."

Brock pulled out his phone. While he waited for an answer, Lorelei explained the cipher and how to use text to glean the position of the remaining parts of our multicache.

"Our ordered triples indicate the paragraph, word, and letter. When we stand in front of the timepiece, you'll figure it out."

"No answer," Brock said. He slid his phone into his pants pocket. "It's four fifteen now. Can we give her a few minutes?"

CHAPTER EIGHTEEN

The sub-zero wind howled through the entry doors as they swung open behind us.

"Sorry, sorry." A tall, broad-shouldered woman marched up the ramp. She wore a black suit, a crisp white shirt, and a blue chiffon scarf knotted at her neck. Her black brogues slapped the pavement as she raced up the incline, jangling keys in her hand. The stark red lipstick popped in her pale face framed by a short, black bob. "My receptionist called in sick and the board president was absent, so the meeting lasted longer than expected. Brock?" She thrust her hand out to Galen. He shook it but nodded at the only other possibility in the vestibule.

"I'm Brock Isaacson." Brock stepped forward and offered his hand. She held on an extra, seemingly uncomfortable, moment. Brock withdrew his fingers. "Mrs. Nygren, this is our instructor, Ms. Katherine Wilk."

So formal, I thought. Mrs. Nygren tipped her head.

"And Ms. Mackey," he said.

Mrs. Nygren raised an eyebrow.

Brock pointed. "Lorelei Calder."

"Pleased to meet you," Lorelei said, juggling a sheaf of papers and her backpack.

"And you've met Galen."

"Yes, yes. Again, I apologize. We now have real money for an actual budget and some of the board members got carried away today with wild ways to spend the windfall." She unlocked the door. "I thought we'd meet on the smoking lounge stage. Follow me. Follow me."

Brock and Galen exchanged puzzled glances behind her.

Our footsteps reverberated in the empty exhibit, an unnerving echo from times past. Mrs. Nygren led our small entourage to an impressive meeting room. We crowded at one end of a twelve-foot oval mahogany table surrounded by chocolate-brown leather desk chairs. The elaborate wall carvings and crown moldings lent an air of historical significance. Soft yellow light emanated from the ornamental sconces, reflecting off a buffed floor ornately designed in black-and-white tile. The rumbling water cooler and desk holding a computer and printer looked decidedly out of place.

"Sit. Sit." She swept into the chair at the head of the table. "Give me more of your marvelous marketing spin."

Brock reddened.

Lorelei shifted her pack onto the floor, extracted pages from a manila folder, and handed them around the table. "This is a copy of what would appear on the geocaching webpage with the title, attributes, description, and a vital hint."

"Explain, again, what a geocache is? Never heard of it. Never."

All three students said simultaneously, "A high-tech scavenger hunt," and laughed.

Brock spun a great promotional yarn.

Mrs. Nygren chewed the end of her pen. Her brow furrowed and her chair squeaked when she bent forward and said, "Take me through this geo-thing."

"If you let us set it up, we can do a walk through."

"Yes. Yes." She clasped her hands together like a tot seeing Santa for the first time. Mrs. Nygren rose quickly, and her chair rolled away from the table, slamming into the computer desk, and jostling the contents. A cup holding office supplies spilled across the top. "Sorry, sorry. This sounds fun." She didn't look like she was having fun as she shoved the pens, pencils, scissors, and other desk paraphernalia back into place.

Brock gave the go ahead and Galen, Lorelei, and Jane disappeared into the exhibit to set up the last two stages.

Brock pulled up the location and demonstrated the use of the GPS from under the eave at the entrance in front of the brochures. He said, "What could you do with a seven and a two standing here?"

We backed away.

Mrs. Nygren looked up at the entrance sign and down at the welcome mat. She cocked her head while reading the sign on the door. Then she pointed to the correct trifold. Brock smiled.

"Location. Location," she said and barreled into the exhibit, correctly following the clues to the clock and the bridge where she signed the log. She read the entry and found the letters, "B. O. W."

She frowned. "The instructions say to get credit for the cache, you have to submit the answer to the question 'How many bodies were recovered from the sea after the *Titanic* tragedy?' How do you log the cache?"

"There are millions of geocaches all over the world and you can log your finds online at the game site." Brock had done his homework.

"What do you think so far, Mrs. Nygren?" I asked.

She rocked in place. "Great, great."

As we trekked toward the bow, Brock defined the quest. "Geocaching is a recreational activity that usually takes you to surprising places. Sometimes you learn something new. Sometimes you can trade trinkets or pick up a travel bug. Once, there was a Kennedy half-dollar. I traded a penny and made forty-nine cents."

Mrs. Nygren stopped short, and if she hadn't erupted in a belly laugh, I'd have thought we were in trouble.

We stepped onto a deck cooled to emulate the frigid temperature the night of the sinking. I scanned the water, searching for floating mannequins. We rounded the corner and Galen and Lorelei stood against the far wall. Mrs. Nygren stepped into the niche where the starboard and port railings met. She closed her eyes and struck a pose, tall and regal. When she opened her eyes, she grasped the rail and hunted.

"This is new." She pulled on a sturdy chain wrapped around the intersecting rails at the point of the bow. At the end hung the shiny blue pendant.

"Gem of the Ocean. Gem of the Ocean," she said with appreciation in her voice.

She turned it over and tipped her head. Then she flipped it from one hand to the other and stopped to scrutinize the edges. Her face relaxed and she peeled the stones apart. A smile stretched across her face.

"Three hundred thirty-four." She squinted and checked the number. "That can't be right."

"It is." Lorelei stood taller. They'd found a fact that even baffled the director.

"Brock?" Mrs. Nygren sought a second opinion.

I almost didn't notice Lorelei's shoulders sag. Checking up on her stung, I could tell.

"True, true," he said.

Jane rolled her eyes.

"Well, well," said Mrs. Nygren. "I like it. I give my permission to do your thing."

Galen said, "We'll get the listing online and running—"

Lorelei finished, "We'll let you know."

CHAPTER NINETEEN

Typical of Minnesota winters, unpredicted snowflakes flitted through the headlights. When the weather hovered at freezing, slippery patches of black ice could show up on the roadway at any time. I tested the brakes with a light tap and a red car peeled by. Our headlights barely caught its Lexus emblem.

Jane blustered. "Idiot driver!"

I slowed even more.

Jane inhaled. "Ronnie claims the destruction of the wreath is a misdemeanor, probably done by kids." I strained to hear her soft voice. "An investigation isn't worth the time and manpower that he needs to take care of real crimes."

"Does he think your break-in is a misdemeanor too?"

"They have my statement. Maybe the miscreants

thought there was something of real value trussed up on the Styrofoam. Even my ring didn't add much to the value of the theft."

She sniffed. "I don't think it was kids, Katie. Ronnie's just such an—" She gasped. "Look out!"

The voices in the van went silent.

Brake lights flared in front of us and swerved, then twisted and spun. When the dancing ceased, the lights beamed at an odd angle, flickered, and went out. I crept closer, swallowed hard, and willed my heartbeat to slow down.

Jane punched in three numbers on her phone. "A car slid off the road at …" She leaned forward as we neared the small green indicator. "… mile marker thirty-seven on county road four." I heard mumbling on the other end. "I don't know if an ambulance is needed. You'll stay on the line? We'll be there in seconds."

I rolled to a stop and put on the emergency flashers. An eerie glow illuminated the kids' faces, eyes wide, mouths agape. "Stay here," I cautioned releasing my seat belt. Jane nodded a 'let's do this' and we opened the doors.

The front of the car had speared a pile of snow and the rear bumper hung onto a slim patch of pavement, rocking precariously. The dark-red car's wheels spun over the narrow ditch, unable to make purchase.

As Jane reached for the driver's door, the engine revved and I yanked her back. She dropped her phone and scrambled to dig it out before it was swallowed by the soft snow. "Hello," she said, brushing snow from the mouthpiece. "I don't know if anyone is hurt. The car is stuck, and we haven't been able to see inside yet." She listened. "Yes, please send help."

The front door of the car creaked and a round bundle tumbled out and dropped to the ground.

"Stupid car." The driver aimed a foot at the wheels and Jane pulled her away. "What do you think you're doing?" The driver yanked her arm out of Jane's grip.

Jane's hands went up in surrender. "The car might fall if you upset the balance. Be careful. Did you leave it running?"

A pale face, wrinkled like an apple-doll, leered out from under a black fur hat. Angry words erupted from the vermillion lipstick slash at her mouth. "That's no business of yours and keep your hands to yourself."

Jane stepped up to the roadbed and continued her phone conversation.

"We called for help," I said. I recognized the rotund woman from the gala, the one trying to sneak a peek at the encaustic that wasn't there.

Her glare forced me to start back up the hill.

"Where do you think you're going? Get me out of here," she ordered. In my haste to obey, I slipped down the ditch. My boots collided with her footwear somewhere under the snow. She landed on top of me.

"You clumsy—" Before she finished her outburst, our two young men lifted her and guided her over the snow. Lorelei gave me a hand up.

"Thanks." We followed their footprints out of the ditch.

Brock and Galen flanked the woman who sat in the back seat of the van, her hands braced on the frame. She was no Cinderella, but Brock replaced her shoe anyway. I swallowed a chuckle. Galen brushed at the snow on the arm of her coat.

"Are you sure you don't need an ambulance?" Jane asked. "They can send one along with the tow truck."

The face seethed behind puckered lips and squinty eyes. "I don't need an ambulance." She caught Lorelei gazing at her. "Girl, what are you looking at?"

Lorelei was fast on her feet. "I-I'm admiring your beautiful coat. Mink, isn't it? The headwrap matches perfectly." Brock's mouth fell open and Galen stifled a snort. Lorelei championed all creatures and loathed fur but conjured up an Oscar-worthy actress gene, playing the part we needed to keep the peace.

"Yes, they do. Thank you for noticing." The woman's supercilious tone softened. "You have exquisite taste. What's your name, girl?" She patted the seat next to her. Lorelei crawled over the bulky passenger and sat.

"I'm Lorelei Calder. And these are my classmates, Brock Isaacson and Galen Tonnenson. Ms. Mackey is our history teacher." Jane nodded. "Ms. Wilk—"

"Yes. Yes." The woman waved in exasperation and pointed at Jane. "You there," she said. "How long before they'll be here with assistance?"

Jane caught herself before her eyes rolled any farther when she realized the driver deigned to include her in the conversation. "Fifteen minutes, Miss ..."

"Daniella Jericho." She raised her head and two of her chins disappeared. So did a few of her wrinkles. "Close that door, young man. It's freezing." She batted her eyelashes, blinking weird smoke signals in baby blue eye shadow. My stomach churned.

As the door clunked across the track, Brock raised his eyebrows. The door trapped Lorelei inside. Galen barked a laugh and Jane and I joined him.

"Poor Lorelei," said Brock, his face contorting as he tried not to smile.

Galen's phone dinged. His laugh stopped in his throat as he read a text. "Dr. Bluestone says it's a comminuted fracture." Confusion filled his face. "She broke multiple bones and needs surgery."

Brock's phone dinged. "It's my mom." He moved behind the van to return her call.

Jane's phone dinged. She smiled. "It's Drew." She stepped to the front of the van and put the phone to her ear.

I stamped numbness from my feet and willed my phone to make a sound. I patted and rubbed heat into my arms. I stepped from one foot to the other and pulled out my phone, but it still didn't ring.

When the strobing lights of the tow truck and a police car pulled up behind the van, the door slid open, and Ms. Jericho pivoted in the seat. She extended her gloved hand to Galen who assisted her as she stepped down.

All cooing smiles, she addressed the police officer appraising the predicament facing her car. "I simply don't know what happened officer."

We could tell him what happened.

She turned to us. "Thank you, dears."

Where did that come from?

"I've got this now." She took the officer's arm and gushed. "My, what strong arms you have!" I think Red Riding Hood's wolf got a bum steer.

Jane's eyes grew large. Galen wiped the smirk off his face with his mittened hand. Lorelei shook her head. I threw a questioning look at the officer. He took down Jane's phone number, checking it against the call collected by dispatch and said, "I know how to get hold of you. It's cold and getting colder. Go ahead and get out of the snow. But be careful. We've been to several pileups in the last half hour."

* * *

Ida's decorations pulsed like a homing beacon. Light beamed from every window, flashing trapezoids on the snow like animated boxes.

I bounced over ice chunks up the driveway. I couldn't wait to see how Dad's trip went.

A crisp layer of frost covered the steps. I gripped the railing and took one stair at a time, hauling myself closer to the doorknob, mentally itemizing points to talk over with Dad and Ida.

A biting wind wound around my neck and down my back. I shuddered. The door flew open in front of me. I slipped and jerked one way as Dad said, "Hi, darlin'."

My feet slid out from under me. My hands slapped the icy pavement and I landed in a heap. More embarrassed than hurt, I waved Dad off. "I'm okay. And thank goodness you're here." I crawled back to the top step. Dad held the door and I rolled inside, laughing and crying at the same time.

"Katie?" Ida stood at the sink, drying dishes. The look on her face shifted from concern to relief. "How are the roads?"

"They're pretty iffy. We met with Mrs. Nygren at the history center, and she's going to allow us to place a geocache in the *Titanic* exhibit."

Ida tsked.

"What's wrong?" I removed my heavy winter gear.

"She chaired the board meeting today and her micromanagement skills rubbed everyone the wrong way. I should've been there." Ida leaned against the counter and in her most disapproving voice said, "I received four testy phone calls and one grouchy voicemail on our way home. Yvonne means well, but her financial acumen leaves a lot to be desired. She has no idea what's needed to create a sound budget.

"We've operated on a shoestring with no extra funds. Now that there's a little money, she doesn't seem to want to spend any of it. But as a non-profit, we need to have a solid plan, invest in our information technology, and build a robust infrastructure." She'd rotated a Dutch oven in her dish towel, drying it for the duration of her tirade. I took the cookware from her hands and tucked it away on the shelf above the refrigerator. "Thank you, dear. I knew you were good for something." She and Dad shared a hoot. "Yvonne even brought up the idea of estate planning for those of us on the board, expecting us to name the history center as a beneficiary. That's not a bad idea, except her approach was tactless. She has promised to secure future gifts from a couple of sources." She exhaled, crumpled the dish towel, and set it on the counter.

I picked up the towel, refolded it into a neat rectangle, and lined it up parallel to the sink. Bad habit.

Dad poured a bottle of red wine into a decanter on the counter and removed two glasses from the cupboard. He reached for a third, but I shook my head.

"Soup? Hot chocolate?" Ida asked, busying herself at the stove.

"Sure. Thanks."

When she turned back to me, she crossed her arms. "You look like you're ready to burst. Out with it."

"On our way home, we witnessed an accident on the county road between Columbia and the history center. A fancy car whizzed past us, driven by a maniac, and plowed into a snowbank in a ditch right in front of us. No one was hurt but Daniella Jericho is some piece of work."

"That doesn't cover the half of it." Ida snorted.

Dad's eyes bounced back and forth between us.

"She's got a bit of money and thinks she's better than everyone else. But I'll say this for her. She doesn't like coming in second. Her after-event donation rivaled Grace's and will go a long way to provide educational opportunities at the center for visitors of the student persuasion. I still credit Grace with leading the way to record-breaking philanthropy earmarked for the children at the hospital."

My face crumpled.

"What?" she said, her brows furrowing.

"Carlee's a patient there."

"What happened?"

"She fell and broke her ankle and needs surgery, but her dad …" My voice hitched saying those two words. "*Her dad* told us she should be fine."

She handed me a cup of something warm and directed me to the table. Dad pulled out my chair and I sat. "Thanks."

I took a sip of the beverage and sighed. Hot chocolate spiked with a touch of Bailey's warmed me from the inside out. I sipped slowly. I could only have one. I had to teach in the morning.

A bowl of her butternut squash soup landed in front of me. I took three greedy spoonfuls, then said, "How did it go with Elizabeth?"

CHAPTER TWENTY

A strange look passed between Dad and Ida, but before
I could ask what that meant, the doorbell dinged.
Maverick barked and lunged toward the entry. I nabbed his
collar and whispered. "Quiet."

"I'll get it," Ida said.

I scratched under Maverick's collar, and he leaned in
for more. Then he laid down at my feet and put his head on
his paws, but his eyes darted between me and the doorway.

Cold air preceded the caller Ida dragged into the
kitchen. "This is a pleasant surprise." She plunked the
man into a chair at the table and said, "Coffee, tea, or …"
She shifted her eyes to the decanter. "… something else
entirely."

"Got a beer?"

When he removed his knitted cap and unleashed an untidy head of hair, I sucked in a breath. The cup of hot chocolate sloshed on its way to my lips. Maverick's head came up. Last evening's late-night visitor sat at my kitchen table. At least I wasn't alone this time.

I petted Maverick. He relaxed a smidge.

"Meet Jordan Quintz." Ida pulled a can from the fridge. Jordan nodded. "This is Harry's daughter, Katie."

"My Auntie said I owe you an apology." His eyes searched Ida's face.

"I can't imagine why." Ida inclined her head toward me as she poured more wine. "Katie?"

Jordan looked warily at Maverick and then from Ida to Dad to me. "This your place?"

I nodded and got a good look at his face. His itty bitty pale gray eyes sat atop a plump bed of cheeks flushed bright red. His thin dry lips turned down before disappearing altogether. Mousy hair, with a mind of its own, circled his face and his dark eyebrows crawled across his forehead. Okay, I was being petty, but he'd scared the bejeezus out of me and I wasn't inclined to be complimentary.

Ida handed Dad a glass of wine and set a can of Surley in front of Jordan. I took a sip of chocolate to calm my nerves although I knew it was probably the smooth Bailey's providing the warmth and relaxation.

"I'm sorry if I caused you any trouble." His recitation sounded rehearsed. He popped the top on the can and took a long swig.

Ida raised her head. "What trouble?"

"Auntie Grace went ballistic when you didn't come for supper." He took another huge gulp. More likely, she'd needed the distraction of her friends to bolster her courage and cover the awkwardness of having someone she scarcely knew stay with her.

"I left you a message with our regrets—" Ida began.

"I might have forgotten to pass along the message." His voice sounded as whiny as it had when Miss Grace had hauled him home last evening. "So, I went out."

"What are you babbling about?" Ida's fists went to her hips.

At least he had the wherewithal to look embarrassed. "They make great margaritas at that Mexican joint, and I had a few. I got a little mixed up when I came home last night. Every yard around here looks the same covered in snow. I thought this was Auntie Grace's place." He nodded at my door. "When my key didn't work, I might've seemed frustrated."

Downright nasty, more like it.

His right hand snaked across the table. "No hard feelings?" He waggled his fingers.

Dad's admonition to 'forgive and forget' pounded in my head as three pairs of eyes locked on me. I relented and leaned forward.

A grin flashed across his face. "I wouldn't want to upset my new neighbors before ever setting up shop." My hand halted on its way across the table, but it was close enough for him to grab and crunch my fingers. "Thanks. Auntie Grace will be happy to know you've accepted my apology."

"I didn't know there were any homes for sale in this neighborhood," I said, massaging my knuckles. Maverick's head came up again.

"I'm not buying. I'm moving in with Auntie Grace."

"Oh," Ida said.

Jordan glanced at the clock, threw back the last of his

beer, and rose. "Gotta run."

He disappeared in another blast of arctic air and Maverick stood and looked at me as if to say, *Good riddance*.

Ida eyed me suspiciously. "What was that all about?"

My ears grew hot, and my face flushed as I remembered cowering behind the door. "He tried to break in last night. I called the police and Ronnie came. Although he wasn't very helpful, it should be on record. And poor Miss Grace had to haul him home."

Ida's eyes looked like green saucers. The knuckles on Dad's hand went white as he gripped the stem of the goblet.

"It's fine. Really."

Ida's phone buzzed. She checked the screen and her brow furrowed. "It's Phillip's assistant." She pressed a button and answered somberly, "Anita, how are you?" She stepped out of the kitchen.

"Dad, how's Elizabeth?"

I couldn't read him. He examined his hands for an answer. He took a sip of wine then carefully placed the glass within the triangle formed by his thumbs and forefingers. "Ida and I carted home a carful of my belongings."

I glanced around.

He chuckled. "I thought we'd be a little crowded so I offloaded it in Ida's office where it will be out of the way, and I can take time to sort through it." He savored a sip of wine. "It felt like we were severing a business partnership. Elizabeth's so methodical. When I asked her why, she said it was all on her and that I shouldn't concern myself. But Katie, she's no longer the woman I married." He sipped again. "She already has a renter. She'd like me to get everything out as soon as possible."

After a long pause, I asked quietly, "Is there something else going on in her life?"

He shrugged. "She insists it's just work, and we could use a break. Absence makes the heart grow fonder and all that."

Ida bounced back in, her mood brightened a bit. "Anita's been at a self-imposed retreat, remembering Phillip, working, and designing. She had developmental photos of Phillip's pieces and found some canvases of earlier drafts they'd worked on. She's been studying with Phillip for a while, and she thinks she can recreate the piece that Grace purchased." Ida's face lit up. "She wants me to bring my keepsakes over right away so she can get started on my complementary encaustic. Even with the tragedy of his death, she's going to try. Isn't that wonderful?"

I nodded.

"Good. Let's go. We'll take your new car." She marched into her apartment.

"Isn't it a bit late?" I said, and hoped Dad would put a halt to our evening excursion.

"It's Ida, the steamroller." Dad placed his hand over mine. He gazed out the window. "It stopped snowing."

I winked at my dad. "Wanna join us?"

He let go of my hand and grunted. "Not for all the sun in San Diego."

I armed myself against the cold, zipping my jacket and pulling my cap down over my ears. By the time I'd cinched my boots and tugged on my gloves, Ida stood at the door, tapping her foot.

She clutched my arm on our short walk through the fresh, fluffy white wonderland. Yard lights and streetlamps glinted off the crystal carpet, winking like tiny diamonds.

Faint notes of Christmas music lilted from the Farley's house.

We slid into my new wheels, Dad's pride and joy, and rolled onto the street where the glaze of ice sparkled on tree limbs and mailboxes. "Maybe we should wait for better conditions."

"Nonsense."

Nothing moved. We didn't see a vehicle or person or animal. Even the branches were still.

"We could walk faster," Ida said in a teasing voice.

"But not any safer." I gripped the steering wheel so tightly my fingers tingled.

"Take a left." She dictated the turns and we crawled through the empty streets. "Ronnie called with more questions about finding Phillip."

My heart sped up. "What hadn't he already asked?"

"He wanted to know about our teacher-student relationship, what happened at the gala, and why I stopped bidding. He asked if I'd heard any rumors about money Phillip might be coming into. All quite confusing."

We skidded to a stop at the light controlling the last intersection before Anita's house. When I touched the gas pedal, the wheels rotated without gaining traction and the weighty back end swerved. I let up and Ida's head struck the headrest.

"Sorry. Maybe we should turn around."

She shook her head and clenched her box. We both took a deep breath and rolled past the last few houses.

Anita opened a side door, and we entered an enclosure built with tall windows and skylights. The black-haired woman from the gala looked down on Ida. Sturdily built, she had the broad shoulders of a swimmer and the grace of a dancer.

"Who's she?" she asked.

"Katherine Jean Wilk, my driver," Ida said and smiled. "Katie, meet Anita Jones."

Anita sniffed at the hand I offered. I retrieved it, examined it for some sign of its offensiveness, and stepped back. Ida set her box of treasures on the narrow wooden table in the entryway.

"What do you have for me, Ida?" Anita said, pulling on a pair of white cotton gloves and rubbing her hands together.

They hovered for a moment, then Ida opened the lid. Anita clucked and stirred the contents with her finger.

"These are wonderful. You're sure you want to part with them?" For a second, her eyes seemed to blaze with gold.

"Yes. I can't wait to display them in a piece."

Anita drew the delicate fabric and brittle papers from the tin. She extracted the buttons and tugged a jeweler's loupe from her pocket. Closing one eye, she scrutinized each as if it were a gem. She returned one button with a kind of reverence and arranged the rest of the items on a tray.

"Do you really think you can reconstruct the encaustic for Grace?" Ida asked.

Anita nodded. She couldn't tear her eyes away from Ida's mementos.

"That would be wonderful."

"Would you like to see?" She sounded like a little girl looking for approval.

She carried the tray and led us through a maze of easels propping up completed canvases. Anita had learned a lot from Phillip McCall. We stopped in front of one covered by a canvas tarp. Anita set the tray on a worktable. She grabbed the corner of the fabric and flung it over the top, revealing an extremely close reproduction of Miss Grace's encaustic.

"This is one of our original constructs, but I haven't finished building up the levels of wax."

Ida blew out a stream of air. "You've done a beautiful job. It looks exactly like the one at the gala." Ida lifted her chin. "*You* did the one at the gala."

Anita blushed.

"Why would Phillip claim credit for your work?"

"That wasn't his intention. We worked on it together."

I squinted and curious characters took shape, bleeding through the ultra-polished semi-transparent wax, perhaps mapping where embedded items might be placed or a color change could occur. I cocked my head. The lighting shifted and the characters disappeared.

Anita lined up Ida's items on the worktable. "I should have a good start on yours tomorrow as well."

"Anita?" Ida's voice lost some of its cheerfulness. "Who would have wanted Phillip dead?"

"I have absolutely no idea." Her tone had changed too.

Ida blushed. "I didn't mean to insinuate—"

A phone trilled and Anita's hospitality gene shut off. She checked the screen and let it ring as she picked up what looked like a hair dryer and a brass sculpting tool. "I've got work to do. Please show yourselves out."

Ida picked up the tin and the button rattled as she tiptoed toward the door. Neither of them took notice of me. I tilted my head again and caught another glimpse of the curious symbols on the canvas, then turned and slalomed through the labyrinth of art, marveling at the volume of her work.

Ida stood next to the car, bundled against the cold, and gazed into the starless sky, swaying to imagined music. I depressed the unlock button on the fob and, when she didn't move, opened the passenger door for her and guided her to the seat.

The car idled for a moment. I asked, "What's going on?"

Ida shook her head. "Art is a hobby for most of my students, an avocation, and they rarely follow in my footsteps. It's not for lack of talent, but usually economics and motivation. I've applauded all my students and their triumphs in any field, but I understand and am more personally vested in the artists because I recognize the obstacles they face. Bobby worked especially hard and, with his rare gift, succeeded in the art of moviemaking. He accomplished much in his short film career, and his skills at drawing and painting were nothing to scoff at. When we lost him …" Her voice caught. Robert Bruckner's death still knocked the wind out of her. "We lost a role model. He shared his talents and reinvested in our community. Phillip was just getting his wings and hadn't yet learned to share his gifts. Now it's Anita's turn and I hope she follows in Bobby's footsteps. They are all indeed gifted."

"Was Anita also one of your students?"

"No, but I take pride in having taught her teacher."

"You are gifted as well."

She shook her head.

"Your art is hanging all over town."

"I'm fortunate that my paintings have been so graciously accepted, but I'm only a good artist. When I nurtured

Bobby, when I encouraged Phillip, when I support Anita, a piece of me lives on."

She looked out the window. I put the car in gear and Ida hummed carols on our slow drive home.

We stopped in our driveway, delighting in the animated red, blue, green, and gold Christmas lights beaming in ever-changing patterns through her front window.

Then a shadow darted from my kitchen table. *Maverick*!

"Little scamp," Ida said, and a smile stretched across her lips. "Or not so little."

By the time we made it inside, Maverick had nestled in his kennel, acting the perfect puppy.

"Dad," I called. "Dad?"

I might have heard a soft click and checked his bedroom door. Closed—now.

"Chicken," I muttered to myself.

Ida cradled Maverick's face in her hands and gave him one giant smooch. "Goodnight. Sleep tight," she said. She yawned contagiously and waved on her way out.

I could only shake my head. I still had scores to record but instead I wondered what allowing Phillip McCall to take credit for her wonderful art had cost Anita Jones. She was hiding something.

CHAPTER TWENTY-ONE

I kept one ear on my science club students' conversation while I prepped for the next day. The puzzle sounded fun and doable.

"Ms. Wilk?" said Lorelei. "Would you check this out one last time before we publish it?"

I knew there wouldn't be any errors in the geocache post, but I sat at Lorelei's laptop and read the listing, reviewed each word, and referred to my photos, searching as if I were on site at the exhibit.

"Brock?" I asked. He pretended not to hear. "Brock?"

"Brock," Lorelei said with the sharpness of a tack.

"Yes?"

"'Claim a one-dollar rebate on your regular-price ticket when you bring your stub bearing the initials written on the inside cover of the log found at stage three to the gift shop.' Did Mrs. Nygren give you permission?"

His head bobbed up and down. "Yes. Yes," he said impishly. "If someone wants to find the cache, she's up five dollars, and if they don't, she's out nothing. And she said the cacher might buy something at the gift shop or even become a supporter. After we publish the cache, we're heading out there to make sure it all works like we planned. Kindra hasn't seen the finished cache yet, so she'll be our test case."

Lorelei's forefinger hovered over the submit key. Pairs of expectant eyes watched me. I gave the nod as Jane crashed through the door.

"Sorry about that," Jane said, breathing hard. "What's happening?"

"We launched the 'Gem of the Ocean,' and we're going to the exhibit to make sure it all works." Brock beamed.

By the look on Jane's face, I think she had something brewing too.

The kids waved on their way out. I dropped in, and almost out of, the roller chair behind my desk. I thought Jane might laugh, but she was lost in her own world.

"Give," I said.

She slid into the chair next to mine and growled. The look on her face stopped the laugh I might have had. "Christianson returned the pieces of my wreath but because of the value listed on the gala program, he has chosen not to pursue its vandals." She placed air-quotes around 'pursue.' "The destruction at my house and supposed robbery is an open case but in light of his demanding ..." Again, with the air-quotes. "... caseload, it has been relegated to the back burner. And he calls me

Janie. Nobody calls me Janie."

"What does Drew have to say?"

"It's standard operating procedure to prioritize cases, the more serious cases demanding attention and resources, so he started asking around, but his task force commander assigned him a new case today." She snarled.

"What about his leg and crutches?"

"Perfect cover." She crossed her arms. Her eyes glistened and her voice softened. "I miss his smile already."

"Then let's hit the road and you can join me for supper."

Her eyes grew large. "Who's cooking?"

* * *

"It's bubbling." Dad tugged on an oven glove and pulled out the baking sheet with four ceramic crocks filled to the brim with French onion soup and not so much as a drop sloshed over the edge as he delivered them to the table.

"I've starving." Jane plopped down in a chair.

Dad picked up his spoon and Ida cleared her throat. He set the spoon down and bowed his head.

"For what we are about to receive, let us be truly grateful," she said.

"Thanks for having me." Jane took a big spoonful and closed her eyes. "This is delicious. Like everything else you make, Ida. Do you think we can salvage some of the pieces and make a new wreath?"

"I have some ideas. It's such a shame someone took the time to pull it apart though."

"It's as if the robber didn't know his gems and precious metals and had been fooled into believing it was more valuable," Dad said. "I was," he mumbled between slurps.

"We can redo it and the new one will be better than the original," said Ida.

"I plan to leave this one up all year."

When my spoon grazed the bottom of the bowl, I sat back, expanding my full stomach. I moaned when Ida topped off the scrumptious dinner, delivering four light and airy, deep, dark chocolate souffles to the table.

Ida's pocket played an Irish tune, and she danced a snappy jig. She retrieved her phone and answered it with a lilt. "Anita."

Her voice took on an edge.

"What? Oh, no. We'll be right there. Don't worry."

CHAPTER TWENTY-TWO

Ida stared at the logo on the base of the refrigerator.

"Ida? What's wrong?" Jane asked.

Ida lifted her chin and pulled back her shoulders. "We have a memorial to attend." She bulldozed around the kitchen. Pointing her finger at me, she said, "Refrigerate the soup." She slammed a box of cling wrap on the table. "Harry, cover the salad." She banged the soup crocks in the sink. "Jane," she said. "Rinse these." And, horror of horrors, she snatched the remainder of the magical soufflés before we could finish them and tossed them in the trash.

Maverick's head rose and he stole a worried glance at me.

"I'm in no state to drive," she said, slowing the pace of her cleanup.

"Where do you need to go?"

"The Johnson Funeral Home. Paula McCall had Phillip cremated and is holding a memorial tonight in ..." She glanced at her wrist. "... thirty-two minutes. Paula called Anita as a courtesy. I guess she isn't Phillip's ex yet and she has complete control of the funeral arrangements. Anita is beside herself and I promised we'd attend." Her eyes implored.

"I'll drive," I said.

"I'll go with you." Jane said, getting no argument from me.

"I'm chaperoning," my dad said with a wink. He yanked off his sweatshirt and headed to his room.

"I need to change. Be ready in ten." Ida dashed off and her door thumped closed.

Jane and I put the dishes in the dishwasher, swiped the table, and ran a vacuum across the floor before Dad returned, dressed in his church clothes. We donned our winter gear and waited.

I removed the keys from the hook as Ida barreled through the adjoining door and my jaw dropped. She wore a midi-length red-and-blue peasant dress, a green patent leather belt and matching boots. Golden bangles marched up her arm and four-inch hoops dangled from her earlobes. She'd touched up her makeup and wound a daffodil-yellow turban around her curly red hair.

Maverick's head came up again and he blinked.

Ida wriggled into her down coat, grabbed my arm, and forced me toward the door. "I'm celebrating the life of an artist and friend. Let's go. We're picking up Grace." She caught the look on my face. "Now."

Ida, Jane, and I took the front seat and we swung by Miss Grace's. Jordan Quintz earned a few points by the gentleness he showed, escorting Miss Grace to the car. He settled her in the back seat before hopping in next to her.

The defroster couldn't keep up with the fog of six heavy breathers crowded into the space. I scratched the frost building up on the inside of the windshield and inched down the quiet streets.

We parked between a dark sedan and a battered truck in front of the funeral home. Jordan gave Miss Grace two hands, helping her slide across the seat. Then he cradled her arm, and they took slow steps over the salted walkway. Ida wrapped her arm around Dad's, and they walked side by side. Jane and I brought up the rear, sneaking each other curious looks.

The taciturn mortician held the beveled glass door with her white-gloved hands, nodding like a butler. I signed the guest book and picked up a memorial program with a photo of a plant on the cover. Inside I found a poem, an ink sketch of Phillip, an agenda for the evening, and a truncated obituary. We followed the lighted hall to the room at the end where soft music played in a minor key.

Wilting floral arrangements lined the front of the room behind the dais. I sucked in a quick breath to avoid the cloying fumes of flowers close to the end of their usefulness. The unending sweetness of the lilies and heavy perfume of the carnations smothered me in sad memories. I had a startling image of Charles and gasped. I took shallow breaths and tried not to draw attention to my suffocation. Dad gently smiled in understanding and I exhaled my memories.

The mortician tugged at her white collar and glanced at the clock on the wall.

Anita stood to the right in front of six abstract paintings mounted on easels. She stepped up to Ida and said, "Stop by my studio tomorrow. I've made headway on the encaustics."

"I'll give you a call before Grace and I show up."

The woman standing in front swiped at her eyes as Miss Grace stepped away from their embrace and Ida moved forward. The woman shook Ida's hand and Ida introduced my dad. She took his hand, then crumpled against his chest. "I don't know what I'm going to do now." He patted her head, eyeing Ida for an escape. The spikey heels on her black boots put her at five eleven and she looked directly into Dad's eyes. "Thank you for coming."

Ida yanked my arm. "Katie Wilk, Jane Mackey, this is Paula McCall."

I made quick work of shaking her soft, clammy hand. With the sky-blue eye-shadow and pink lipstick, she looked pretty in a baby-faced sort of way.

She sobbed again. "He was such a good man. He worked so hard, but the trials of an artist's life were too much." Her glance went over my shoulder. She inhaled and prepared for another mourner.

Daniella Jericho waddled into Paula's clinch, and they looked like Sumo wrestlers, rocking each other back and forth to see who would win the takedown, weeping and howling.

Trying not to stare, I inspected the cards attached to the flowers and furrowed my brow. One read, Louise, you will be missed. Another read, the world has lost a kind woman. Could Paula have reused the floral arrangements?

The clergyman cleared his throat. As the four of us took our seats behind Miss Grace and Jordan, Paula held Daniella at arm's length. Secured by both shoulders, Daniella didn't have a chance with her short, chubby arms, until Paula let her go.

Paula said, "Let's get this show on the road." *A little cold,* I thought.

Paula dropped into a chair at the front and the clergyman stepped to the podium.

"I never met Phil McCall—"

"Phillip." Multiple voices made the correction.

"Phillip." The minister coughed. "But his wife requested we sing "Jesus Loves Me.""

I was grateful Ida's beautiful alto overshadowed his out-of-tune scratchy voice.

The celebrant's vague recitation could have been used at any number of nondescript memorials. The only connection he made was in choosing the pronoun—he. After six minutes (I checked) he concluded by saying, "And you are all invited to the fellowship hall for coffee and Phil ... Phillip's favorite Christmas cookie."

With ten of us in attendance, we couldn't slip out unnoticed.

Dad dissolved instant coffee crystals in the hot water he poured from the dispenser at the end of the table and sipped. His upper lip curled, and he put the cup down.

I bit into Phillip's favorite cookie, but the taste of the oversweet, dried crumbs told me he'd never had one of Ida's holiday treats. In fact, I was pretty sure my baking was better and that's not saying much. I wrapped the remains in a napkin and headed toward the trash receptacle near Paula who had her arm draped around Miss Grace's shoulder.

"You'll land on your feet." Miss Grace saw me. "Are you ready to leave?"

"Whenever you are."

She stepped away from Paula. Anita took her place but the words she exchanged with Paula didn't look comforting. They looked angry.

CHAPTER TWENTY-THREE

After another long, but exhilarating day in the classroom, I didn't relish another trip out in the cold, but I couldn't let Ida go alone. I checked my watch for the eleventh time. "I thought we were going to take Miss Grace to look at Anita's encaustics?"

"I've been texting and calling Grace all day." Ida paced, stopped, examined her phone screen, and paced again.

I stuffed my gloves into my pockets. "Maybe she forgot. I hear creative types can be somewhat scatterbrained at times."

Ida snorted and, as she rarely forgot anything, it was warranted.

She stopped in her tracks. "You heard her. 'Let's have Katie take us tomorrow after school,' she said. 'Sure,' you said. Well, it's tomorrow. And Grace is not answering."

"Do you ever ignore phone calls and texts?"

"Never. I …" The worry lines on her face relaxed as she consulted a memory. "Sometimes."

"Let's just walk across the street and talk to Miss Grace."

"Grand idea. You do have them on rare occasions, don't you?"

I answered with a snarky buzz of my zipper overheard by Maverick who inserted himself into our outing. I clipped on his leash, and we followed Ida into her kitchen.

"In December, I never go anywhere emptyhanded." She plated a variety of holiday goodies, covered it with plastic wrap, and tied a red ribbon around it. She handed me the dish and tossed Maverick one of her homemade doggie cookies. He knew a good thing.

She slid her feet into heavy boots, pulled a cap down over her ears, wound a scarf around her face, and yanked her midi-length down jacket closed. We aimed for the door, ready to brave the plunging temperatures.

"Just a second." She disappeared and came back cradling a bottle of wine. "Her favorite. Now we're ready."

Maverick dragged me across the street to the Loehr driveway and Ida hustled to catch up.

We stood on the sidewalk and admired Grace's elegant blinking fairy lights.

"What do you think it's telling us?"

I scrunched my brow. "Telling us?"

"Think—a subliminal signal code. That's cryptography, right? It's your forte."

I thought for a second and barked a laugh. With her stern look and left eyebrow raised, I disguised my chuckle with a cough. "What do *you* think it says?"

"Two messages. Happy holidays, of course." She crossed her arms and set them on her stomach. "And buy, buy, buy." Then her frown melted, and she joined me in the merriment. Maverick shifted from paw to paw and wagged his tail.

When Ida took her next step, Maverick took two and cut in front of her. Her legs flew out and she tumbled to the ground. I didn't hear the wine bottle crack, nor did I feel the burgundy splash. All I could hear was Ida's whump to the pavement.

I knelt next to her. She didn't move.

"Ida?" I put a hand on her shoulder. She unclenched one eye and peeked at me.

"Am I alive?"

She opened her other eye and rolled from side to side.

"Stay here and I'll get help."

She sat up and patted her body. She touched her bright red nose and then put her hands on her cheeks. "I think my triple padding kept everything safe. Help me up." She reached out her hand and rocked back and forth.

"Are you sure?" Adding my weight to Ida's momentum, she bolted upright.

"I'm fine." Her face lit up. "You, on the other hand, are a complete and utter mess."

Then I felt the liquid on my face and the cold piercing slivers through my pants. I looked down. Wine dripped from everywhere. I shivered.

I gave her my arm and held on while she checked her various parts.

"I'm fine." She confiscated the cookie plate. "Go change." She brushed a few red droplets from the top of the cling wrap and took measured steps toward the door.

I cautiously collected three large glass shards and

tugged Maverick toward home. "Please, Maverick. I need to change." We made it as far as the garbage can in our back yard. I tossed in the pieces of the bottle, and began a fruitless game of tug-of-war with Maverick to get him into my apartment so I could clean up. He sat unmoving, while I cajoled, jerked, bribed, and heaved.

Maverick leapt to his paws and bounded from right to left. I gripped the leash and stumbled behind him. In answer to a bone-chilling howl, he dragged me across the empty street and up the sidewalk to Miss Grace's front door. Maverick stood on his hind legs and what came to mind was the cost of painting over the trail of nail marks scratched into the wood.

Whimpers filled the air usually bursting with live music. We followed the puddles from footfalls across the tile.

Ida had collapsed on the polished wood floor with her head in her hands.

A Tiffany-style floor lamp spotlighted our eighty-plus-year-old neighbor slumped over the keyboard of her immaculate white grand piano. Not a strand of Miss Grace's white hair was out of place. Drop earrings matched a double strand of pearls that cut a white line against her collar bone. The French-manicured nails of her right hand curled into a piano chord we'd never hear. Black mules peeked from beneath a fitted, long turquoise gown that shimmered with beads and sequins. With the empty snifter on the coaster next to her left hand, she looked ready to perform, emulating Dean Martin or Frank Sinatra from the Rat Pack, famous heartthrobs of her youth.

Music lay scattered on the bench and the floor around her. The end of the reel-to-reel tape slapped a continuous rhythm.

If Ida hadn't been keening, I'd have thought Miss

Grace was asleep. But no one could have slept through her sobbing. I knelt beside Ida and put my arm around her. Maverick sat, tilted his head, and blinked his soft brown eyes.

"I know, boy. We'll take care of her." Miss Grace had died where she most loved to be, at her beloved piano.

Something crinkled beneath my knee. I pulled out an old black-and-white photo. The grim faces stared at the camera, and I frowned in return before I flattened it and slid it under the lamp on the end table. I scratched once under Maverick's chin, then pulled out my phone and punched in a number.

"Erickson."

"Pete?"

"Katie? Sorry, I didn't read the caller ID. How are you? What's that noise?"

"That's Ida." I choked on my words. "Pete, I think Miss Grace has passed away."

The silence hurt.

"Where are you?"

"Ida and I are in her music room."

"I'll be there as soon as I can. I'm calling Dad, I mean, Ronnie. Sorry, I'm just not used to him being in charge." He hung up.

Maverick lapped tears from my face. Sweat rolled down my back. I unbuttoned my jacket and raised Ida to her feet. I walked her to the living room and seated her on the sofa. She cried softly. "Maverick, stay with Ida."

Cool air seeped in around the thick frost growing like a crystal fungus at the corners of the door. It squeaked as I shoved it closed. A sheath of ice coated the windows and distorted the view with its opacity. It wasn't long before the lights of the county coroner's van bounced into the Loehr driveway. The door groaned and it seemed to take forever before Pete retrieved his case and unfolded himself from the driver's side. Then Susie popped out of the passenger seat. He nodded as I opened the heavy oak door. A former piano student, Pete was familiar with the layout of Miss Grace's home, and he walked into the living room adjacent to her favorite chamber where she had created beautiful music. Susie stopped in front of me and, without a word, grabbed me in an unprecedented one-arm embrace, then we followed Pete.

"Why is it so blazing hot in here?" Susie unwound her scarf and stuffed her gloves in her coat pockets. Until then, I thought my internal temperature gauge registered the heat in an emotional response.

Maverick and I leaned against the wall. He panted. Ida nestled in Pete's protective arms, her shoulders convulsing. Susie stepped into the music room. The supplies in her bag clinked when she set it on the floor. The clock on the wall ticked away the seconds.

Then the sirens came in waves.

Temporary Police Chief Ronnie Christianson barged through the door, barking orders to the officers who followed him. When he saw me, he tromped close and spat, "What are *you* doing here?"

"We found the body."

He almost sneered. "I ask again, what are you doing here?"

My shoulders straightened. I raised my chin a hair. "Ida and I wanted to visit our neighbor with a plate of cookies and a bottle of Christmas cheer." I had nothing to show. We'd left the tray of cookies on the floor next to the piano, but he took notice of the dark splotches staining the front of my jacket and my jeans and raised an eyebrow.

"Ida slipped on the ice. The bottle broke and the wine splattered." I had to think 'short sentences' so that I wouldn't say anything I'd regret.

"Step outside and wait. I need to get a statement from you." Ronnie turned his back on me and marched to Pete and Ida.

In a short time, Ida joined Maverick and me outside. She trembled but didn't say anything. When fifteen minutes passed and her lips turned blue and my fingertips tingled, I knocked on the front door. I didn't receive an acknowledgment, so I opened the door and stuck my head inside.

"Hello." I stepped farther inside.

"Ronnie?" I followed muffled voices to the music room.

I heard Pete say, "She'd known for a while."

I stomped my feet to get attention. The solemn exchange ceased and the intense stare of five pairs of eyes made it difficult to breathe, but when I worked up my courage, I said, "Chief, I'm taking Ida home."

* * *

An hour passed and we'd neither seen nor heard from Ronnie.

"We should fix something for Ida to eat. I think we might have some of her chicken soup in the freezer."

Dad opened the door and stared at the stacked plastic containers. He sighed. "Which one?"

"I used red covers for beef, orange for poultry, yellow

for seafood, and white for vegetarian."

"Good to know you haven't changed."

My face heated. My shoulders sagged. He knew me well. I liked the order. Then he chuckled. I shook my head and removed an orange container from the freezer. While it warmed on the stove, I reorganized the remaining foodstuffs.

I chopped a carrot, celery stalk, and onion to add and freshen the stew, a trick I learned from Ida.

The doorbell rang.

"I'll get it, Dad."

I expected Ronnie. I got a surprise.

CHAPTER TWENTY-FOUR

I s she here?" Jordan's nose dripped and his red eyes darted from one corner of my kitchen to the other. It could have been tears or it could have been a cold, or it could have been brought on by the onion.

"Who are you looking for, Mr. Quintz?"

"Call me Jordan. I'm looking for Ida. I'd like to speak with her. She's known my aunt longer than anyone else and ..." He searched the room behind me. "You've heard she died, right?"

"I'm so sorry for your loss. She was a special lady." I choked up and tripped over the last two words.

Jordan's eyes glistened, and then he skirted by me when he noticed Dad at the stove.

"Harry." He swallowed my dad in an overly familiar

bear hug. "She's gone."

Dad's left-hand patted Jordan's back. His right hand dangled a large spoon over the hot pot, his arm pinned to his side by the embrace.

"I was just getting to know her," Jordan said, and rocked my dad back and forth. "And I miss her so much already."

My dad mumbled a response and Jordan released him.

"I need to talk to Ida. She's not answering her phone or her door. I thought maybe she'd be here." He craned his neck, looking over Dad's head into all the living space he could. "Is she?"

"No. I'm afraid she's cut herself off for the moment. Her loss is traumatic—"

Jordan spun on me. "And mine isn't?"

I stepped back.

Maverick's bark startled Jordan and he hung his head. "I'm sorry. I wasn't prepared to lose her after just meeting her." He looked up, penitent. "Please tell Ida I'd like to talk to her. I know they were close."

Maverick yapped again and a voice howled from somewhere outside, "Gra-ace. Gra-ace."

I cracked open the door and crept onto our porch. Jordan shoved passed me, forcing me out of his way, and I had a much better view.

Daniella stood in the headlights of her car, wrapped in the black fur jacket and matching headpiece, shaking her fists at the sky, crying out.

Jordan took another look behind me before he clattered down the steps and into the street. It seemed like anger flitted across Daniella's features, but then her eyes locked on mine. I had to have imagined it. Jordan took her hands in his bear paws, and he looked down at her. They spoke for a moment. Then he led her up the sidewalk and they disappeared into Miss Grace's home.

I closed the door and shuddered.

In the kitchen, Dad ladled warm soup into a porcelain tureen. "What do you make of that?" he said as he refitted the lid.

I shrugged. "I couldn't say. But Ms. Jericho? She's the crazy driver we stopped to help after she drove her car into the ditch. The rich one who sat at Miss Grace's table at the gala."

Dad shook his head. "Coming?" He headed toward the adjoining door.

I rapped before I turned the knob. "Ida?" We kept the door between the apartments unlocked for easy access and I'm glad we did.

Something always simmered on her stove or baked in her oven, but not today. Dad centered the tureen on her kitchen table, placing it just so. Maverick darted between us and dashed into the living room.

She sat on the couch hugged by the dark.

"Ida?" I flipped the light switch. I heard the deep intake of breath and her long exhale. "Dad warmed some soup. It's on your table. You should eat."

She looked at me with grief so deep I could see her heart beat, then her eyes drifted to Maverick. He sat in front of her. She clasped his head in her hands and gently massaged his chin.

"I just got my friend back and now she's gone," she said.

I sank into the seat next to her and hugged her. "You've made great memories. And I got to watch the extraordinary dynamic duo of Columbia."

"But our fight—"

"Not a fight. You both wanted the same thing, and you solved your differences."

She stopped kneading his chin and Maverick nudged her hand. His ears perked up and then the doorbell rang.

Kindra, Brock, Lorelei, and Galen huddled on her stoop.

"You didn't answer your door, so we thought we'd try here," Kindra said, shivering.

Brock flashed a bright smile. "Mrs. Nygren called. Sixteen visitors to the *Titanic* exhibit used our cache-code for a discount and look." He held up his phone. "We've logged nine favorites."

Ida's Christmas lights flickered on, and she joined me at the door. Her lips smiled though her eyes were someplace else.

"Don't stand outside. Come in and have a cup of hot chocolate and tell us all about it." Once a teacher, always a teacher.

The four bodies bustled inside and hung their coats on the rack. Ida threaded her arm through Lorelei's and patted her hand and the rest followed their pied piper of goodies to her kitchen.

Dad lifted his shoulders and hands in a don't-ask-me gesture and headed after them. Maverick cocked his head and left me holding the door, gazing across the yard at Miss Grace's house. Dim lights shone through the front room curtains and two windows on the upper floor, looking like a ghostly grimace.

Laughter shoved my gruesome thoughts aside and I decided my sweet tooth needed tending.

Ida would do anything for her students and mine. She

smiled and told a story.

"I guess I could be a bit sneaky. For one of my art juries, the piece needed to be utilitarian. For example, we could decorate a hat rack, or a coat stand. I painted a stool. I used them all the time—"

"Of course, you did," Dad said, tipping his head to gaze at my students over the rims of his glasses.

Four pairs of eyes searched Ida's kitchen.

She opened her pantry and slid a wooden step stool across the floor. A four-foot-tall handle was secured to the solid square base. "I never expected it, but this piece won the regional competition."

She smiled. The light scuff marks of repeated use didn't mar the jewel-toned painting and the students circled the piece and oohed and aahed.

"The auctioned pieces raised funds for the elementary school library and a second-grade teacher bought it as a special reading throne for her kids. On a birthday, or when a student did a superior job at a classroom activity, they won the right to sit in the chair."

In order to get the full effect, Brock leaned over the rail and stared down at the flat surface. He closed one eye and then tilted his head. "Where are her clothes?" he asked.

Kindra gasped.

The others jostled for the right vantage point to see what Brock had seen and when the giggles subsided, I closed one eye and could just make out the figure of what could have been a naked female hidden among the flora and fauna.

"The stool was just the right size and the teacher used it for about three weeks before one of her students did what Brock did. Just goes to show you never know what might be hiding in plain sight." Ida became reflective and the big smile withered. "Come to think of it, the young man was Phillip McCall."

Lorelei broke the stillness. "Brock, can you read a few of the comments from the cache?"

He pulled up the website and brushed his fingers over his phone screen. "Most of them just wrote TFTC."

"What does that mean?" asked Dad.

"Thanks for the cache," said Lorelei.

"This one included a long note, 'Caching with Bronco today. Started in Little Falls and ended in Columbia. Another big day through multiple counties finding great caches. We concluded our day visiting a gold nugget in the guise of a history center. This is a favorite for sure.' This one reads, 'Awesome. What we enjoyed most was seeing this historical gem—the *Titanic* Exhibit—in the middle of nowhere. Who'd have thought!'" Brock glowed. "By George, I think we've got it!" he crowed with a slight British accent.

Ida sealed four small individual baggies stuffed with special treats and handed them around. Her phone buzzed. She stared at the face and pocketed the device. "Spam risk," she said.

CHAPTER TWENTY-FIVE

CJ Bluestone sat at my kitchen table, rotating a cup of hot tea. "Carlee's surgery went well."

"Thank goodness."

"They're keeping her until tomorrow." He looked deeply into the tan liquid. "I have an important delivery today, and I am unable to stay with her." He looked up. "Could you stop by and see her?"

"Of course."

He exhaled and sat back. "I didn't think parenting would be so difficult."

Dad took that moment to glide into the kitchen. He snorted. "Little kids, little problems. Big kids ..." He caught my stink eye and poured himself a cup a coffee. "What do you have going on today, Doc?"

"Halvorson Farms has a cow ready to deliver but she had complications last time, so my presence has been requested. They've scheduled a hemilaminectomy for Buster, and Sheba is expected to whelp her goldens in the next twenty-four to forty-eight hours."

"We'd love to visit Carlee, wouldn't we Dad?"

"Anything you say, darlin'."

CJ promised to keep in touch and get our take on Carlee's condition.

Ida loaded a box of gingerbread cookies, snickerdoodles, million-dollar cheesecake bars, peanut butter cups, divinity, and fudge to make our visit to the children's ward successful and I agreed. She also sent a box of holiday reading geared for kids of all ages.

"They have such a shortage of books. Please leave them with Rachel. She'll know what to do. And tell her, if all goes well, I'll be by for caroling soon."

She reached for the door and Dad said, "Ronnie hasn't stopped by again, has he?"

"No," she said. "But they haven't arrested anyone yet."

The door closed behind her.

I grabbed the goodies and Dad tilted his head as we walked into the cold. "Who did it? And don't give me that look. I've seen the wheels turning. Talk to me."

"I'm just thinking out loud. McCall took advantage of several people. Yvonne Nygren almost had a small mutiny on her hands when the blank canvas was unveiled at the gala. Fortunately, Anita Jones finessed a plausible explanation for the switch and made an acceptable substitution—one of her own pieces—and it's obvious to Ida Anita's the better artist. McCall's wife, Paula, almost missed out on the fruits of his success, which also might have happened to Anita." I pulled into the parking garage. "Daniella Jericho is everywhere and she's made a friend of Jordan Quintz, Miss Grace's long lost relative."

"They all attended the gala."

"Jordan too?" We entered the hospital.

"He sat with Grace, Pete, and Susie," Dad said as he pushed the button on the elevator. "You just weren't focused."

The aroma alone gave me a sugar high and I'm certain if I'd have been by myself, I'd have been mobbed by the other visitors trapped in the elevator smothered in chocolate, peanut butter, and vanilla fumes. Ida's skill in the kitchen was unsurpassed. Fortunately, Dad never left my side.

A tan puppy slid to a stop in front of the elevator doors, clutching an orange stuffed toy in his mouth. He dropped it and sat, panting. Dad picked him up and set him in Ricky's open arms.

"Thanks," the little boy said with a smile like a crescent moon. "I'm Ricky and this is Tucker."

"Hi, Ricky. I'm Harry." He tilted his head toward me. "And this is—"

"Hi, Katie." As if it was a big secret he whispered to Dad behind his cupped hand. "We've met." He screwed up his face, searching his memory. "You came caroling too?"

Dad nodded.

Ricky had more color in his cheeks and clearer, brighter eyes.

"Hi, Ricky. Would you like a Christmas cookie?"

He looked over his shoulder at Anita. "Can I?" She nodded, smiling at his enthusiasm. "Thanks," he said.

I waved two fingers at Anita. She returned the greeting.

He grabbed the largest gingerbread cookie, but before

he could take a bite, Tucker jumped onto his lap. Ricky held him at bay. He squirmed in the chair and took a treat from the nylon bag clipped to his armrest. Tucker snatched it and trotted over to a well-worn patch of carpet before nibbling.

"Did you come to sing again?"

"Nope. We came for a visit. Do you know Carlee?"

"I signed Carlee's cast … twice. Once with a snowflake and once with an eighth note. We both take piano lessons. And she knows some magic tricks," said Ricky. "C'mon. I'll show you where she is."

He wheeled his chair to the last room down the hall, farthest from the elevator, and knocked.

"Who is it?" sang a voice from within.

"Guess," said Ricky.

"Go away," she said. Ricky's contagious giggle snagged Dad and me and then I heard the chortling from behind the door.

"I come with snacks," he sang.

"Is it George?"

"Nope."

"Is it …"

They exchanged a string of meaningless names until the little boy whined, "It's me, Ricky."

"Come in, Master Ricky."

Carlee beamed from the bed. "My dad said he was busy today, so I was prepared to hang out with my little buds, but I thank you most sincerely for visiting. Galen left about fifteen minutes ago." Her eyebrows raised and she pointed to a ceramic vase filled with beautiful pink flowers. "And Lorelei said she'd try to visit too."

"We brought treats to share."

Fully cognizant of the Wilk culinary aptitude, the fear on her face only disappeared when I assured her the treats were made by Ida. She grabbed a bar and so did Ricky.

"I guess I'll let you go," he said around a mouthful of crumbs, and he rolled out the door.

"What a sweetie." Thoughtful, her eyes misted. "He's so brave. His mom said he might have to stay over Christmas. She brings Tucker to visit every day."

I silently counted my infinite blessings.

"What else do you have?" Carlee tilted her head.

Dad tipped the grocery bag and the top few books slid out and onto Carlee's bed.

"Books! Let me see." She pawed through the bag. "I can't wait. My little buds will love these—*A Visit from St. Nicholas*, *How the Grinch Stole Christmas*, *The Christmas Pig*, *The Polar Express*, and Ricky will think this one is a hoot." She held up *Santa's Underwear*.

Dad snagged it. "Let me see that one."

Carlee rooted around for the last book, crinkling the bag, and gently extracted a novel. She hugged it and hummed. "I've always wanted to read the real story. I've seen all the movie adaptations." She turned the book for me to read the cover.

"That's one of my favorites too. And I live with a Scrooge," I said, gauging whether Dad was listening.

He tore his eyes away from the amusing words on the page and worked a Dickensian scowl onto his face. "Very funny."

"I think you'll love *A Christmas Carol*."

Ricky quickly rolled into the room but not before sneaking a glance over his shoulder. "She's back," he hissed.

Carlee threw herself onto the pillows and pulled the

white bedclothes up to her shoulders. "Shut the door, please," she said urgently.

Ricky wheeled himself farther into the room and I closed the door with a whisper.

Dad removed his glasses and stared at Carlee. "What's going on?"

Ricky couldn't contain himself. "The black fur ball keeps coming back and asking to see Carlee. I almost blew it the first time, but I heard Carlee's dad tell her some of the same things my mom tells me, and it reminded me not to talk to strangers. And let me tell you. No one is stranger than that lady."

"Who is she? What does she want?"

"I dunno, but Nurse Rachel moved Carlee in here after the first time she showed up and swore me to secrecy." He crossed his heart and held up three fingers.

Dad and I exchanged looks. Ricky understood the look. "You aren't a stranger, Katie. Can I show them, Carlee? Can I?"

Carlee pulled the covers over her head, and we heard a muffled, "Okay."

Ricky opened the door and positioned his wheelchair so he could stick his head out far enough to see down the hall. Dad grabbed onto the doorframe and peered over Ricky's head, and not to be outdone, I leaned over Dad. We had a clear view all the way to the nurse's station. Rachel stood with her arms crossed over her chest listening to a blustery tirade by a short woman in a black fur coat.

Daniella Jericho.

A throat cleared behind us and toppled our spying totem pole.

CHAPTER TWENTY-SIX

I picked myself up off the floor and dusted my bruised ego with as much dignity as I could muster and I followed the blue booties and the green scrubs to a wry smile, a scruffy chin, curling black hair, and chocolate-brown eyes.

Pete Erickson's right eyebrow rose, and my heart thumped once and then thumped off when I remembered Susie. I looked past him to make sure the elf hadn't followed.

"Morning, Doc. Have a cookie." Dad to the rescue.

"Don't mind if I do." After one bite, his eyes closed, and Pete moaned in delight. "Ida has made the best snickerdoodles since for-e-ver."

"What makes you think I didn't make them?" I set my fists on my hips.

He snorted and raised both eyebrows. It was worth a try. I relented. Then he examined the scene. "What are we doing here?" he said conspiratorially.

Ricky whispered, forcefully, "She's back." He grabbed Pete's hand and hauled him into the room. Pete's foot caught on a wheel, and he teetered over me for a second before Dad pulled him upright. Dad to the rescue again—maybe.

"Is this the visitor Rachel has been hounding me about?" Pete asked. Ricky nodded. "I have to take a look."

"It's Daniella Jericho," I said.

He briefly glanced down the hall to make sure. He closed the door and leaned against it. "You can come out now, Carlee." She lowered the linen. "Do you know Daniella?" She shook her head. "I wonder what she could want."

Carlee looked at me. I looked at Dad. Dad looked at Pete and Pete watched Ricky scarf down a piece of Ida's satiny fudge until all that remained was a brown smudge on his chin. A sharp rap interrupted our staring contest.

Pete inhaled. Carlee tossed the sheet back over her head. Dad closed the lid on the box of treats. Ricky rolled his chair forward to use as a battering ram against whoever might be on the other side of the door. Pete opened it but blocked the interior.

"Dr. Erickson," Rachel said officiously. "Officer Rodgers says he's here to deliver papers to a juvenile patient we might or might not have."

"Hi, Dan. Can you give them to me?"

"Doc. I'd prefer to deliver them myself, but you can sure witness the delivery."

Pete stepped from the threshold. We could've looked guilty of something as mundane as holding an illegal card game but instead we were caught red-handed stealing cookies from the box on Dad's lap. Rachel huffed. Dad grinned and offered the box. Officer Rodgers closed his eyes and hummed after his first bite of the fluffy white divinity. Rachel looked right and left and snatched a peanut butter cup before she stomped away.

"Dan, you know the Wilks." Officer Rodgers nodded. "And this scamp is Ricky. You've got to watch out for him." Pete ruffled his hair and Ricky giggled.

"Carlee Parks—"

"It's going to be Carlee Bluestone soon." Her head popped out from under the covers.

"Carlee Parks," Officer Rodgers said again. "I'm required to deliver these papers into your hand, inviting you and your representative to a reading of the last will and testament of Grace Loehr to be held immediately after the burial service which has been expedited to Monday afternoon at three thirty."

Chewing stopped.

Officer Rodgers took another piece of divinity and said, "Have a nice day."

Tears formed in Carlee's eyes, and I wished CJ wasn't miles away. Ricky's mouth fell open when Dad set the treat box in his lap. Then Dad sat next to Carlee and patted her hand. "We're all here for you, doll."

She snuffled and pulled the pages out of the envelope. Tears pooled in her eyes. "Can you read it?" she said, thrusting the papers into Dad's hands.

He scanned them. "The first page is a copy of a request for the funeral to be held as soon as possible because one of the beneficiaries has time-sensitive duties elsewhere."

"Who made the request?" I couldn't imagine anyone in that much of a hurry.

"That's odd. It says the request came from Jordan Quintz. I thought he said he was moving here. Doc, are you finished with the autopsy? Anything hinky?"

Pete gave him *the* look. "You know I can't discuss that with you, Harry."

"So that's a maybe. The reading of the will at the office of Dorene Dvorak is scheduled immediately following the service, the particulars of which are spelled out in detail, and she included an accounting for everything Grace had prepaid." He read the next few pages. "She wrote her obituary for the newspaper and created a memorial video. Grace selected the music and musicians she wanted for her service, and the pallbearers—Pete, you and Katie are on the list." I sucked in a breath. "She named the officiant, the eulogist—Lance Erickson." Dad looked up to gauge Pete's reaction. If he was surprised, he didn't show it. "She appointed readers and chose scripture passages. Her burial plot and headstone are bought and paid for. She even chose the clothes she would wear. And Carlee, dear." He removed his glasses. "You're one of Grace's heirs."

"Let me see that." She grabbed the pages and her eyes flew across the words, her lips a blur as she silently read. "I'm not the only one." She handed the pages to me.

The beneficiary list included the Midwest Minnesota History Center, Jordan Quintz, McCall's Studio for the Arts, and some I didn't recognize, but the last name on the list caught my eye—Ida Clemashevski.

The door swung open. I jumped, anticipating being caught by Daniella.

Instead, a lilting voice said, "Who's having a party without me?

Lorelei waltzed into Carlee's room, getting smaller by the minute, and handed a huge box of chocolate truffles to the patient. "You're looking great! How are you feeling, really?"

"That's our cue, Dad. Get well, Carlee. And you, be good, Ricky."

Dad's forlorn look could only mean one thing. I deprived him of his favorite treat—more chocolate—and I'd have to make it up to him.

Pete caught up to us before we were claimed by the elevator. "Harry, I don't want you to think I don't trust you, but you know how rumors get started. I can't talk about Grace. I can say with complete confidence, and I won't be divulging any secrets if I tell you Phillip McCall died with strychnine in his system. Tragic end to a creative genius."

"Did you know him well?'

"Not well." The serious look he gave me could mean anything. "Katie, keep yourself safe. And watch out for Ida."

The elevator doors opened, and Dad and I stepped in. I wiggled my fingers and Pete disappeared behind the doors.

"Was he trying to tell us something without telling us something?" Dad asked.

"I'm not sure. But let's head out to the history center. I have a few questions for Mrs. Nygren." Dad perked up so I was safe for the time being as long as I scrounged some chocolate.

The ship loomed large in the frosty gloom. I gave Dad my phone and the app took him to the doorway so he could attempt our geocache. He counted seven columns then down to the second row and pulled the brochure. We paraded up the gangplank behind a dozen or so guests.

"Looks like you have a crowd today," I said to our ticket taker.

Derek sat, happily raking in the money. "Yeah, but kind of ghoulish. There was talk of murder and some heard about the two old biddies' fight—"

My ire curled around my ears. "It wasn't a fight."

"Just telling you that it's been great for business."

"Any geocachers?" Dad asked.

"We've had a few come through and they loved the mystery and the solution, so good on ya."

"I'm here to try it out." Dad dug out his wallet, but Derek waved us through.

"No money from you, thanks. And I'm sure Mrs. Nygren will be happy to see you. She's hanging out by the bridge."

We knew the way to the grand staircase. Dad decrypted the cypher and then verified where we needed to go next with the map guide on the wall. When we mounted the steps to the bridge, we saw Mrs. Nygren but she didn't seem happy. Neither did the short fur-covered woman talking to her. The deadly venom in Daniella's eyes stopped me in my tracks. Dad plunged forward.

"Ms. Jericho, I've heard so much about you."

Her look relaxed a bit when she shifted her focus to Dad. He could be quite charming.

"Do I know you?"

"Not yet." He extended a hand. "Harry Wilk."

"We'll talk later, Yvonne," she said over her shoulder. A fake smile covered her face, and she snaked her hand around his arm and led Dad toward the First-Class Dining Saloon.

"I was just telling my daughter," he said with a nod in my direction, "how fortunate we are to have such generous benefactors of the health care system, the arts, and the history center in a town this size, built by hard work and maintained by caring individuals who can afford ..." Their voices drifted as they disappeared into the exhibit.

Mrs. Nygren sniffed and looked like she might cry.

"What's wrong?"

She hesitated. Then it all came pouring out. "The hospital board planned to donate a percentage of the pledged funds in lieu of rent. With Grace gone, it'll be difficult to collect both her substantial pledge *and* Daniella's." The tears began to flow freely, and she swiped at them with the back of her hand. "There were no back-up provisions for payment when someone dies. If there was no formal gift made in Grace's estate plan, her donation will be zero and Daniella worded her pledge to match Grace's." Her voice squeaked. "I don't know what will happen to the exhibit now."

"But the history center is named in Miss Grace's will." Oops. I overstepped.

Mrs. Nygren stopped crying. "Do you mean we *will* collect the pledge?"

"I don't know the terms." What could I say? Then I spotted Officer Rodgers stepping briskly our way.

"Katie?" He looked confused by my presence. "Yvonne, I have an invitation for you or another representative of the history center to attend a reading of Miss Grace Loehr's last will and testament, Monday after the funeral service at the offices of Tupy, Dvorak, and Sticha. Have a good day, ladies."

She clutched the envelope to her chest with a little disbelief and a lot of relief. The invitation could save the day.

"I need to find Daniella."

"And I need to find my dad."

They hadn't gotten too far in the exhibit. Dad took one

look at my face and disentangled himself from Daniella with a promise of catching up soon.

"Officer Rodgers is delivering the invitations, if you can call them that. I think we should be home for Ida. I don't know how much more she can handle, but I don't think she expected to be a beneficiary of Miss Grace's estate."

We made tracks, as they say, going as fast as the road conditions allowed, but we were still behind Officer Rodgers. We pulled into the drive, and he nodded as he walked to the end of the sidewalk and got into his cruiser.

Ida sat at her kitchen table, staring.

"Ida?" I put water on for tea and dug around in her cupboard for her favorite, Earl Grey. Dad trooped in carting another favorite, Midleton. He poured a short glass and set it in front of Ida. She picked it up, examining it from all sides and finished it off in one gulp followed by a shudder. Dad poured another.

"Why on earth would Grace name me in her will? Why?"

"You were her friend."

"But she ignored me for decades and we were just getting reacquainted."

"From all you've told us, she was a good soul. She wanted a life of performance and for many years, she got that."

"She lived the dream." Ida sipped at her second glass. "I understand the bequest to Carlee and Ana, and maybe even the Quintz family, but what could she possibly want to leave me?"

That was the question.

CHAPTER TWENTY-SEVEN

Ida guided Jane with minimal directions to rebuild her holiday wreath. I provided hot water for tea to go with the cookie snack. After attaching each bauble, Jane stood back and tipped her head right and left before adding something new. When Jane picked up an oval pendant with a soft green patina coating the copper sheath around a polished stone, she stared at it as it hung from the chain in her hand. She tried it out in two or three places before Ida moved to her side.

"May I see that?

Ida gently stroked the filigreed casing. "This is lovely. Where did you get it?"

"This old thing? It came in the box Ronnie gave me. Wasn't it yours?" Jane scrunched her eyebrows.

"I don't remember." Ida positioned the gem so it would be noticed, dangling loosely, and Jane lashed it to the Styrofoam with florist wire. When they'd used up the rest of the jewelry, Ida provided sparkly gold and silver ribbons and delicate lace to fill in empty spots.

Dad held up the completed decoration for us to admire. "This is better than the original."

Afterward, Jane and I slipped on aluminum snowshoes and took a quick spin through the waterfowl protection area. I pointed out where the pieces of the wreath had been scattered.

She shivered. "I still feel violated. But I don't think anything else is missing. Drew finished installing the security system and I'm back home. No more weird phone calls but I still tiptoe through my apartment, trying to catch a thief lurking in the shadows."

"Did you tell your dad?"

"Had to or Drew would. He's coming to Atlanta with me for a few days during Christmas break."

I frowned. Of course she'd go home for Christmas, but I'd miss her. "When do you leave?"

"December twenty-fourth." We silently padded over the soft new snow. "I read the latest article. Pete identified strychnine as McCall's cause of death, and the journalist made it sound like Ida had a motive to kill McCall. Did she have the means or opportunity?"

"Jane!"

"Think about it. Almost everyone heard him call her a cheapskate when she stomped out and he didn't seem pleased with her taking credit for his art education. Where was she on Friday night? Would she have had the drug to give him?" She held up her mitten when I started to object. "I know Ida and you know Ida, but there are those who would like to find her guilty of something."

"Like Ronnie?" I asked.

"If McCall was killed, who could possibly have wanted him dead? We have to get a little creative here because we don't know much, but I'd say his assistant, for one, took a lot of guff at the gala that night, first after the unveiling and then when she found the mannequin."

"There's always the significant other. Emotions can be inciting motivators. Ida thought Paula and Phillip McCall were divorced."

"Any new love interests? Business partners? Maybe someone connected to the gala? Heirs to a fortune he might have hidden somewhere?"

"I didn't know him that well, but I could ask Ida. He did look out-of-sorts Friday night, don't you think? Scared? Anxious?"

"Now that you bring that up, maybe. Or he may have been surprised. He donated his art for exposure, to get his name out there. He wasn't expecting the bid to go sky high. But he did look startled when the auctioneer unveiled the *blank* canvas." She stopped hiking. "Maybe Anita didn't tell him she swapped the pieces."

"Jane, what if he'd inserted some kind of contraband in the piece and Anita replaced it."

"What do you mean?"

"Anita promised to reconstruct Miss Grace's piece and make a second one for Ida, attaching special mementos, relics, and souvenirs. What if McCall had something else embedded in the original wax piece? Like jewelry or drugs or special papers."

Jane didn't move. Then she swiveled her head. "We're stretching here."

"Maybe." We picked up our pace. *Maybe not.*

"I'd like to be able to point a finger at Daniella Jericho. She's a piece of work and missing a pleasant gene or three."

I thought the same about Jordan Quintz, but that was just because he'd scared me.

When my back yard came into view, we saw Maverick bounding back and forth behind the fence.

My phone chirped. "Hello?"

"Sheba hasn't delivered yet and Dad is still out at Halvorson's." Carlee took a deep breath. "He'd like to stay there and monitor Buster too but then can't promise to return before the reading of the will tomorrow. Can you please go with me? I don't want to go by myself."

"Do you need a ride there?"

"No, thanks. Galen will take me and that will give him something to do. He's driving me crazy."

I sensed the hint of a smile. "I'll meet you after the service."

"Great."

"How's your leg?"

"I'm fine, but you might have to drive a wheelchair."

I hoped it came with an instruction manual.

CHAPTER TWENTY-EIGHT

My substitute sauntered in late, giving me mere minutes to pick up Dad and Ida. With the great number of mourners still in line when we arrived, the service didn't start on time, and I was able to take my place across from Pete.

In his tender eulogy, Lance Erickson reflected on the generous life of Grace Loehr, a musician, humanitarian, teacher, and friend. I'm not certain anyone knew she had provided music scholarships every year for three outstanding piano students. Her undercover philanthropy included replacing the stained-glass windows in the parish hall and underwriting the summer vacation bible school. The high school music directors knew where to go if they needed to purchase instruments for students without resources. I thought Lance had finished, but he choked up while trying to introduce Carlee.

Galen wheeled her to the front and handed her the microphone. She held it at her side for a long time before she brought it to her lips. "Miss Grace came into my life when I least expected and most needed her." Her voice cracked. "She took in my sister Ana and me, knowing only that we'd been horribly deceived. She offered us food, and clothing, and a beautiful place to lay our heads while our future was sorted. Miss Grace listened to us and when she spoke, we knew it would be profound. She was a performer of first order and shared her gift, teaching us lessons we'll never forget. I plan to be a pianist, just like her." Ana stepped up to the front and put her hand on Carlee's shoulder. Carlee kept her eyes on Ana and started to sing. Ana joined her and the transcendent blending of their voices took me with them, "Somewhere Over the Rainbow."

We exited the church to a recording of Frank Sinatra singing "My Way" and Ida handed me a wad of extras because I'd run out of tissues.

Galen had Carlee bundled next to my car. "Do you want me to go with you?"

"Thanks, but no," she said. "You have to train and be ready to start wrestling after the Christmas break. Ms. Wilk is going with me." He lifted her into the passenger seat and collapsed the wheelchair, stowing it in the truck.

The look he gave me would have withered a wiser woman. "She'll be fine. Promise."

"And my folks and I will be there too." Ana said, walking up and standing next to the open door.

Galen reluctantly turned and walked back to his car.

Ana and her parents followed me through the snow-

slicked streets, parking in the lot adjacent to Dorene
Dvorak's office on Main Street. Ana's dad lifted Carlee into
the wheelchair. The tenderness he showed both girls was
filled with apology. It was his vengeful first wife who had
wreaked havoc on their lives.

Dorene's assistant seated us around a large table in a
conference room and offered bottles of water. "She'll be
right with you," she said as she closed the door and muffled
the rapid-fire cadence of a busy office. We timidly cleared
our throats, cracked open water bottles, and avoided
looking at one another.

Dorene blew in with a stack of papers and positioned
herself in the middle of the table. "Grace Loehr will be
sorely missed," she said and sat. She placed cheaters on her
nose and met the eyes of each one of us. "You each have
been named in Grace's will with a specific bequest. There
is a no-contest clause. If you challenge the terms of this
document, you will receive nothing. Any questions?"

I thought I understood why Carlee and Ana had been
given a gift, but Miss Grace had certainly gathered a hodge-
podge of disconnected individuals. Jordan Quintz rocked
in his chair. Paula McCall nestled deeper in her seat and sat
back. Daniella Jericho repositioned her fur coat. Yvonne
Nygren looked at the hands in her lap, shredding a tissue.
Dad leaned toward Ida who sat bolt upright.

"Before her death, Grace Loehr created an endowment,
ensuring continued support of the area arts. That is not
part of her estate."

Someone sucked in a breath.

"Which is still substantial. Let's get down to it. Shall
we? All the provisions must be met before the settlement
will be made."

"Carlee and Ana share the house and all its contents, except items specifically identified, if they would live in it until graduating from high school. They take possession one week after this reading," she said. I approved.

"The Steinway goes to Jordan Quintz."

Jordan's face contorted. "What if I don't want her big, ugly, white, grand piano? Who cares if she thinks I'm a great musician? What am I going to do with that albatross? What's it worth?" He turned on the girls. "Who are you anyway? What did you do to my great-aunt?"

I leaned forward, planting my face in front of him. "Leave. Them. Alone."

Dorene kept reading. "Grace's estate will pay two-hundred-fifty-thousand dollars for a set of four completed encaustic pieces donated to the hospital."

Paula sniffed. "We toiled, scrimped, and scraped for years, and now, when Phillip's lost to me, his art is finally receiving the recognition it deserves."

"Miss Grace's estate will make good on her pledge to the Midwest Minnesota History Center and add an additional quarter of a million dollars after Mrs. Nygren inventories and certifies the provenance for the artifacts registered at the center in the *Titanic* exhibit." Yvonne's eyes grew large behind her glasses. Dorene handed her a thick folder. She had her work cut out for her.

"After that time, Ms. Jericho, you will be held legally responsible to match the gift."

Daniella wriggled uncomfortably in her seat. She lost the smug look she'd had. She might be required to come up with the funds.

"Lastly ..." Ida blinked. Dad took her hand. "Grace Loehr bequeathed sheet music, books, and recording equipment, plus an undisclosed amount of money, to Ida Clemashevski if she plays the holiday piece she performed at their last competition forty years ago."

Dorene gazed over her glasses at the shell-shocked faces around the table. "There is one more condition to be met or her prior will goes into effect."

Jordan sat forward, hopeful. "What's in the prior will?"

"I can't tell you."

"When was it written?"

"Before this one."

Paula said, "What's the condition?"

Dorene surveyed the room. "Grace wrote, 'You must determine who killed me.'"

Carlee and Ana gasped. The air left the room. Silence. Daniella shuffled her shoes. Jordan slid his chair forward. Yvonne sniffed.

"She was killed?" Carlee wrapped her hand around Ana's.

"You mean, no one gets anything until we find out who killed her? How do we know anyone killed her?" said Jordan.

"There's more." Her eyes lingered on the page. "You have five days, beginning today."

Jordan slammed his hand on the table. I jumped. "God did it. Done," he said it.

Dorene continued to read. "With irrefutable proof."

The door to the conference room banged against the wall. Pete stepped in followed by four police officers who surrounded the table.

"Grace Loehr was murdered. The drink we found on her piano was laced with strychnine," Pete said solemnly.

A larger man shoved past Pete. Metal handcuffs

clanked in his right hand.

"Now, Ronnie," Ida began in a reprimand. She stood. "That's no way to enter a room."

He stood a full foot taller than Ida. With a glint in his eye and a satisfied smirk on his face, he dangled the bracelets in front of her. Temporary Police Chief Ronnie Christianson said, "Ida Clemashevski, I am placing you under arrest for the murders of Grace Loehr and Phillip McCall."

Jordan whacked the table with both hands. "Well, Miss Dvorak. Now we know."

CHAPTER TWENTY-NINE

My heart pounded in my ears and drowned out the rest of Ronnie's recitation. I heard Dad's warning words, "Don't say anything, Ida!"

Jordan's hands flew up. "There you have it. Ida killed Grace."

"Ida didn't kill anyone," Dad said.

I closed my eyes, opened them, and pleaded. "Pete, you've got to do something."

"I think I've already done too much." The lovely brown in his eyes faded. He turned and followed Ronnie and Ida.

"We'll reconvene in five days." Dorene grabbed the file and gave me a penetrating look. "Proof." She nodded and exited.

Carlee, Ana and her parents, Dad, and I waited until

the rest of the heirs filed out. "Dad, what do we do now?"

"You're going to figure out who killed Miss Loehr," said Carlee. "Means, motive, opportunity. Who? And why? But first, we have to see Ricky." Even with everything else going on, thoughts of the imp could bring out a smile.

Ana and Carlee embraced. I trundled the wheelchair through the snow over the sidewalk one block to Columbia Community Hospital. When I stopped at the doors, Dad took control of the wheelchair and said knowingly, "It can't hurt you. Come on darlin'."

When the elevator doors to the children's ward opened, Tucker galloped our way but sat at the toot of a whistle. Rachel cocked her head and one side of her mouth turned up in a half smile.

"We came to see Ricky."

"He's on his way up from his last treatment before Christmas."

The elevator doors whooshed. Ricky looked zapped until he snapped his fingers and Tucker landed in his lap. They rolled toward Carlee, playing a momentary game of chicken, Carlee trying to pass a much quicker Ricky.

Anita Jones followed Ricky off the elevator. She didn't seem surprised to see me. "Carlee's an angel, isn't she?"

"Hey, Mom, Carlee brought the sequel to the book." He lowered his voice an octave. "The book which shall not be named. Can we read it?"

Anita said, "Just once, though. I don't want you to drive Rachel crazy." She whispered. "He feels better when he rests after his treatment, but he misses his friend."

"Excuse me," Dad said. "The first book was a hoot. I've got to hear the follow-up." He slid a chair next to Ricky.

"Ricky's such a good kid, but I'm sure he's a handful. This must be difficult."

"Yes, he is. But with the settlement to the McCall Institute, I'll finally get paid and that will go a long way." Anita's ears turned crimson.

"You haven't been paid?"

"It's all good now." A harried look haunted her eyes. I waited for her to say more. "McCall promised he'd help me make a name for myself and when I finish the pieces for the institute, Paula said she'd help make it happen. But, for now …" She pasted a huge grin on her face. "Ricky's coming home, and I've got some Christmas shopping to do." Anita beamed, trying to contain her joy at hearing her son's uproarious laugh. "Excuse me."

Dad gave up his chair and Anita joined Ricky and Carlee.

"Don't you want to hear the story, Dad?"

"I already read it. Why so serious?"

"I just had a strange conversation with Anita, Ricky's mom."

"Wasn't she the screamer at the gala? You know, the one who found the mannequin floating in the ice pool."

I nodded. "And she might be a whole lot more."

Rachel took her place next to me. She crossed her arms in front of her. "We could use a rousing round of "Jingle Bells" before you leave."

When Carlee closed the cover of the book and handed it to a beaming Ricky, we sang two carols and made our way to the exit.

The elevator doors slid open, and Paula McCall stepped off. Her tan flats slapped the linoleum tiles all the way up to Anita and we heard her say, "We have to talk."

CHAPTER THIRTY

Dad didn't have any desire to know what Paula had to say and ushered us out of the hospital. I dropped Dad and Carlee at my apartment and picked up my furry friend.

Maverick and I interrupted Jane retooling her memory box at her kitchen table. She'd removed the staging items and had begun the task of cleaning the niches and substituting some of her own mementos. Before I could tell her about Ida's arrest, she cleared her throat. "Look at this," she said, a little disgusted. "I have to find something to cover up these doodles. And I really don't like this fishing lure. I think I'll use my mom's ring and maybe my broken angel. What do you think?"

I nodded when a few doodles jumped out at me.

I nabbed a pen and note paper and copied the marks. "These look the same as the ones on the encaustic Anita was completing for Grace. What do they look like to you?" Jane shrugged. "I have to ask her if they mean anything." I shoved the paper into my coat pocket.

"Did you hear about Ida's arrest?"

"It's all over the news. How can anyone possibly believe she's guilty?"

"If she's convicted, Ronnie will use it to bolster his position as the most likely candidate to succeed Chief Erickson. When he arrested Ida, he threw out his chest and pulled himself up to his full height, a foot above her. I think Ida had been his piano teacher—"

"Between Ida and Miss Grace, they probably gave lessons to half the forty-and-under population of Columbia."

"But Ronnie's eyes sparked anger and maybe a bit of revenge. It looked like he wanted payback for every tortured half-hour of life Ida had commandeered to forward the integrity of his musical training." I marked the word integrity with air quotes. I took off my coat and plopped into a chair. "And I saw Paula McCall at the hospital. She went there to see Ricky's mom. Guess who that is."

Jane said, "Anita Jones."

"How did you guess?"

"She has that motherly look." I was bewildered. "Honestly? Carlee introduced us when I visited her Saturday afternoon. What do you think Paula wanted?"

"With McCall gone, she's the new head of McCall institute. Anita's happy about the bequest because she might finally get paid."

"She's earned it. McCall wasn't very nice to her at the gala."

"A lot has to happen before she gets paid, though." How could I tell Jane that Miss Grace predicted her own death? "Miss Grace had written that the provisions in her will would only take effect if we could prove who killed her."

Jane dropped into a chair. "How could she know? You have to call Pete." I shook my head. "Suck it up for Ida."

I steeled my heart, searched my favorites, and punched in his number. A female answered, "Dr. Erickson's phone. He's occupied now. May I take a message?"

I heard his voice in the background. "Who is it, Susie?"

I thought I could see her eye roll. "It's Wilk." She snorted. "I'll take a message."

"No. I'll take it now." The was a banging and a rattling as if the phone fell or was dropped. "Oops." Right, oops.

"Katie?" Pete said in a rush.

"I can't help Ida without your assistance. You know she didn't kill anyone. Did the same drug kill both?" He breathed heavily. "Pete. Please."

He muffled the phone a bit but through it I heard, "Susie, be a darling and get me a notepad and something to write with. Katie's sharing Ida's lefse recipe with us." When Susie's tromping footsteps faded, Pete whispered, "Strychnine. Ida's in big trouble Katie. She and Grace did have a disagreement at the gala."

I tried to jump in and tell him that they'd reconciled, that they'd even hugged. But he continued with, "And add enough flour so that it won't stick. I can't wait to try this one. Thanks." He hung up.

"Strychnine." Jane already typed it into her phone. "It comes from nux-vomica, an exotic tree. And Ida sure does love her flora." She eased a sheet of notebook paper from a pile of school supplies and sorted through the pens standing in a mug covered with numbers and math symbols that read, "Solve your own problems." She lined up the pen parallel to the top edge of the paper and leaned over the table. "It allows you to think better, I know. And you've got some thoughts brewing. Write. Them. Down."

I picked up the pen. Nothing came. I tapped it against the paper. Jane delivered a cup of tea. On the cup was a sketch of Ruth Bader Ginsburg and a quote that read, "Every now and then it helps to be a little deaf." I drew a circle and wrote Grace Loehr inside. I sniffed. Writing her name made her absence more real. Around it, I wrote the names of the legatees and beneath each their inheritance. Paula — money, Anita — money, Jordan — piano, Yvonne — money for the center, Carlee and Anna — house and money, Daniella — I had no idea. I floundered again as I performed mental gymnastics trying to work out the murders.

Jane's eyes narrowed. "You can't honestly believe Carlee and Ana are suspects. They didn't even know they were in her will."

"Maybe she was killed by someone else *because* they inherited the house. Jordan Quintz expected the house to go to him and he wasn't happy about the bequest. You never know what random, insignificant, seemingly irrelevant datum will lead us in the right direction."

"Then you're missing a suspect." She waited. "You never know what random, insignificant …" I stared at the page. In letters half as tall as any others, I reluctantly penned, "Ida."

My phone pinged. "CJ is coming to get Carlee and he'd like to have a word with me. Sounds kind of serious."

Maverick and I sped on foot through the neighborhood,

passing happy Christmas displays oblivious to my growing apprehension. Why would anyone kill Miss Grace? Who would kill Phillip McCall? Ida couldn't kill anyone, but something besides her had to connect the two deaths.

When Maverick yanked the leash, I'd discovered I'd stopped in front of Carlee and Ana's new home. The living room lights bled through the dark red drapes and cast a forlorn signal on the snow. Faint musical notes floated so near I could almost make out the melody. Fairy lights twinkled in the yard, an invitation perhaps.

As if he could read my mind, Maverick plunged through the snow mound, and I skied behind him until I touched the clapboard siding. My hand skimmed the slats up to the window on the same side of the house as Miss Grace's music room. I caught Maverick's attention and put my mitten to my mouth. The blinds didn't quite meet the sill and I peered into the room.

I heard two voices. I assumed Jordan still occupied the house or would until Saturday. But who could be with him?

A shadow grew larger, and Jordan tromped into the room. He slid books from the shelves, one at a time, opened and shook them. At first, he returned them to the shelves, but then he tossed them on the floor at a frenzied pace. When he stopped abruptly and pivoted my way, I ducked. I stopped breathing. Sweat drizzled down my back. In the quiet, Maverick's panting sounded like a chugging train.

We bolted.

CHAPTER THIRTY-ONE

Maverick bounded up the steps and in through the door Dad held open, joining CJ's young puppy, Renegade, in a race around the kitchen. CJ whistled. Renegade sat. Maverick sat. I sat. I had to learn that trick.

"Tell me about the will," CJ said. The dogs dropped onto the carpet in the doorway. With their heads on crossed paws, their big eyes ping-ponged back and forth, waiting and watching.

Dad pulled a warm baguette from the oven and filled four bowls with one of Ida's fragrant beef stews. While we savored the delicious supper, Carlee and I told CJ more than he wanted to know. When his spoon scraped the bottom of the bowl, he asked, "Why would Carlee and Ana get her house?"

"I think Miss Grace wants the two of you—" Renegade's paws slapped across the linoleum and slid to a stop next to Dad. "Excuse me. The three of you to move out of your dinky apartment. She owned a modest home with a kitchen and a yard and neighbors. She never had children of her own and adored Carlee and Ana. She took pride in being able to provide something special for the girls. They went through quite an ordeal."

"Do you think Carlee is in danger?"

I shivered, thinking how close we came to losing both girls to an evil man who methodically trafficked girls on the fringe. But he chose the wrong girls. They had an entire brigade take him to task. CJ rescued Carlee and Ana the first time on sheer principal because of the man he is, but now his concern ran deeper.

"The provisions of the will are dependent upon proving who killed Miss Loehr. I heard, from a reliable source, that the cause of her death was strychnine." Even at the best of times, CJ was hard to read. Knowing Carlee could possibly be at risk made his face implacable.

"I'd like to meet Jordan Quintz."

"Da-ad," Carlee said. The look on his face could have melted a snowman at thirty degrees below zero. "Thanks for dinner. But we've got to go. I have homework." She shrugged into her coat and gloves. When she came out from under her stocking cap, she caught the disbelieving looks on our faces. "Lorelei brought candy, puzzles, chuckles, gossip, *and* assignments."

CJ lifted Carlee from her wheelchair. Dad collapsed it and rolled it behind them. Before they reached the door, Maverick and Renegade roared to life. CJ and Dad stood stock still while the dogs snaked between them toward the back door. CJ whistled and the dogs sat. I nabbed their collars, pulled both pups behind the table and knelt next to them. Then we heard the knock.

Dad leaned the wheelchair against the wall and pulled open the door. In his most deferential voice he said, "Chief Christianson. What can we do for you?"

My curled fingers tightened around the nylon and I whispered to the dogs, but it could have been to Dad too. "Be good."

"I received a complaint from Jordan Quintz. He thought he heard someone creeping around outside the house." Funny. I didn't think Ronnie made similar inquiries when I caught Jordan trying to break in here and I knew who the guilty party was. "Lo and behold, we found tracks to and from the window and one belonged to a dog. They ended at the street but we're canvassing the neighborhood for witnesses." He eyed Maverick and me. "Katie, you wouldn't know anything about that would you?"

"I'm sorry Chief Christianson. That was my dad," Carlee said. Her dad hitched her higher and cinched her closer. "I asked him to check out the house and make sure the doors were secure. You know it may be mine soon, and I don't really know the man staying there. Did you see anybody, Dad?" He shook his head from side to side, with all honesty, as *he* hadn't seen anybody.

"And I suppose you scoped out the Loehr home with Ms. Wilk's dog?" Ronnie pointed to Maverick who hung his head and looked, to me, as guilty as a dog possibly could. Renegade took that moment to break free from my hold and sidle next to CJ. She sat and cocked her head, batting her beautiful golden eyes at Ronnie.

"Meet Renegade," said CJ.

"Ah-ha. Please call in if you see anyone *else* sneaking

around." He handed a business card to Dad. "I think the Farleys are organizing a community watch. Maybe you can join them. Can I help you, Dr. Bluestone?"

"Thanks, but I've got her. However, if you would carry the wheelchair, then Harry would not have to go out in the cold."

Ronnie took the chair from Dad, and they were out the door.

"What gives, Dad? You have an odd look on your face."

Dad took a deep breath. "Dorene called." He stopped talking. Maverick nudged his hand. "The bond could be a lot."

My insides turned to jelly. "Ida won't get out on bail?"

"It sounds like Ronnie will do everything he can to keep her in jail. But it's time to 'fess up. What did you see at Grace's?"

"I saw Jordan, but he should be there. I kind of peeked in the window and I saw him searching through some books and papers in her music room, tossing them around and throwing some to the floor. I didn't see anyone with him, but I thought I heard someone." I shrugged. "He was looking for something. I think it's time we paid Mr. Quintz a condolence call."

My phone buzzed. "It's Pamela." I accepted the call. "Hi. You're on speaker with my dad and me."

She took a deep breath and launched into a tirade atypical of our neighbor. "Ronnie paid us a visit. He scared Emma and I was so angry that I wasn't thinking when I told him I hadn't seen anyone at Grace's. But Katie, I saw you. What on earth were you and Maverick doing? Why were you peeping through the window? What has gotten into you this time? I owe you and Maverick, and will always owe you and Maverick for taking care of my Emma, but I want to know what I'm getting myself into."

For the third time, I recounted the terms of Miss Grace's will, adding Carlee's little white lie.

Pamela breathed heavily. "I'd do anything for Ida too. That horse's patootie. What's Ronnie thinking? He can't believe that Ida's a murderer. It looks like he's trying to arrest someone for the high-profile crimes, which might give him a leg up in the search for a chief." She growled. "Sheesh." I heard a small voice in the background. "Mommy's fine, honey. Go back to bed and I'll be right there.

"Katie, I've got to go. Can I sign you up for our neighborhood watch? I need to submit a list to Ronnie to get him off my back."

"Absolutely."

I heard a sharp intake.

"Pamela? What's wrong?"

Her voice cracked. "Pull up the Columbia *Sentinel* Master Gardener files from a year ago. Look for Ida's winning entry." She called out, "Coming, honey." Then said, more quietly, "I have to go."

Dad keyed the information into my laptop and shook his head. "Now what are we going to do?"

Ida beamed from a full screen photo in the special section from the online version of the Columbia *Sentinel*, parting the shiny, deep green leaves of a tall plant in a clay pot and held her hand under a round fruit, resembling an orange. Dad summarized the caption. "She took first place in the exotic plant category."

CHAPTER THIRTY-TWO

As the month neared winter solstice, fewer hours of daylight somehow translated into fewer productive hours in my day. Not possible mathematically, but the fifteen hours between sunset and sunrise usually appealed to my hibernation gene. Rather than burrow deeper under covers, I planned to act as if the sun had risen and accomplish as much as I could. I wouldn't be able tell the difference when I sat at my desk in my interior classroom. No windows, no sunlight anyway. With good intentions, I plodded through the quiet halls and stepped around the corner toward the math pod.

Brock's head popped up from a whispered conversation he was having with Kindra. "Hey, Ms. Wilk."

"What are you doing here so early?"

"The workout equipment is available to all off-season students before school." On the mend from a shoulder injury, Brock took advantage of the open gym and exercised regularly to ensure he was back on the pitcher's mound in the spring.

Kindra encouraged Brock with a nod, and he said, "You should check out our cache."

"I will."

I logged into our geocaching account and spent the next ten minutes shackled to my computer, reading the less-than-raving reviews: 'wasn't what was expected,' 'who cares,' 'why do we have to email an answer to the cache owner,' and 'don't waste your time.' I'm certain the disparaging comments hurt.

Instead of prepping for the day, I sought comfort among the biographies of mathematicians I had stashed on the shelf, paging through the historical snippets to locate an amusing anecdote or unexpected fact for my students. Rifling through my collection, I hit upon one of my favorites and coordinated my interactive whiteboard with a little bit of trivia.

When my students finally settled into their seats, I brought up the specs of a World War II airplane. "Too many aircraft were shot down and unable to make the return home during the war." I changed the screen. "This drawing of a plane riddled with red bullet holes indicates the concentration of damage sustained on the undercarriage, the wingtips, and the tail of many of the planes that returned to base. I'd like you to break up into four groups, take a few minutes, and answer the question: where would you reinforce the armor on these planes?"

After a fun exchange within the teams, they indicated

they all had answers. A spokesperson from the first group walked up to the whiteboard and circled the obvious areas in need of more protection. The other groups agreed. "They'd have to reinforce the plating over the areas hardest hit with gunfire. We can see it. Is that what they did?"

"The military experts agreed with you …" Then I dropped my bomb. "Until Abraham Wald, a mathematician and statistician …" I stopped and gave them time to grasp the significance of this individual's vocation. "… introduced the *survival bias* phenomenon, the logical error of concentrating on things that survived instead of things that didn't. The ground crews observed the damage on planes that made it home. Wald postulated the Allies should armor the areas where there were no dots at all because the planes sustaining hits in those places never returned." My students groaned. "Sometimes it's what you don't see that's just as important as what you do see."

After school, I returned my Wald file to its chronologic timeslot. But before I realigned the stack of files, I looked more closely at the illustrations of ancient computation systems. I removed the files, wondering why they looked familiar, and slid them into my briefcase.

I hadn't heard from Dad or Ida and after a quick run through of our mock trial case, I zipped home for news.

Maverick didn't greet me at the door. My footsteps echoed in the empty kitchen. The ticking of the clock on the wall counted out individual seconds. I piled my school things on the counter and knocked on the adjoining door. Dad answered, drying a white porcelain tureen. I followed his eyes and tilted head toward the living room where Ida sagged into the couch. Her sallow complexion set off her brittle red hair. The green in her normally vivid eyes looked gray. Her small feet dangled above the floor and a black monitor encircled her ankle. She gripped the arm of a baggy, ugly-Christmas sweater with one hand, and held a folded newspaper in the other. She rocked as she read.

She looked up at me and tears filled her eyes. I knelt in front of her, crushing the paper and cupping her cold hand in mine. "We're going to figure this out."

"Those poor girls stuck in jail," she said. "They didn't have anyone to vouch for them and they must stay in that awful place. When I get this straightened out, I'm going to figure a way to provide funds for those who can't afford it."

"Ida," I sighed. In the middle of a murder investigation, the number one suspect is worried about everyone else. "We are going to get you out of this. Have you thought of anything that will put us closer to finding out who killed Miss Grace?"

She shook her head and the tears spilled down her cheeks.

"I'm going out to talk to Mrs. Nygren. Can we have a meeting of the minds when I get back?"

Dad said, "We'll work on our end."

I headed out to the history center, my thoughts clouded by the realization that Carlee and Ana could be denied the house, the history center might have to go without funds to update, Jordan could be our neighbor, and Ida could go to jail. I knew she didn't kill Miss Grace. Someone just had to prove who did and time was spinning out of control.

I parked Dad's car and pulled out my caching app. The GPS directed me under the eave and the answer to the pair of numbers jumped out at me. Someone had painted a horizontal arrow next to the second row and a vertical arrow above the seventh column pointing to the answer in the Honour and Glory pamphlet slot.

Derek glanced up and waved me through, continuing to read the book he held in his hand. I took the visitor route to the staircase and kept my eyes open for Mrs. Nygren. She'd be easy to spot in the empty halls, but I made it to the bridge without encountering anyone. I opened our journal expecting to see the cipher, the initialed heart, and the signatures.

I tore the defaced first page out of the book and crumpled it into a tight ball.

CHAPTER THIRTY-THREE

I removed the lewd sheet of instructions for the third stage and replaced it with something close to the original until the kids could fix it. It was a good thing they monitored the posting so closely.

I delved deeper into the center through a third-class berth, across the spotless *Titanic* deck, past a yellow line of demarcation, looking for Mrs. Nygren. Throwing caution to the wind, I quickly looked into the cool water room. I zipped my jacket and bundled my scarf around my neck to ward off the frosty air. Water sloshed over the sides of the pool but, thankfully, I didn't find anything or anyone. I exited through the double doors, into the Monongalia County archives.

Sickly green paint peeled from the walls and the dark

wooden floor creaked. When I brushed by, dust rose from the glass cases housing artifacts from the scions who lived around Columbia near the turn of the century over one hundred years ago. Hidden moth balls perfumed the air, barely covering an age-old mustiness. The lights dimmed and brightened, indicating closing hours. I picked up the pace and rushed through the exhibits, passed a vignette arranged with mannequins dressed in pioneer clothing bent over boiling pots. Next, golden-eyed wolves surrounded a snowbound wagon hauling a frightened family. Hunters in coon-skin caps cast furtive glances into a mural with many pairs of buffalo eyes staring back. A mule dragged a pile of skins on a wooden frame. The radio station figured prominently in local history, and I stopped to admire the replica of an old production room. Vinyl records surrounded a broadcaster wearing a tie-dyed T-shirt, baggy jeans, a beard, long gray hair, and small oval wire-rimmed glasses, hanging onto a large silver microphone in a low-tech analog recording studio.

I pushed aside fabric curtains and passed through a room filled with sculptures, paintings, beaded jewelry, and hand-woven wall hangings created by local artists, out into a dark hallway.

Light leaked from beneath one door, and I knocked.

"What? What?" came the distinctive reply.

I stepped into a room in chaos filled with overturned cardboard boxes, metal tins, plastic tubs, and opened file drawers. Mrs. Nygren stood in the middle, brushing back tendrils that stuck to her forehead and cheeks. The grimy marks on the tip of her nose and her chin made her look like a chimney sweep. A sheen of sweat rested above her lips.

"Can I help you with something?" I cast my eyes

around the room and spread my hands, palms up, meaning no threat.

Mrs. Nygren sank to the floor. "I made quite a bit of headway on the inventory list. Bobby realized his dream when he built this exhibit, and he organized the borrowed and leased pieces with precision." She shoved a file into my hand. "Owner, detailed description, value, length of lease, and location in the exhibit." File A described a deck chair located in plexiglass case E-1, valued at $150,000, on loan from a private collector for one calendar year.

"This meets Miss Grace's requirements, doesn't it?"

"Some. Some. But I can't find any of Bobby's personal pieces."

"Robert Bruckner's pieces? None of them?"

She shook her head. "They are smaller pieces, mostly jewelry, but I can't find any of them. I don't know if he moved them and never had time to record the new information before …"

"He was killed." I finished her thought and shuddered.

Tears filled her eyes and she nodded. Maverick found Robert Bruckner's body and I shivered, remembering the bloody paw prints I followed to the scene.

"I've searched all the cases housing jewelry with no luck. I don't know what else to do. They're simply lost."

Or stolen, but I didn't want to bring that up.

"May I see what's missing?"

Mrs. Nygren had drawn heavy black lines through three-fourths of the items listed. The remaining articles belonged to Bruckner, including three pendants, a pair of cufflinks, a brooch, a collar pin, diamond earrings, a money clip, coal, assorted fragments of dinnerware, and a piece of the ship. "Do you have a more detailed description of what's missing? Maybe I can help."

"Yes, I—" The overhead lights crackled and turned dark. "Hold on. We keep blowing the old fuses, but the generator will kick in." The lights turned back on. "Goodness, it's closing time. You should go. Go. Follow the blue lighted path to the ticket counter. You can get out without setting off the alarm for another thirty minutes."

"Can you email me the list with the descriptions?"

"I don't see what good it will do."

"You never know." I jotted my email on a purple square sticky note.

As I backtracked the way I'd come, I could have sworn the yellow eyes of the stalking wolves viewed me as prey and I picked up my pace. My anxiousness magnified every groan in the old building. It felt alive.

Derek held the door and walked out with me.

There were four vehicles in the parking lot. Derek jumped in a beater truck and waved as it bellowed and growled to life. My wheels rested in the circle under a parking lot lamp. I dreamed it might be warm. Mrs. Nygren needed a ride. But that left the dark-colored Lexus that looked like the one belonging to Daniella Jericho. I drove home, wondering if she was still wandering around inside.

Maverick waited inside the door, gripping the leash in his slobbery mouth. Before I could close the door, he pranced into the back yard. "I get the hint."

I snapped the leash onto his collar. He dragged me down the drive and across the street, following our old tracks to the window. "Maverick," I hissed. "We can't be here."

Then I heard the front door slam.

CHAPTER THIRTY-FOUR

Jordan marched around the side of the house in a T-shirt, jeans, and boots. "You."

"I'm sorry. My dog—"

"Don't give me that. I'm calling Chief Christianson."

"Wait, please. I just wanted to offer my condolences." I had to think fast. "But my dog has a good nose and decided to check out the tracks. I also wanted to see if there's anything I can do for you."

"Like what?"

"I know you were surprised by the terms of the will. You are family. Maybe I can help you go through the house and if there are things you'd like, you could ask for them. Carlee and Ana are just so happy. You don't know what they went through, and the house is a blessing." I didn't want to tell him about the vile woman who thought she could make money on them.

"You can come in, but don't get any funny ideas. What about him? He'll be good?" I nodded and hoped he'd be good.

I left my winter gear by the door but kept Maverick on his leash as Jordan started the tour. He never glanced at the cabinets loaded with knickknacks as we trekked through the living room. The familiar first floor brought to mind the lovely music that always filled this house, and I could hear Miss Grace's fingers dancing across the keyboard. I knelt next to Maverick and laid my forehead against his.

Jordan disappeared. I sat on the loveseat where Ida sat after we found Miss Grace and noticed the edge of the crinkled photo I'd stuck under the lamp. I tugged it free and polished it against my sweater. Maverick rocked back and forth. Before he could lunge anywhere, I slipped the photo into my pocket and laced my fingers around his collar. I looked around the room. The books and papers were back on the shelves, but lined up unevenly and haphazardly, maybe done in a hurry.

Jordan reentered, carrying a beer. "I don't even know where to start." He tipped his bottle toward her beautiful piano. "I looked up what to do with that old monstrosity and it would cost a gold bar to move. I don't play piano. It's worthless to me but if those girls want it, I'll sign it over for five grand."

I thought that sounded fair, and I think with CJ, Dad, Ida, Jane, and I at the ready, we could afford it. It belonged in this room.

"Do you know the terms of her previous will?"

"Sorry, I don't."

"Let's start upstairs."

I heaved a sigh. I didn't want to know the provisions of the preceding will. It meant we'd failed to complete our assigned tasks, and Ida would be going to jail.

"Stay." Maverick slumped to the floor. I dropped the leash. I ran my hand along the polished wood of the banister, following Jordan.

He opened the door to the room at the top of the stairs, revealing white walls with a single bed covered in gray, a white dresser, white nightstand, a goosenecked lamp, and white dotted Swiss curtains. Four white wooden fir trees, in graduated sizes, lined the mantel above the gas fireplace in the corner.

"This is a guest room. The drawers and closet are empty," he said. He'd been here alone and knew the contents of the entire house. We'd have no way of knowing if he'd already found anything of value. But honestly, I thought, Carlee and Ana wouldn't want his family things.

Fluffy white towels hung from silver metal rings in a sparkling Jack-and-Jill bathroom joining the white room to its mirror image. The addition of a tufted gray-velveteen seat lodged in a bay window and glittery white snowflake cutouts on the mantel stepped up the minimalist decor.

The next room was three times their size. Decorated in soft blue and white, it had a cottage feel. Royal-blue shams covered the extra-large pillows piled on the crisp light-blue bed linen. A huge white pile rug outlined the living space around the bed. Gulls swooped over a sandy beach under a sunny sky in a blown-up photograph that hung over the bed. A chaise lounge upholstered in irises faced a wood-burning fireplace packed with charred birch logs. Streetlights leaked between the wide slats of the blinds covering the window. Jordan turned up the rheostat on the recessed lights in the tray ceiling, flooding the room with harsh light. The warmth of the room faded.

"Help me go through Grace's stuff." Jordan ran his fingers over the seashells and sharks' teeth in the crystal bowls on the dresser. Then he opened the drawers, one at a time, and rifled through the contents. He turned toward me. "Are you going to help?"

"How about if I just witness what you do? I wouldn't know what to look for." And I couldn't invade Miss Grace's private space.

"She can't care, you know. But whatever. You can watch and *guarantee* I don't take anything." He slammed the bottom drawer. He took one book at a time from the neat stack on the nightstand and held it by its cover, shaking it. Nothing fell out and the stack nearly toppled. He opened a walk-in closet door and pulled a string, illuminating neat rows of folded sweaters and pants, long dresses sheathed in plastic, shoes paired on metal rods, jackets, shirts, and skirts lined up by color—darkest to lightest, and hatboxes piled to the ceiling. "Someone will have to go through this junk. I haven't found anything worth keeping."

A second door led through a bathroom to a small office. Jordan plunked into the soft leather chair and opened and shut the desk drawers, pretending to inspect the contents.

Back out in the hall, I slowed in front of a closed door. "My room," he said, urging me down the stairs. "After you."

Jordan searched a half bath, and the kitchen.

"What's behind that door?" I asked.

"That's the utility room." He waved dismissively. "You watched. Now you can tell them I didn't take anything! Right?"

I nodded. *You didn't take anything this time.* I wondered where Miss Grace kept her personal belongings, photos, records, or jewelry? I knew she had some as my hand went into my pocket, and I felt the edge of the old picture. I meant to return it but was distracted when a growl rumbled from the front room.

CHAPTER THIRTY-FIVE

Maverick charged the door and launched into a full-on, loud, and aggravated bark.

"Shut him up," Jordan yelled, reaching for the knob. With a glare at Maverick and me, he opened the door.

"Maverick, sit." I scratched his ears and the top of his head. He stopped the ruckus, sat, closed his big brown eyes, and leaned into my hand.

Daniella teetered on the top step. Jordan grabbed her fur coat and hauled her inside. "Daniella." He looked back at me. "Nice to see you again. What can I do for you?"

I yanked on my boots and shrugged into my coat. "We'll finish our walk. Thanks for the tour."

Two pairs of piercing eyes bored into my back as we stepped carefully down the steps. Maverick towed me to the sidewalk, but even at this distance I could hear raised voices. Maverick bent his head toward the path we'd beaten to the window, and I tightened my grip. "No, you don't, doggie-mine." We headed back to our apartment.

Chilled from our jaunt around the neighborhood, I stacked logs and lit a fire. I recorded assignment scores by the flickering firelight and checked my lesson plan for the next day, trying to quell a nagging feeling. I gazed at the yellow, red, and orange blaze licking the crackling wood, working through the suspects in both murders, which amounted to nothing.

McCall had taken advantage of Anita's desire to be accepted into the art community, but she had no reason to kill Miss Grace. Paula had almost missed out on McCall's windfall. Yvonne had benefitted more when McCall and Miss Grace were alive. Daniella was a pain and could have killed anyone. She knew Paula, Yvonne, and Jordan. Jordan knew Miss Grace, and he was an heir. There must be something.

My hand grazed the photo in my pocket, and I removed it. The grim faces of five young girls with identical bowl cuts and straight bangs stared back at me. The plaid pinafores over white blouses with puffy sleeves and Peter Pan collars, white gloves, frilly white anklets, and Mary Janes completed the school uniforms. I turned over the photo and, in the dancing flames, caught indentations. Long ago someone had written something on the back, and I detected time-worn letters. I moved the photo to eye level and skimmed my fingernail over the ridges then searched for a pencil and lightly shaded the back. The graphite settled in imperceptible depressions and six words appeared: Lauren, Michele, Lisa, Nicole, Jordan Quintz.

Jordan was a girl?

Many thoughts scurried through my brain. This could be a different Jordan. Jordan could be pretending to be a man. Jordan could have altered her appearance. I typed Jordan Quintz into the search engine and frowned at the long list generated. I typed in Jordan and Lauren Quintz. The list grew. I refined my search parameters, and landed on a two-year old obituary for Jordan Quintz, sister of Lauren, Michele, Lisa, and Nicole.

When Jane didn't answer, I left a message. "Call me." I paced, wondering how to share my concerns.

I called CJ, and Carlee answered. "Hi, Ms. Wilk. Dad's with the animals but he'll be back soon. Care to leave a message?"

"Just have your dad call me, okay."

Drew was someplace, maybe undercover, and Pete was someplace else, maybe under cover. I read the entire notice of Jordan's death, recounting adventures to India and Australia, eating foods alive with wriggly things I wouldn't touch, bungee jumping, parasailing, rock-climbing, white-water rafting, and avid story telling. Her sister noted 'with her penchant for spinning a good yarn, we didn't believe she was dying until that final day when God took her breath away.' She was survived by her loving sisters and her travel companions.

While I mulled over who might be across the street, my phone buzzed. Before I could tell Jane about Jordan, she said, "I got another weird call."

We decided she'd stay with Dad and me until Drew returned, or we figured out what she had that someone else wanted. I pulled out the couch and had just finished making the bed when Dad walked in.

"Jane coming?"

"Yes. How's Ida holding up?" He shrugged. "Dad, I need your advice about something." He took a seat next to me and I let him read the obituary. Then I handed him the photo. "I picked this up at Miss Grace's. I don't think that man is Jordan Quintz."

"There could be more than one—"

"I assure you there are many more than one but look at the names on the back of this photo and compare it to the list of survivors in this obituary."

He looked skeptical. "Who do you think he is?"

"I think if I did a little digging, I might be able to ferret out some answers."

"Darlin', you can't stick your nose where it doesn't belong. Two people have died."

"We know that Ida is not responsible. I don't trust Ronnie. He won't even consider other suspects. We have to do something." Dad rubbed his temples. "And Jane will be with me."

"That's not necessarily a good thing. I can't have either of you getting hurt. I'm going to check on Ida." His hand grabbed the doorknob of her apartment. "Promise me you won't investigate." He disappeared next door.

Minutes later, Maverick woofed, and I went to the door, opening it as Jane's hand came up to knock. She barreled through the door lugging an overnight bag and the jeweled wreath she'd just recreated. She cradled the memory box under her arm, swinging a black Dior satchel from her shoulder. She squatted and everything toppled to the floor—it didn't have far to go. "I'm almost finished with my wreath *and* my memory box.

"Listen to this," she said. She pressed play on her phone and a distant voice intoned, 'Give it up.' "I reported the call to Officer Rodgers, but he can't do anything until we can figure out who it is. This recording isn't even considered threatening."

We tossed around a few possible solutions as we hung up her clothes and secured her lovely belongings up and out of Maverick's reach. We sat at the kitchen table with mugs of hot chocolate and a plate of broken cookies between us, all that remained of my Ida stash. She nibbled a cookie and scratched behind Maverick's ears, then she turned the photo over in her hands and saw the names. I spun my laptop screen for her to read and her mouth dropped.

"Who's our guy?" She commandeered the keyboard, and her fingers flew over the letters. When she waved me next to her, the cursor hovered over a social media page honoring the memory of Jordan Quintz. She pulled up older posts wishing her a missing-you-happy-birthday-friend. She scrolled through the collection of photos—a fair-haired Jordan standing drenched beneath a waterfall, a helmeted Jordan flying through a blue sky, a long lean Jordan reclining on a beach towel as waves inched their way over her slender toes. We compared the photos and agreed the faces looked similar.

We scanned several posts and froze after spotting our Jordan Quintz in a group photo taken in Australia. What game was he playing?

"I have a mind to go over there right now and ask him."

Jane texted wildly and put a calming hand on my arm. "Wait until I hear back from Drew. Maybe Grace knew everything. After all, she had this photo of the girls. Drew will know what to do."

A gravelly voice from behind me said, "What to do about what?"

I blanched as Dad's words of warning washed over me.

"Harry!" Jane skillfully deflected his question, closing the laptop and hustling to give my dad a hug. He grunted and she said, "I'm staying with you until Drew gets back."

"Then I insist you take my room."

"But I'm already firmly ensconced on the cozy couch where I can snuggle in front of the fireplace and wake up to the piney fragrance of your Christmas tree. I'm afraid it'd take a crane to move me now. Thanks, anyway, but I won't unseat the king."

He grinned and yawned.

Maverick stretched his forelegs and Jane cued, "Who's the queen?"

My stomach growled. The three of them gazed at me. "Cookie crumbs anyone?"

Dad shook his head from side to side. He lifted the tote he carried. "Ida was in a frenzy. She fixed a batch of ham-and-cheese sandwiches, made more gingerbread and sugar cookies, and taped directions to the top of a pan of cinnamon rolls for morning. I'll warm the sandwiches and you can set the table."

I poured more hot chocolate.

Jane scrounged around in the cupboard and found a bag of chips. "Do you think Ida would like to join us?"

"I hope she's asleep. She's had one heck of a day." Dad said, dishing out sandwiches. "When we finish eating, I'll clean up the kitchen and you two do your thing."

Jane kept up a smoke screen with the prattle of stories about her growing up. I held my aching sides and tears streamed down Dad's cheeks, listening to her babbling conversation while we finished the scrumptious meal.

Dad's preoccupation with Ida's plight had him clanging the dishes. "Do you need any help, Dad?"

"Nope." Crash. "I've got this." Bang.

Jane set up her memory box and opened a small can of paint. I emptied my briefcase, organizing the hours of the day.

After a few minutes, Dad said, "I'm going to check on Ida again."

"Tell her we miss her." I opened the top file.

"Jane?" I felt my eyebrows rise. "Jane."

"Give me a sec. I'm almost finished."

I tore my eyes away from the figures on the page in front of me. "Wait." I clambered from my seat, tripping on Maverick who'd come to attention. "Look."

Jane dipped her paintbrush in a can. A drop of green paint clung to the hairs, but she didn't make another stroke. "It looks like the markings on my shadow box."

I rubbernecked around the baubles she'd inserted, trying to locate the strange symbols.

"Where are they?"

"I painted over them."

My shoulders slumped until I remembered I'd copied the symbols and stuffed them ... where? I searched my briefcase. I fanned through the pages on the table. I rummaged through my pockets and came up with the crumpled square.

I knew what I'd find. "These could be ancient numerals. But for what?"

Maverick lifted his head and gave a friendly bark. I almost stopped her, but Jane had more faith in my dog than I did, and she opened the door on our local Grand Central Station.

Susie shuffled along in front of Pete. "We know you're sticking your nose where it probably doesn't belong, and

Pete was only doing his job but now he's feeling like he contributed to Ida's arrest. Tell him it isn't so."

Pete stood on the top step, hands in his pockets, collar up against the cold, his curly hair gently tossed by the wind. "Have you found anything to clear Ida yet? She couldn't have murdered Grace. Ronnie is reading the facts the way he wants and I—"

"*We* want to help," Susie said.

"C'mon in."

I grabbed a deep breath and ran down what I'd learned at the reading of the will and what might have been motives for Miss Grace's murder. Jane nudged me. I laid the photo on the table.

"Who are they supposed to be?" asked Susie, checking her nails.

Jane displayed the social media page dedicated to Jordan Quintz. Pete zoomed in for a closer look. When the churning behind his eyes stopped, he stared at me. "You don't really know what this means."

My temper sometimes flared at unanticipated times. "Maybe I should just ask him," I said with a huff. "And what about these?" I flattened the square and matched the unusual markings to my files on the history of math.

"They look like scribbles to me." Susie grumbled. "I don't think you have anything that will help Ida. She did have an argument with Grace. She had motive, means, and Grace lived across the street." It's a good thing Susie reached into her purse and pulled out a tube of lipstick. Then the laser looks wouldn't harm her.

"Pete," Jane said. "You're awfully quiet."

"Tell me again why Daniella sat in at the reading," said Pete.

"She accompanied the history center director. I thought she came to see if she still needed to match the pledge dollars."

"She was not a beneficiary?"

I shook my head.

Pete tapped his forehead. "Jane, can you pull up the obituary for Fred Jericho?"

A craggy face filled the screen. The cold, bottomless eyes drilled right into me, and I cringed. Jane scrolled down and read the article.

"Pete," Susie said. "Isn't that the guy who closed down the parochial school here in Columbia?"

The hint of a smile reached Pete's eyes. "I think he made some teachers second-guess their calling. He dropped antacid in the fish tank in third grade and put graffiti on the walls in eighth grade but ended up designing popular gaming apps. Daniella married him about fifteen years ago. She lived the high life until he died and left everything to an order of nuns to start a school in the mountains of Peru."

Susie shook her head. "She doesn't have any money?"

Jane's eyes shifted between Susie and Pete.

"I don't know. She could have squirreled away funds, but her main source has dried up."

Susie crossed her arms over her chest. "Well, her fur coat has seen better days." Jane nodded. Takes a fashion maven to know one.

"Then she wanted to show up Grace at the gala, but might not have been able to honor her pledge?"

Pete didn't speak. He looked like he wanted to escape.

"What are you thinking, Pete?"

"Grace came to see me with some unusual symptoms." He breathed deeply. "She was terminally ill."

Susie stopped fidgeting. Maverick got up from his spot on the floor and looked back and forth. I almost choked.

"Are you saying Miss Grace committed suicide"

Pete shook his head. "No, but it's the reason her will is so current. And it may be a reason for someone to help things along."

A throat cleared. Dad stood in the doorway to the kitchen, frowning. Caught. "Hi, Doc. Susie." A look that could have held a dagger landed just shy of the table and he said, "We've got to solve Grace's murder. I'll put the cocoa on."

"You're quiet and that scares me, Katie," Pete said "What are you thinking?"

I rotated the laptop and typed the information before spinning it back.

"Jeez, I forgot."

Susie bumped his head as she bent to get a closer look at the caption below the photo of Ida hugging her winning plant. "Nux-vomica grows in Southeast Asia and contains strychnine."

Then we made plans.

CHAPTER THIRTY-SIX

Jane drove us to school while I scribbled notes filled with questions, circles, connecting arrows, and missing pieces. I needed to compare the crude symbols to the pictogram pattern on Anita's encaustic.

We were nowhere near proving Ida's innocence, but the rocky path had some offshoots to explore. Susie had local sources to quiz about Daniella's financial stability. Pete thought he could talk to Ronnie and determine if he had any desire to pursue other suspects. Dad promised to keep an eye on Ida. Jane made an appointment to meet with Paula at the McCall Institute. And I hoped to talk to Mrs. Nygren after school, but the day didn't go as planned.

Icy roads contributed to a ghastly pile up and Pete and Susie worked through the night caring for over a dozen injured patients. Then, following the arrest of their immediate faculty supervisor for tax evasion, the fellowship team requested their presence at an emergency evaluation and reformation of their instruction schedule.

Ida disappeared and Dad sent me frantic text messages, but she'd shared her plans to rehearse for the evening's music fest for the children at the hospital with Officer Rodgers. Rachel arranged for the atrium piano to be transported upstairs to the commons area and Ida supervised its tuning. When she arrived home to change into concert attire, a dress long enough to hide her new ankle bracelet, she begrudgingly invited Dad to attend the evening performance.

In the middle of our mock trial run-through, Ronnie called, requesting Jane cancel her apartment alarm that had been going on and off for over an hour.

I intended to talk to Yvonne, but Carlee rolled up in her wheelchair with hope-filled eyes. "My dad is still working and there's a Christmas sing-along at the hospital. Could you take me to visit Ricky?"

Her eyes lit up, pleading in a way I couldn't resist. And I could keep an eye on Ida.

Packed to capacity, the elevator spilled the passengers who were greeted by a jolly Rachel, a small green elf tooling around in a wheelchair, and a skinny Santa hauling a huge bag over his shoulder. A high school *a cappella* group entertained first, the director waving his baton wildly, working hard to motivate the singers and keep their attention away from the cider and colorful cookies mounded on the table in front of the nurses' station.

I looked three times at the costumed high school juggler and magician who performed amazing tricks that garnered kudos from adults and kids alike. Galen wore the mask and cape of Zorro, but Carlee giggled and confirmed he had four magic tricks that worked every time and that was his entire repertoire.

Santa made the rounds, handing out treats and making a huge effort at a belly laugh. When he stood in front of me, I whispered, "Santa, you need more padding."

"Yes, darlin'." He handed me a small box and winked. I opened it. I clamped my lips and shook my head. Leave it to Dad to give me a box of chocolate kisses. Anita furrowed her brow when he handed her a shiny green, padded envelope. She emptied the envelope and lifted the lid on a blue velvet box. Her eyes flew wide then sparkled. Before she closed it, she tipped it toward me and revealed the contents—the fine gold pendant with a small diamond on a serpentine chain. Elizabeth had missed out.

"This can't be for me." But there was no mistaking the name printed in black capital letters on the front of the envelope.

"It's Christmas." My smile took up so much of my face I could barely see over my cheeks. *Dad.*

"Anita," I said, still smiling. "What happened between you and Phillip?"

She turned gray.

"Are you all right?" I led her to a chair. "Can I get you a drink?"

She nodded but when I returned with the apple cider, all that remained of Anita Jones was the green envelope. I picked it up and its contents shifted. I stuffed it into my bag and zigzagged through the murmuring crowd as the bright notes from the piano quieted the voices.

Ida swayed, the gold and pearlescent sequins on her

dress sparkling in the lights. Her fingers danced through unexpected harmonies and challenging arpeggios, and her entire body stretched from treble to bass and back. The physical gymnastics mesmerized her audience as she wove odd themes and familiar melodies with spectacular ornamentation. I picked out the first few notes of an evocative "O Holy Night" and a stunning "Silent Night." The voices rose together singing, "O come, let us adore him" and grew until she gracefully slowed and concluded, dramatically draped over the keys. She moved away from the bench and took a little bow. Tears glittered on her cheeks, and the pint-sized piano student who took her place banged out "Jolly Old St. Nicholas."

She retired to the nurses' station and crumpled. Dad rushed to one side, and he steered her into a chair I nabbed.

"Forty years ago, I found that score on the music rack of Grace's beautiful white Steinway. It laid perfectly beneath my fingers and before I finished the piece, Casimer was seated by my side. He didn't leave it until the day he died, but it seems Grace never forgave me."

Dad took her hand. "Yes, she did. She thought she wanted what you had, but she wanted a life of musical performance. She forgave you the first time she played Carnegie Hall, but she was too proud to ever admit it to you. The last few months were some of her happiest. I know. She told me."

"Oh, Harry." Ida put her head on his shoulder. We wrapped her in her coat and Dad trundled her out behind the Christmas revelers. Galen caught my eye, pointing out a giggling Carlee and Ricky. He pantomimed that he'd get her home.

I pressed my bag, feeling the outline of the gift box and

joined Dad and Ida in the elevator. "Anita forgot her gift from Santa." Dad winked. "After I drive you two home, I'm going to drop it off and then swing by the history center to see if I can catch Mrs. Nygren."

"Tell Yvonne I'll assist with the inventory," Ida said.

I needn't have worried about remembering how to get to Anita's. Trouble lights lit the yard filled with three fire engines, two police cars, and an ambulance. Anita stood in the snow, her arms hugging her shivering body, staring at the spectacle.

I gently touched her shoulder. "Anita?"

Her eyes stared at the enormous gray-and-white icicles forming on the eaves and walls of the addition to her home housing the forest of easels. "If I hadn't taken some pieces to the history center, they'd all be gone now. The ceiling in my studio fell in and most of my supplies are ruined. I guess I'm lucky. The fire was contained, and our living quarters are untouched." She fell to her knees. "What if Ricky had been here?"

I swallowed hard and choked back tears of my own. I lifted her and brushed off the snow.

"But he wasn't. He's safe." I eyed the blackened mess and deep ruts freezing in the yard. "We'll get this cleaned up. Ida knows people. You might not be able to work in your studio for a while, but we'll make it right. Do you have a place to stay tonight?"

"I can stay with my sister, but I'll need to get some things."

"Does she live in Columbia?" She nodded. "I'll give you a ride."

"Thank you." She requested permission to enter the premises and was directed to the policemen standing near the wall that sustained the least damage.

If possible, the look I got from Temporary Police Chief Ronnie Christianson would have turned me into another pillar of ice. A young fireman accompanied Anita inside, giving Ronnie time to tramp across the yard. "You again. What do you think you're doing?" he said with disgust. "Where there's trouble, you're not far behind."

I lifted my chin. "What trouble?" I wouldn't be intimidated, much. "I'm giving Anita a ride to her sister's."

"We'd like her out of here before the fire marshal arrives."

"You suspect arson?"

Ronnie squinted and his chin jutted out, like he was trying hard to contain his nasty words.

"We'll get out of your hair as soon as Anita grabs a few things." Thankfully, it took her all of five minutes to pack a bag, but, under Ronnie's steely glint, it was a long five minutes.

Her sister lived halfway to Ida's. Before she got out of the car, I extracted the gift box and handed it to her. "Santa never makes a mistake."

CHAPTER THIRTY-SEVEN

I heard Maverick before I saw him. His frantic nails scratched the wood on the inside of the door. "Hey, fella." He skirted past me and into the yard with furious yapping. I peered into the dark beyond the golden circles under the neighborhood lights for evidence of a squirrel, or cat, or bird, or any other living creature and came up empty. "C'mon, boy." He finished marking his favorite tree and hightailed it into the apartment, proud of doing his job.

Dad and Ida drank cocoa at the kitchen table. She smiled softly behind the steam above her mug, cuddled in a bulky sweater that bunched up around her neck. Dad dipped a peppermint stick in his mug, sipped, and hummed. "What did Yvonne say?"

"I didn't get out to see her," I said.

Dad's brows took a nosedive. "Where've you been?" he said, sounding like a dad.

"Anita Jones had a fire in her studio …" They both sucked in a breath.

"Oh, that poor dear." Ida looked ready to cry again.

"She's okay. The studio—not so much. I dropped her at her sister's while they investigate the cause of the fire. I'm going to give Mrs. Nygren a call. Maybe she'll see me now."

"She will. The clock is ticking," Ida said.

In more ways than one.

"You'd better take Maverick with you. He's been pouting all day and I think he'd like the change of venue."

When we connected, Mrs. Nygren apologized for not emailing me a copy of the list of objects she needed to organize. She'd be at the center for another few hours and said I could text her for admittance when I arrived.

Maverick sat in the passenger seat, riveted by my every word with nary a dissenting opinion. We didn't come to any astounding conclusions, but I figured out I needed to talk to Paula McCall along with the bogus Jordan Quintz. My to-do list grew.

Mrs. Nygren answered my text with a call. "Come to door five on the east side of the building. It isn't locked, and it's closest to my office."

"I brought my dog with me. He's a good boy. May I bring him in?"

"Of course, of course. I love dogs and there isn't anything he can get into."

I wasn't so sure about that, but Maverick and I made tracks through the crisp clean snow.

Door five squawked as I pulled it open. We tiptoed down a dark tunnel toward the orangish shaft of light streaming from a room at the end of the hall.

"Mrs. Nygren?" Her office looked almost as bad as Anita's studio, though dry. Papers, beige and maroon files, and manila envelopes stuck out of drawers that couldn't close. A mound of garbage rose on the floor in front of the trash can. Stacks of boxes lined one wall and overturned empty boxes piled up next to the opposite wall. Necklaces hung on the corners of the computer screen, and pieces of jewelry hid most of the keyboard.

The printer stopped whirring and Mrs. Nygren collected copies from the tray. She skimmed them and, without looking my way, shoved two sheets at me. "None of these items are here. I've looked through the entire *Titanic* exhibit, in the safe, and in the storage unit. I can't imagine where they are. I distinctly remember polishing this jade and diamond piece for Miss Grace to wear the night of the gala and wondered how it could be worth so much in its condition, but it was one of the Bruckner originals, not a reproduction. I didn't get it back." She stared at her reflection in the window, then shifted her eyes to mine. "I don't know where else to look."

Thumbnail images accompanied the detailed descriptions. Only one item was checked. "Where did you find the cufflinks?"

"I lent them to the man who hosted Table Seven. He pretended to be Thomas Andrews and he was so thrilled to use them he donated five hundred dollars for the evening's wear. He returned them on Monday after the gala. But I can't find anything else."

Maverick slumped to the floor. My finger traced the

lines down the page and stopped on the blurry photo of a pendant. It looked like the necklace Jane hung as the new focal point of her wreath. "Miss Grace never returned the pendant?"

"I forgot all about it until I read the list. By that time—"

"Ida helped Robert Bruckner put the finishing touches on the exhibit. She might have an idea where else to search."

"Thank you. Thank you. I still have two more days, but I'll take all the help I can get. No matter what, I will have to report the loss and—" She sniffed. "That will be the end of my job."

"Do you have a number where I can reach you?" She entered her contact information on my phone.

If the jade on Jane's wreath belonged here, we had our work cut out for us. Was it the same piece? How did it get onto the ice? Who took it from Miss Grace? Maybe Mrs. Nygren was trying to hide the fact she took the items.

Maverick's pose shifted to that of a sphinx, eyes and ears alert. Mrs. Nygren and I turned and watched. He stood and gave one huge woof, and Paula McCall appeared in the doorway.

"I see you're busy. I can come back tomorrow, Yvonne."

"Don't go. I'm on my way out." I secured Maverick's leash. "I'm very sorry for your loss, Mrs. McCall. Thanks again, Mrs. Nygren."

"You can call me Yvonne, Katie."

"Thanks, Yvonne."

Maverick loped beside me, and we jogged to the car.

* * *

The only illumination at 3141 North Maple came from

the fairy lights aglow on the Christmas tree in the back window of my apartment which, I hoped, meant Ida slept, nestled in her bed.

Dad's door was closed, but Jane bolted upright when Maverick jumped on her mattress and lapped her face.

"Whoa, big fella." She giggled but couldn't wriggle away from his mile-long tongue. She dropped her phone and I heard Drew shout, "What fella?"

She picked up the phone, said some lovey-dovey words, and smooched at the speaker a dozen times before saying goodnight.

I flicked the switch on the table lamp and plopped into the cushiony chair next to her. "Look at this." I pointed to the sheet that included a note about a jade and diamond pendant.

Jane scratched under Maverick's chin, distracting him from giving sloppy kisses. Her jaw dropped as she read the description. She skated across the bed and stopped in front of the wreath hanging on the inside of my front door. She compared the paper in her hand with the genuine article, looking up at the necklace and down at the explanation and photo, and up and down again. "This is it," she said, a little awestruck. "How did it get with my wreath jewelry?"

I cocked my head, waiting for her to remember.

"Oh, right. Ronnie brought it over with all the other pieces." A bright light went on in her head. "But who took it from Miss Grace?"

"That is the question. Do you think we need to call Ronnie?"

We looked at each other and said at the same time, "No."

Jane inhaled. "I can't deal with him tonight."

"Me neither."

She read the rest of the list, and I told her about my evening, the concert, the fire, Yvonne, and Paula.

"We'll have to talk to Daniella tomorrow too." Jane yawned. "I'm bushed. It's time to call it a day." She sank back onto the pillow.

I pointed to Maverick and snapped the leash on his collar. I donned my headlamp cap and reflective vest, which felt mildly comforting, and we stepped outside. I glanced across the street. "The music room lights are still on, Maverick. Let's go talk to Jordan, the phony, right now."

I marched up his steps, raising my fist as if to knock. Maverick pawed the door and it swung open with a screech. Maverick pulled loose and I took three rapid steps after him, calling, "Hello, Jordan? Hello? Anyone here? Maverick!"

During the day, the collection of figurines in her glass cabinets smiled benevolently. At night, in the beam from my cap, the menacing grimaces from Alice and the Red Queen and Dorothy and the Wicked Witch of the West tracked my every step. My pace slowed to a crawl, and I backed into the glass case that held Miss Loehr's precious piano music boxes, releasing a few notes. The dissonance sent goosebumps up and down my arms. Or maybe it was the polar temperature of the night.

"Maverick," I whispered, tiptoeing to the dining room where I switched on the lights. The credenza doors flopped open, revealing empty shelves. I tripped on one of the three overturned chairs. Linen spilled from the hutch drawers and fell to the floor. The cutlery that used to fill the velvet-lined silverware box could have been hiding anywhere in the upended room.

I punched in Jane's number and got voicemail.

"Maverick, where are you?" I took a few more steps toward the music room. "Jordan? Hello?" I said with more courage, creeping, one foot at a time, into the lighted room.

A black hole gaped in the alcove the bulky antique reel-to-reel tape recorder used to fill. I skied on a slippery slope of music scores and books until I slid on a tape reel and skidded into the piano bench next to Maverick. I picked up the reel, thinking I'd save myself from being taken down on my exit. He gave me an expectant look and raced out of the room. His paws padded up the stairs. I pocketed the reel and I chased after him.

I gasped at the chaos I found in the twin rooms at the top of the stairs. The mattresses stood upright against the wall and bedding heaped on the floor.

Maverick rocked from paw to paw, waiting for me to catch up. As soon as I grabbed for his leash, he danced out of reach and into the master suite. The room had an orderly disorder, different from the rest of the house. Someone had been looking for something, hadn't bothered to conceal the search, but the contents remained in their respective places.

Stacks of clothes, still on their hangers, lined the wall. Fancy gowns peeked through jagged slits in their long transparent plastic protective sheaths. Shoes had been removed from the rack but lined up in pairs on the floor. I stepped over a jumble of headpieces.

Then, I heard a moan. I caught Maverick before he made his escape and hung on tight when he stood outside Jordan's room raising a ruckus. I pounded on the door. "Jordan? I'm coming in."

The door clattered against a stack of dirty dishes. The

room smelled like week-old sweat and month-old liquor. Clothes covered every surface, but not as if someone was looking for something. More like, a messy person.

Maverick barked and jerked me toward the source of the groaning—a figure on the floor.

One eye opened in the red and purple swollen face and peered at me. "You."

CHAPTER THIRTY-EIGHT

Jordan was strapped to a gurney, conscious and yelling a string of blue words, a diatribe against the unsafe welcome he received in Columbia, telling whoever would listen he'd been attacked. Ronnie Christianson exchanged words with the emergency technician, thumped the ambulance, and it carted Jordan away, sirens whining, red and white lights pulsing against the windows on every house down the street. Ronnie swaggered up the drive. He pointed a finger at me, hitched up his pants and said, "What are you doing messing up my crime scene?"

A woman, Ronnie's height, stepped up behind him and said, in a voice as soothing as honey, "It's not your crime scene, Officer. Christianson, isn't it?"

"Yes, Chief," Ronnie said, his obsequious voice didn't

quite reach his eyes. "I'm needed inside. Excuse me."

Chief? A copper-skinned woman, bundled in a long puffy coat and swaddled in layers of knitted scarves, snugged deeper into her winterwear. She stomped her feet in black furry boots that looked like bear paws.

Her eyes followed Ronnie into the house, then she turned to me and said, "How do you do, Miss …?"

"Wilk. Katherine Jean Wilk. But everyone calls me Katie. And this is my dog, Maverick."

She put out her hand. Although I couldn't feel her fingers through the leather mittens, I did find reassurance. "Acting Chief West. A mutual trial." Her dark eyes glittered with understanding. Of course, that could be how she got criminals to let their guard down. A beautiful, intelligent woman as a boss, I wondered how Ronnie had taken the disappointment.

"How did you come to find the victim?"

"The door was open." She waited. A long time. She was good at interrogation. I was ready to confess. To what? I didn't know.

"Is it always this cold in December?"

I forced a smile. "Yes, it gets pretty cold. I mean, no. Not all the time. Maybe, occasionally." My smile defrosted and sagged. "This weather is not unexpected just unwanted at times. It's great for winter sports like cross country skiing, ice fishing, and snowmobiling." I blathered on about the weather and words of a song rang through my head, "If I only had a brain." Sweat trickled down my back and formed prickly needles in the arctic air. I shivered. "Where did you come from?"

Her unblinking gaze made me look for something to do and I scratched the top of Maverick's head. He leaned in and his empathetic eyes reminded me, *you have a brain, use it.*

"You were saying?"

I stood straight. "Maverick is a search-and-rescue canine trainee and has a knack for finding people." She didn't need to know they could be dead people. "He budged his way inside and I chased after him. The first floor was in shambles. I called out and no one answered. Maverick rushed up the stairs and I followed. We found …" I balked at calling him Jordan, but I didn't have another name for him I wanted to share out loud.

"Katie?" Jane called and raced across the street. "What's going on now?"

"Jane Mackey, meet Chief West."

Jane processed the information. Her eyes enlarged slowly and so did her smile. "Congratulations. I'm so happy to meet you." Then I read trouble on the map of Jane's face. "Wave at your dad. He and Ida are watching from the front window."

I did as I was told.

"Chief West, did you discover the guy's real name?" Jane just couldn't keep a secret.

"You don't think that's his name." Chief West smiled. "Lance warned me about the two of you. Well, you're correct. His name is Lloyd Wicheck."

"How did you find out who he was?"

"After Miss Loehr was killed, we were made aware of Wicheck's real identity and his purpose for nondisclosure."

Ronnie knew and never said anything. He couldn't still believe Ida was guilty.

"Although Miss Grace couldn't remember ever meeting Jordan, she had a photo of the Quintz family and knew they were all girls and she'd informed her attorney of her suspicions while updating her will."

I cleared my throat. "I might have seen the photo."

One of Chief West's eyebrows rose. Through a stiff smile, she said, "Miss Loehr planned on catching him in a lie, but he confided in her—"

"And he killed her," I said, my tongue working faster than my brain.

"And told her everything. He was engaged to Jordan when she died. Although Jordan and Miss Loehr had never met, the real Jordan admired the woman. Jordan wanted to be just like her. She even planned to invite her to their wedding. She thought her family pretentious and snobbish, having severed ties with Miss Loehr decades earlier because they had no patience for a country girl with aspirations for performing classical music on stage of all things. They told Jordan, in no uncertain terms, she'd be cut off if she contacted Miss Loehr."

"Lloyd, on the other hand, is a bit of a malingerer. He originally came to Columbia to share Jordan's dreams with Miss Loehr but got sucked in by the thought of all that money and attempted to deceive her. He figured she didn't have anyone else. He might win her over and share in her prosperity. I think Miss Grace liked having him around and appreciated hearing stories about the relatives. She put aside her anger at his attempt to dupe her. In the end, she carefully altered her will to benefit the people she loved."

My voice sounded as if it came from a far distance. "And those who loved her." I took more time with my question. "Do you think he *might* have killed Miss Grace?"

"No. He had a better chance to win her over if she'd lived. But promise you'll leave the investigating to us."

CHAPTER THIRTY-NINE

In a rush to walk before school, I declined to wear the neon-yellow reflective vest but clipped the flashing light to Maverick's collar. He loped and dragged me behind, skimming the ice sheet on the sidewalk. Preoccupied by Dorene's impending deadline compounded by the suspects in Miss Grace's death and Chief West's warning, and my fear of falling, it took a horn toot, bouncing headlights from an oncoming vehicle, and a yelp from Maverick to jar me back to my surroundings in time to avoid colliding with an equally distracted driver. The car behind me swerved at the last minute to avoid hitting us, laid on the horn, and sped away.

A truck pulled over on the opposite side of the street. My heart pounded and my ragged breath formed frosty plumes of mist.

"Are you all right, Katie?" asked a concerned voice.

I gulped the biting air and slowed my breathing. "I am now. Thanks, Pete." My insides somersaulted. It had to be the adrenaline.

He hopped from the driver's seat and drew nearer. "I didn't think that car would see you until it was too late. Black does not make you very visible. You could've been hurt. Luckily, Maverick wore a flasher and a reflective vest. What are you doing out this early?"

I stared in disbelief. "Maverick and I walk every day. Winter daylight occurs during school hours so we need to get out when we can." I sounded preachy. I glanced around and softened. "Columbia looks so calm before dawn. How far do you think we've walked?"

"Too far. Hop in. I'll give you a ride back." He strode to his truck and climbed in.

When I didn't move, the window slid down and he said, "It'll take you at least thirty minutes to get back from here."

Maverick tugged on the leash. I looked right and left and we crossed. We scrabbled into the cab. I sniffed Susie's scent and all my thoughts evaporated. It would be a long ride. Then Maverick broke the ice. He licked my cheek, and I couldn't sit still. I squirmed and released a giggle. Pete joined in.

We both spoke at the same time.

"Have they rearranged your workshop times?"

"Do you have any news about Ida?"

Pete's question carried much more weight than mine.

"We don't have much time to exonerate Ida and prove who murdered Miss Grace and probably McCall. Tell me what you've come up with."

I rattled off as much as I could before he stopped in front of Ida's. "And to top it off, we've been warned by the acting chief of police to stay out of the investigation. I think she's testing us."

His eyes widened. "How is Ronnie taking it?"

I shrugged. "Chief West has quite a commanding personality." I took a deep breath. "Do you have any information that could help Ida?"

"No, but now that we're back, we'll see what we can dig up on Daniella."

I'd almost forgotten the *we*. Worse than that, I'd almost forgotten about Daniella.

A mouthwatering aroma greeted me when I reentered the kitchen and was handed a plate of berries and cream, bacon, and French toast. Jane sat next to Ida, studying Yvonne's list of artifacts. Ida nodded. "I remember the necklace now." She and Jane carried the wreath to the table and carefully removed the pendant, shuffling the remaining baubles to fill the empty space. "You don't believe I took it, do you?" Her confidence waned.

"Absolutely not," Dad said. "But there is something odd about where it appeared."

Jane dropped the pendant into a mesh bag and found a place for it in her purse. "We can deliver the gem to Yvonne after school and ask if she's learned anything about the other pieces. If she hasn't, we'd better be thinking about where they could be. Ida, is there a hidden box, a cabinet, a safe, or something in the *Titanic* exhibit?"

Ida looked thoughtful. She drew her brows together, and shrugged. "Bobby installed a working safe in the purser's office for authenticity."

"It seems all too convenient that you should just *happen*

to find this piece." Yvonne sounded like she didn't trust us. The feeling was mutual.

"This necklace appeared among the pieces of Jane's wreath Officer Christianson fished off the frozen pond. It's the only one we found from your list."

Her hard stare relaxed. "I'm sorry. I only have two days to unearth the rest of Bruckner's artifacts. I should thank you though. This necklace is worth twice the sum of the values of the other pieces combined."

"Which is what exactly?" Jane asked.

Yvonne tilted her head in a 'wouldn't you like to know' slant and changed the subject. "Anita came to check on her encaustics and said Ricky is going home for Christmas."

"That's great."

She sank into a desk chair on rollers, dropping her head back against the neck cushion. "I've run out of ideas."

Ida's possible news bubbled out of Jane. "There could be another safe in the *Titanic* exhibit."

Yvonne stood quickly and the chair rolled back, striking the metal file cabinet. She rummaged through a thick stack of papers on the desk, tugging free a blueprint covered with notations, numbers, pen and pencil marks, coffee stains, and water rings. She hung over the plan, muttering to herself, "Another. Another?"

We tiptoed out of Yvonne's office and piled into Jane's car. "My alarm went off again last night. If I'd have been staying there, I'd be a wreck." Eric Clapton's *Wonderful Tonight* played from Jane's phone, and she giggled when answering. "You're on speakerphone. Say hi, Katie."

I said, "Hi, Katie," and Drew groaned. Then I tried not to listen for the next fifteen minutes until she dropped me off at home.

I fed Maverick and let him wander outside while I checked on Ida. Dad huddled on her couch, alert, guarding the stairs. "She's been sleeping for most of the day. I think she's depressed. I am."

"Do you think she'd like a return engagement at the hospital? Everyone loved her music, and it would get her out of the house. I'd like to visit Ricky, so she can go with me."

"I'll get her. We can grab something to eat on our way back."

Fifteen minutes later, she floated down the stairs draped in a forest green-and-white striped caftan. The hair gathered on top of her head spilled over a matching headband. She touched a spot on the band, illuminating a dozen or so twinkling lights nestled in her red curls. Another blinking strand hung around her neck. She shimmied into a long furry coat and seized the handle of a valise. "Let's get a move on, Katie. I'm not getting any younger." She lowered her chin and glowered. "And neither are you."

The warmer temperature during the early part of the day softened the snow and melted some of the ice which refroze in abnormal and unpredictable bumpy formations in the frigid below-zero temps of the evening. We bucked and bounced down the streets.

"Careful." Dad braced himself with one hand on the dash and the other pressed against the roof of the car. "You'd better let us off in the circle drive at the front."

By the time I parked and jogged back to the doors, my aversion to entering a hospital was eclipsed by my desire to thaw my iced fingers and increase circulation to my frozen toes. I shivered on the elevator ride but when the doors opened, the music seemed to warm me from the inside.

Children, parents, visitors, and staff surrounded the piano and sang softly. Ida swayed from side to side, her fingers gliding over the black and white keys. I was so caught up in the image of her performance, the warmth enfolding us, and the pleasant resonances, it almost didn't register when she shifted melodies, keys, tempo, or volume. Her eyes sparkled, embracing everyone with a gentle smile. This was not the music of a murderer.

A throat cleared next to me. "Anita's in the lounge, Room 499. She'd like to talk to you," Rachel said, watchful eyes glued to her young charges.

"Thanks."

I found Anita pacing and wringing her hands. "Happy Holidays, Anita. Yvonne tells me Ricky will be going home for Christmas."

An immense smile took over her entire face. "Yvonne and her husband have been saints during this whole ordeal. I don't know what I'd have done without them. She encourages me and reminds me what makes Ricky happy so I can stay focused and positive. Her husband helps me with the chores Ricky's dad, Zac, usually took care of. Now I have to figure out how to get Santa to visit."

"That's wonderful." But it didn't explain why she wanted to talk to me.

"His dad's deployment will be ending in May, and we miss him so much." She swiped at the tears pooling in her eyes. She sniffed. "But that's not why I wanted to talk to you. I—"

"There you are." Paula McCall charged into the lounge and gave Anita a huge hug. "I heard they're letting Ricky out for the holidays. I'm so happy for the two of you, but I heard about the fire. Do you need a place to stay? Is there anything I can do?"

Anita brightened, hopeful. "A check would be nice."

"Sorry, hon. I won't have access to funds for weeks. I can lend you a couple dollars until then."

Anita sagged.

"Why don't you and Ricky come stay with me through the holidays. You've spent more time in Phillip's house recently than I have. You can help me out and I can help you."

"Thank you, but no. Ricky will want to be in his home for Christmas. Maybe we can get together before New Year's Eve."

"Good idea." Applause erupted from the commons area. "We must be missing a good show. Let's join them, shall we?"

Delicate plinking from the highest register and the lowest register of the piano introduced the next number. The audience had grown, and I wriggled between Rachel and Dad to view the spectacle. Carlee sat on the piano bench next to Ida and they pounded out a string of holiday duets. Ricky beamed from behind them, ringing joy from sleigh bells in all the wrong places, but laughing in all the right ones.

Ida stood and Ricky took her place. She snaked through the audience to stand next to us. "You look surprised."

"Ricky and Carlee are quite good."

"They had the same teacher for a while."

Before I could ask who, Dad's arm hung over my shoulder. "Happy Holidays, darlin'."

CHAPTER FORTY

I da looked alive, invigorated by the music and cheered by the adulation of her audience, rejuvenated by Carlee's camaraderie, renewed by the decorations, and fortified by Rachel's apple cider. Shimmying across the floor in her loud outfit, with her rosy cheeks and bright eyes, Ida could have played an elf.

Dad was sapped. Then Ida let slip that she'd heard Quintz was slowly recovering, under police protection, on the second floor. Dad jumped at the chance to visit. "The room should be easy to spot."

"But Dad, you look tired."

"Not too bushed to hear what the crook has to say." Dad winked and picked up his pace.

"Crook?" said Ida.

Officer Rodgers tipped an invisible hat when he caught us marching down his hallway. "Evening Ida. Thanks for letting us know you were performing here again. It makes it easier to keep track of you."

Her happy face slipped for a second, but she said, "Of course, Daniel. We'd like to see how Jordan is doing, if that's okay."

He gave me a questioning look and I shrugged. "She doesn't know about Lloyd Wicheck."

"Who?" Dad pulled her a few feet away, but before he could give her the rundown, angry voices rose from within the room. Officer Rodgers turned the knob and pushed on the door.

"Someone has to have them. He promised me. I need them. Where could they be?" Daniella Jericho leaned over the bed and Wicheck scrambled as far away as he could without falling onto the floor. "You've got to know."

"I don't know anything. I don't belong here. I don't gain anything by staying and as soon as they release me, I'm gone for good." The head of the bed nestled into a shallow recess. He crouched in the corner and lifted his hands above his head.

Officer Rodgers lightly touched Daniella's elbow and she jerked it out of reach. "We'll see about that, Mr. Lloyd. Jordan. Quintz. Wicheck." She stalked out.

Ida watched her go, then turned to the man on the bed. "My, what big bruises you have."

Wicheck narrowed his eyes and glowered. "You."

"That's getting old, Lloyd."

He sputtered in response.

"We know the whole story. Did you kill Miss Grace?"

"Katie." Ida objected, but that question had scrubbed the bluster from his swagger.

"No. I liked the old broad."

"You also hoped to finagle a nice settlement from her, didn't you?"

Ida's mouth dropped open. She closed it and it fell open again. Dad led her out of the room.

I stared at Wicheck, and then I connected the dots between a few things. "Did you travel to India with Jordan?"

He squinted before nodding.

"You had access to nux-vomica." His eyebrows knitted together. "Strychnine."

Wicheck shriveled in front of me. "No. It wasn't me. I didn't kill her. I liked her. Sure, I had hopes of getting a little something. After all, she was Jordan's great aunt, and I, I mean Jordan, inherited that blamed piano." He shook his head. "But I didn't kill her."

"I'll let the chief know," Officer Rodgers said.

"Go ahead. I just want my life back."

He wasn't a very good man, and he had access to the poison, but I didn't think he had it in him to kill Miss Grace.

"What did Daniella want?" I asked with as much charity as I could muster.

He picked at the lint on his bedding. "Numbers," he said.

Numbers? I tried to wipe the disgust from my voice. "For what?"

"Don't know. Don't care. You know what? I'm tired. You need to leave now. Rodgers?"

I followed Dad and Ida, punching buttons. The call went to Jane's voicemail. I called Pete. Susie answered. She gasped and said, "Call me in ten minutes." She hung up.

Thanks?

Dad whispered the story to Ida in the atrium in front

of the elevators. She stood erect, her hands crossed in front of her. With every new pronouncement, she seemed to pull herself even taller. By the end, she might have even stood five feet high.

"Is it true? He's not Jordan? Did he kill Grace?" Her rapid-fire questions pierced my heart.

"Yes, it's true. He's not Jordan. His name is Lloyd Wicheck. I don't think he killed Miss Grace, but he used very poor judgment. Miss Grace knew he wasn't Jordan."

"Do you think he killed Phillip?"

Dad and I exchanged looks and shrugged.

"I know I didn't kill anyone. But the deaths of Phillip and Grace are genuine losses for all of us. We'll miss their philanthropic and artistic contributions, and their influence on the community. Their deaths must be related." She sniffed and wiped the tip of her nose. "I miss my friend."

Dad offered his elbow and Ida took it. I snaked my arm in on the other side. We walked to the front door and then out into the cold, still night to the car. We rode a few blocks in silence until Ida said, in an unexpectedly cheerful voice, "When the going gets tough, the tough get cooking. I need groceries."

I hung out in the parking lot while Dad and Ida grabbed the ingredients required for dinner. The three bags were chock full of enough to feed a classroom.

Dad lit the decorations in the yard. Ida set to work in her kitchen, sizzling butter, simmering milk, and boiling chicken stock. Dad chopped herbs, carrots, celery, and squash. Ida directed us to flip, sprinkle, stir, and pour. Frying bacon and onions brought tears to my eyes. She plated cheese, crackers, and stuffed olives and ushered me out.

"One hour," she said. "Find something useful to do."

After I checked my lesson plans for the upcoming week, I put on my coat and leashed Maverick. We stepped carefully around the block, avoiding anything that looked like ice when Wicheck's word shoved itself to the front of my brain. Numbers.

Back inside, I ripped off my stocking cap, shrugged out of my coat, and searched my desk for the note possibly containing the obscure numeric notation I found on Jane's memory box. I dusted off the cryptography desk in my head and the lines, dots, and squiggles no longer looked random. I translated a Roman numeral, a Mayan, a Chinese, and a Babylonian cuneiform into a seven, twelve, nine, and three.

I committed the numbers to memory, but the paper crackled in my frustrated hand. Numbers could belong to an address, a zip code, a phone number, an account, a code, latitude and longitude, measurements, a title; the list was endless.

The encaustic I had seen among Anita's canvases and easels bore similar symbols. I checked the clock. I had thirty-seven minutes, plenty of time for a round trip. Remembering Ida's words to never visit emptyhanded, I plated a few of Ida's shortbread cookies. Maverick whined so I took him with me.

Bright light glowed from every window and overshadowed the gloomy ghost of Anita's studio. A white wreath, like the one I made in grade school by tying slices of plastic grocery bags to a wire hanger, hung on the front door. I leashed Maverick. We approached the door and I knocked. White glitter sprinkled free from the wreath. Giggles and scratching noises preceded a tiny woof. The door opened only as far as the chain would allow.

"Hi, Ricky." I was flabbergasted. "You're home already."

"Mom and Rachel smuggled me out." In a conspiratorial voice, he added, "Don't tell anyone." Tucker licked Ricky's bare toes and he giggled.

"Is your mom home?"

"Nah. She went to get a Christmas tree and some burgers." Maverick shoved his nose in the door. "You brought your dog. Cool." The door closed. I heard the chain slide and the door opened again. "Come on in. Mom said, 'no strangers' but you're my friend. Besides, I wanted to surprise her, but I can't do it myself." He reattached the chain. "This is Maverick?"

"Good memory."

The pups sniffed appropriately. Tucker nipped at Maverick's ear and Maverick chased Tucker out of the room and back. Ricky let out a roaring laugh. Then Maverick slumped to the ground and Tucker did the same.

Ricky wheeled his chair to a closet. Two brooms stood against the open door below a teetering box caught on the hood of a winter coat.

This kid amazed me. "Did you do that?"

"Yeah, but the box got stuck. Can you get it down?"

I set the box between us, and he yanked the flaps. He claimed a ratty Teddy bear, gave it a hug, and tossed it to Tucker who dutifully pulled it under one paw and closed his eyes. Ricky extracted one ornament at a time and, like a little dictator, ordered its placement around the room— higher, lower, to the right, or to the left.

"You play piano very well."

He lifted a crystal tree and inspected it. "I like to play, but

I don't have much time to practice right now. Miss Grace is a fun teacher. Was, I mean." His eyes lost their luster. "I got to open the treasure chest and take a prize every time I did my lesson right." He handed me a glass figurine. "Second to the right, and straight on till morning." He pointed to the windowsill and smiled. We created a miniature winter scene, placing it in front of a window thick with frost.

We had so much fun, I didn't notice the time until my phone buzzed.

"Your hour is up. Where are you?" Dad asked.

"I drove over to see Anita and found Ricky home," I said as Anita stepped into the room carrying two take out bags, scowling. "I'll be home shortly." I pocketed my phone.

She plastered on a sweet smile, baring teeth like a mother wolf. "Katie, what are you doing here?" I heard the warning in her voice.

"Hey, Mom. Look what I found." He proudly held the old bear by one paw, playing tug-of-war with Tucker.

Anita's eyes circled the room. "Ricky, you did this?" Her voice cracked in wonder and appreciation.

"'Course I had help."

She brushed Ricky's hair out of his eyes. "You do remember what I told you?"

"I didn't let any strangers in." He smiled, and then he bolted upright, a little startled. "Is Maverick a stranger?"

Anita took a moment. "Nope. Maverick is Tucker's friend. You did a great job decorating, honey. Can I talk to Katie for a second?"

Ricky tossed the bear and Tucker fetched it. Tucker nuzzled next to Maverick and, getting no response, scampered across the room and returned the bear to Ricky for another go around.

"Why are you here, Katie?"

"I was hoping to see your encaustics. You said they weren't lost in the fire."

"Why do you want to see them?"

"When you showed them to Ida and me, one of them had some marks." Embarrassment registered on her face. "They were barely visible through the wax. It looked like a pattern or blueprint. Did they have a purpose? Can I see it again?"

She lowered her head. "That piece was horrible."

"What do you mean?"

She took a deep breath. "Phillip promised to back me in a showing if I'd collaborate on an encaustic for the gala. He didn't like waxwork. He said he'd put his signature on one of mine and it would get the attention it deserved. But he ruined it with all those black squiggles, so I replaced it with a blank canvas, hoping I could talk him into choosing a different one from among the others I'd created. They are so much better. When the auctioneer unveiled what I'd done, Phillip was so angry, I thought he'd burst. Then he died, and I thought I'd killed him."

I gasped.

"That's not what I meant. He was apoplectic and I thought I'd contributed to his having a heart attack or stroke, but I didn't poison him. I need this job. I have Ricky to think of."

"Won't Paula keep you on?'

"I don't know. She says she doesn't have the funds to pay me what Phillip owed and she's not sure what will be left, even after receiving Grace's generous bequest." Suddenly chilled, Anita grabbed her elbows, then kneaded her upper arms. She gazed at Ricky and Tucker. "I can't even afford a Christmas tree this year."

She shook herself and planted a giant smile on her lips. "But we'll be fine. I'll find another job. Everything will work out. We just have to be careful with our finances." She affected a smile.

"May I see them?"

"See what?"

"The encaustics."

"They're not here."

CHAPTER FORTY-ONE

I couldn't stop eating the Moroccan chicken dish and I leaned back in my chair to make room in my stomach.

When Ida went next door for Christmas sweets, I said quickly, "Anita is meeting me at the center tomorrow so I can look at the encaustics. I've run out of ideas, but there might be a clue there."

"Let's hope so, darlin'."

Ida returned with a gingerbread house surrounded by frosted sugar cookie cutouts, tea cakes dusted with powdered sugar, peanut butter blossoms, crinkles with crevices oozing chocolate, and airy angel kisses.

"You've been busy, Ida," I said, and thought of Ricky, working so hard to give their home a sense of holiday. "Anita brought Ricky home tonight and he looks fabulous."

I should have been ecstatic, but Dad picked up on my reticence.

"What's wrong? Did he seem unwell?"

"No. It's just that Anita said she can't afford a Christmas tree."

Ida looked at Dad who looked at me and all three pairs of eyes glittered with the same intention.

"I'll call Pete to see if we can borrow his truck," said Ida.

"I'll empty the reservoir under the tree." I shoved away from the table.

Dad waved a box of clear wrap. "We'll batten down the hatches."

Dad and I encircled the tree, girding the ornaments and lights for the trip across town. Dad put on the finishing touches, reinforcing the wrap with packing tape. Minutes later, Pete knocked on the door, pushing it open at the same time, eager to play Santa again. Ida held the door and it took Pete, Dad, and me to carry the tree to get our load into the cargo bed. We secured it with a blue plastic tarp, and the four of us shook with jolly laughter. Giving felt good.

"Katie, your dad's exhausted." Ida said. Dad yawned as if on cue, and Pete made sure he made it inside. She patted my arm. "Ricky should be asleep by now and it'll take all three of you to get that tree inside. You'd better go with Pete." My laughter dried up in my throat. She thrust the tray of cookies into my hands and shunted me out the door.

I couldn't stand the quiet in the truck cab. "Can we turn on some Christmas music?"

Pete pushed the button, and I nearly swallowed my

tongue when Wham's *Last Christmas* came over the radio. I sat back and stared straight ahead until reprieved by *Jingle Bell Rock*.

Fewer lights were on at the Jones' house, but Pete could still see the damage done in the yard and followed the tracks as close to the front door as he could get. A bright grin splashed across his face, and I think I would've melted if I could've, but I couldn't. So, I just smiled back. He jumped from the truck and up into the cargo bed. He grabbed one end of the tarp and slipped it under the tree. I held onto the other end, creating a sling, and we hauled it up the steps to Anita's landing. I knocked.

"Who is it?"

"It's Santa and an elf."

The door opened a crack. "Katie?" Then the door opened as wide as her eyes.

"Merry Christmas."

She stepped back and we carried the bundle into the room. She shoved furniture to one side as she said, "You didn't have to—"

"We wanted to. Oh!" I dashed out to the truck for the cookie tray and Pete followed me. He heaved a sack over his shoulder and a wrapped box tumbled to the ground. I picked it up and he winked. We waltzed back in and handed over the goodies. I gave Anita a hug and we were gone.

"Did you see the look on her face? Imagine Ricky in the morning." Giddy, we needed no music on the ride home.

Pete stopped at a light and his demeanor changed. "Anything new on Ida?"

"No. Anything on Daniella?"

Pete looked confused. "I thought Susie told you." He cocked his head.

My ears felt hot. I never called her back.

"Jericho wanted to make amends before he died and must've thought he could buy his way into heaven, so he left his substantial estate to various charities. Daniella's friends confirmed that she'd been cut out of an iron-clad will. He left her with only what he'd already given her. Not bad, really. She had some valuable jewelry, some impressive art, a fancy car, and one of their homes. According to those in the know, she's sold off most of her belongings and exhausted her resources to remain solvent. Lately, however, she's been bragging about coming into some big bucks. She started to spend again."

"Like the matching pledge at the gala?" I'm sure a confused look came over my face too. "How does that help Ida? Daniella didn't benefit directly from either Miss Grace or McCall dying. Pete." I inhaled deeply. "I don't know what to do."

"Just do your thing. You have the knack." He put up his hand to quiet my protests. "Ida didn't do it. The truth will come out."

The light changed and he stepped on the gas. Bright headlights popped on from his left and came directly at us. I shielded my eyes and screamed. Pete stomped on the gas and his evasive maneuvers took us into a four-foot-high snowbank. My seatbelt held tight, but I'd be wearing a black-and-blue sash in the morning.

"You okay?"

I opened my eyes and shuddered. "I think so. You?"

He exhaled. "I'm fine. Where did he come from?" He surveyed our surroundings. He put the truck in reverse. The frozen surface crunched but held fast. He shoved the gear shift into drive and rocked forward. Then he put the truck in reverse again and revved the engine. We pulled free. We bumped over the icy chunks in the street, and I decided I needed to get me a big blue truck—maybe.

A weird ringtone filled the cab and Pete quickly punched the console. "Hi, Susie."

"What are you doing, lover?" The slinky voice came over the speakerphone and I shuddered again.

"I'm playing Santa."

"Without me," she whined.

"It was a last-minute gig and more of a Santa delivery than a performance."

"Do you want me to come over?"

"I'm bushed. Okay if I tell you about it tomorrow?"

"O-kay. Love you. Good night," she said in a sing-song voice.

"Sleep tight."

"Don't let the bed bugs bite."

Pete disconnected the call. I stared straight ahead, afraid if I looked at him, I'd burst into snickers. I heard the rasp of the multiple-hours-older-than-five o'clock shadow as he scratched his chin. I faulted the emotional roller coaster but when he chuckled, I couldn't stop myself.

We bounced up Ida's driveway. "Looks like everyone is down for the night. Are you sure you're all right?"

I nodded. "Good night, Pete." I hopped out and saluted as he backed out. Maverick met me with a giant wag of his tail, a good tongue lashing, and a friendly reminder that he had one more duty to take care of before I could meet the sandman.

He pranced energetically in the snow, and we turned around at the end of the block. "I can't wait to hear what Ricky has to say about the tree," I said, double stepping to keep up. A beam of light raked through the limbs of a craggy tree and cast moving shadows across my entry. I jumped, but instead of finding someone behind me, I saw the light switch off in Miss Grace's house. "I think someone's there, Mav. I'll be right back."

Not thinking too deeply, I scooted across the street, up the front steps, and banged on the door. "Who's there?" I waited and pounded again. "I know you're in there. I saw the light." When no one answered, I tried the knob. It opened with a squeal I thought would wake the neighborhood.

I punched in a number on my phone.

"Katie?"

"Someone's in Miss Grace's house."

"What? I can't hear you."

"I'm checking out Miss Grace's—"

"Get out of there. I'm calling the police," Pete said in a stern voice. He hung up.

"Hello," I called again.

Fast footsteps pounded across a floor and a door slammed at the back of the house. I released the breath I didn't know I'd been holding. My hand inched to the switch on the wall. I flipped it but nothing happened. The cold temperature of the house made the hairs on the back of my neck curl and my breath appeared in warm puffs. The furnace must have been off and if the pipes froze the house would have major problems. I followed the dim gray patches faintly illuminated by the streetlights through the windows and edged toward the door to the utility space. My leg knocked against a sharp corner. I muffled a grunt and thudded to the floor, holding my shin, and prepared to rumble with the nuisance. I peered into the shadows to catch the culprit and spied a child-sized bench.

I turned on my phone light to get my bearings. Miss Grace provided books for her young piano students to read while they waited their turn. Ratty, dog-eared copies of picture books and chapter books, classics and comics packed two short shelves of a bookcase, lined up from thickest to thinnest. My finger trailed across the titles, while the ache in my leg subsided, and stopped on the second to the left, Barrie's *Peter Pan*. It took both hands to tug it free. Then the bookcase clicked and popped away from the wall. I inserted my fingers behind the bookcase and pulled, revealing a wall safe.

And I had numbers.

I sat cross-legged on the floor and propped my phone against the back of the bookcase. The angle of the light wasn't ideal, but it was all I had. Charles used to kid that the role of a cryptanalyst was to decipher digital and analog coded messages without prior knowledge of the key. This time I had a key. I rubbed my hands together to warm them.

I spun the dial counterclockwise and clockwise, stopping precisely on each number, finally returning to zero. I took a deep breath and rotated the handle. It didn't budge. I wiggled the dial. The door stayed fast. My shoulders slumped. Then I looked at the lock again and blinked rapidly. The opening index that looked like a bird track, pointed up from the six o'clock position. The safe was installed upside down. Leave it to Miss Grace.

I pulled myself to a standing position, stood with my back to the wall, and bent over. I reached for the lock. Seven. Twelve. Nine. Three. And back to zero. With a satisfying click, I pulled the handle. Stuffed into the space reserved for a music teacher's stickers, candy, trinkets, and novelty rewards sat a red velvet bag. I stared for a moment, wondering if I'd be contaminating a crime scene but my nosiness got the better of me.

My first grab into the bag retrieved some jewelry and a fork. They clinked when I dropped them back in. I reached for my phone, and my world went black.

CHAPTER FORTY-TWO

I batted at the irksome light blinding me. "Stop," I pleaded. "Go away."

"She's ba-ack," Pete said in a sing-song voice.

I sat up too quickly and faltered, my movements overwhelmed by dizziness and frustrated by my thick winter jacket. Pete grabbed my arm and lifted me. I groaned. "My head hurts."

"Good thing it's so hard." Dad leaned against the doorframe and tried to get a laugh, but his ashen face and darkened eyes gave away his concern.

"Right." I struggled to paste a smile on my face, but that sent nails of pain shooting into the back of my head. I grimaced.

"Darlin'," Dad said.

I closed my eyes and rubbed my head. *What had happened?*

I moaned. "The jewelry bag." I searched the floor for any sign of it and moaned again.

"We've got it."

"You do? What happened?"

Chief West sauntered next to Pete. "We were hoping that you could tell us." She wore the official winter police uniform: shiny black boots, dark pants creased within a millimeter of being blade-sharp, leather gloves, and a short navy-blue zippered jacket sporting her badge. The brim of her cap shielded her eyes, which, I could only guess from the tone of her voice, sparked with some anger.

"The lights are on." I could see.

"The furnace too." Pete's eyebrows rose, waiting.

Short and sweet would have to do since the details were a bit fuzzy. "I saw a light, found a safe, unlocked it, and found a bag."

"You still didn't explain how you came to find the safe and have the combination," said Chief West.

A deep, threatening voice asked, "Were you in on the heist? Was your partner going to cut you out? Who is it?" My dad looked ready to punch Ronnie Christianson.

I squeezed my eyes shut and recounted finding the code on Jane's memory box now covered in green paint, translating the age-old figures into numerals, and Ricky's cryptic allusion to Peter Pan.

Pete said, under his breath, "Second to the left, and straight on till morning but Grace always changed the combination." He knew he shouldn't smile, so only one side bowed up. "I got here as fast as I could and ran into Daniella. She said no one was home. Chief West pulled in behind me and managed to hold her for a few more questions. We found you and you kept mumbling something about a sack. Daniella clutched a sack she said she'd found in the snowbank and couldn't explain or identify the contents. The chief confiscated it."

I pulled at my neckline. The temperature was getting uncomfortable.

"It contains the artifacts belonging to the *Titanic* exhibit." The bag dangled from Jane's hand. She leaned into my dad, her tornadic hair interlacing with his. What a pair they made! Puffy winter coats hung over Dad's red flannel pants and Jane's spindly bare legs. They'd managed to pull on boots, but I didn't see any sign of hats or gloves. "I called Yvonne. She'd like you to deliver it tomorrow." Jane turned to the chief. "Is that okay?"

"Certainly. I know there's a clock ticking, and I know where I can find the evidence."

"Did Mrs. Jericho knock me out?"

The chief shrugged.

I rubbed the knot on my head. "Did she kill Miss Grace?"

"We have no evidence to that effect." The chief turned to my dad. "You may take her home now."

Jane handed me the bag, and supported by Dad and Jane, we stepped into a snow globe. Tiny white flakes danced through the streetlights, peacefully landing on my eyelashes and nose. I lifted my face and caught a few on my outstretched tongue. I tittered, slightly intoxicated by the evening's resolution and Dad and Jane joined me.

Our chuckling ceased when we reached my kitchen and looked into Ida's stern face.

"I'm sorry——" I started to say, but she cut me off with

a slice of her hand.

"You could have been hurt." One hand covered her mouth as she staunched a sob. Then she reached out with both arms. "Come here."

We nearly toppled when Maverick joined the four of us, standing on his hind legs in a group hug. After regaining my balance, I nuzzled his face and scratched the top of his head. "It never would have happened if you'd been with me. Next time."

I yawned.

* * *

Friday commenced with an infuriating alarm. When I finally silenced the din, and wrenched open my eyes, Maverick pressed his cold nose onto my cheek and finished the task of waking me. The wind howled and the gusts rattled the windows. I threw back the curtains and discovered a new world. Who knew there were so many shades of white? It had stopped snowing but, nonetheless, it was difficult to discern the street from the yards, the walkways, the trees, and the mounds covering stationary vehicles. The only movement came from branches arching against the wind, swinging at the offensive flakes, and missing, or the occasional plow exploding the snow sculptures into miniscule particles that resettled into new shapes.

If the road was impassable, the district would text school closings but there were none. Jane and I commiserated over tea and toast.

If the weather held, Jane expected Drew to return from his assignment, so she packed up her things and we caravanned to work.

The weather service provided minute-by-minute updates. The forecasters predicted four more inches of snow and winds to pick up. One minute after we achieved the minimum time commitment and avoided a makeup day, buses were recalled to transport kids home during the narrow window of calm before the storm cranked up. Students dropped off at school, and those who drove themselves, were excused to insure safer travels.

My plan to call Ida and Dad to make sure we were set with supplies for the weekend was derailed by the long list of voicemails left by Yvonne. I listened to the first two cheerful messages but discontinued the third when it turned a little testy. I punched in her number, and it went to voicemail. "Yvonne. I'm on my way. I'll be out before the storm really kicks in."

Yellow and white lights pulsed on top of the massive plow in front of me, clearing the street and giving me a sense of safety. I should have known it was false.

CHAPTER FORTY-THREE

During my drive home, Yvonne left another message. The latest board meeting was running late but she'd meet me at her office within the hour. The center was closed due to the forecast so she gave me the back door code.

Maverick yipped and hopped from one foot to the other. Remembering my promise to bring him with me, I grabbed his leash, stowed two bottles of water, two of Ida's cookies, a dog biscuit, and the red bag in a backpack. I nabbed the reflective vests and my lighted cap as well. We'd be visible for blocks.

Joy-filled carols blared from the local holiday station, and Maverick and I howled along. He sounded much better than I did. Flakes continued to drift, overlaying a sheet of white. When the definition of the road disappeared, I should have pulled over, but I used the mailboxes, the mile markers, and semi-discernable track indentations to stay on the main drag.

We'd almost arrived at the turnoff when the broadcaster broke in on *I'll Be Home for Christmas* with an emergency announcement. Monongalia County, along with eleven others, was under a winter storm warning. Plows were being pulled from the roads, and cars were ordered off the streets. She said to expect the temperature to drop twenty degrees, wind gusts of forty miles per hour, and an additional six inches of snowfall.

At that moment, a truck rumbled past, kicking up a curtain of white. I lost sight of my landmarks, so I turned on my wipers, and tapped the brakes. At the next driveway, I planned to turn around and head home, but the tires slid. The car skidded, moving in slow motion. It slipped off the pavement and skated into a deep ditch. We halted, teetering on a slight embankment. I breathed rhythmically to calm my racing heart and heard a snap. The seatbelt held me in place as the car plunged down the steep hill and I bumped my head—again.

Sloppy kisses tickled me. My eyes fluttered open. Maverick continued to cleanse my ear. "Thanks, Mav, but I'm awake now," I said. I scratched his neck and pulled my comforter around to ward off the cold, but it wasn't a comforter. My eyes flew wide. One dim headlight sliced through the pitch-black scene. We'd come to rest against a downed tree trunk, motionless in the middle of a creek.

"This isn't good," I said to Maverick and rubbed my head.

Then the ice cracked. I gulped. We dropped three more inches to the creek bed. I bowed, thankful the water wasn't any deeper. The car shimmied. Then the headlight flicked off. I turned the key, and nothing happened. My phone had little power and no connection. "We've got to get out of here, Mav." I wrestled to get Maverick's paws through the holes in his vest. "It's cold, buddy. This will keep you a bit warmer. Look, I'm wearing one too." I elbowed my way into the vest and fastened the Velcro strips. I wrapped the backpack strap over my forearm, pulled the stocking cap over my ears, and touched the lamp. "Are you ready?"

The driver's door was lodged against the tree and wouldn't budge. I heaved against the passenger door until it screeched, allowing a ten-inch-wide escape route from which to slither from the ice box into the blizzard. Maverick jerked me out of the way when the car shifted again.

The wind shrieked and blasted my face, pelting me with tiny ice bullets. Water swirled around my ankles. Oblivious to my discomfort, Maverick tramped through the labyrinth of shifting walls of snow drifts that reached his shoulders and towed me toward the history center.

When the wind pummeled me and my pace lagged, Maverick pulled with more determination, jerking me on icy feet through the unfriendly terrain. My teeth chattered. My eyelashes stuck together. I couldn't feel my fingers. I stumbled when he turned his head. Sharp icicles clung to his chest and neck and hung from the corners of his mouth. He needed to get out of the cold too.

There was a lull in the raging storm and the form of a ship materialized a mere football field away. Maverick stopped. I urged him to continue. I stood in front and pulled on the leash. He sat, immovable. "C'mon, Maverick. I'm sure I can scrounge up a treat." His ears perked up, but he wouldn't stand. "We've got to go. It's right there." I pointed.

"This is not the time for tug-of-war," I said through gritted teeth. He growled, and I stopped pulling. He looked past me, into the woods. His hackles stood erect. "What is it, boy?" I turned slowly and peered into the depths.

I caught movement out of the corner of my eye and whipped around. Maverick rumbled at a threat I couldn't see, and I spun again. Shadows darted between tree trunks. When they stopped, four unblinking golden eyes locked on us. Maverick's growl grew and I dropped to his side.

"Leave them alone and they'll go home." I used soothing words and stroked his head. "Easy, Maverick." I turned off my headlamp. If I couldn't see them, they couldn't see me, right?

Maverick jumped up and roared. A loud, gravelly yowl answered. He yanked the leash from my numb fingers, and I fell into a snowbank. I screamed, "Maverick!" as he disappeared from my sight.

"Maverick," I sobbed. I shoved off the ground and staggered in his tracks.

The snarls and barks and howls and cries moved away then stopped abruptly. Images of a bloodied and battered Maverick filled my head. I tripped and sprawled on the ground next to a broken limb. I picked it up and held it like a staff, poking the air in front of me and testing the ground, softly calling, "Maverick."

The crunch of my footsteps through the snow nearly covered the whimper. Brandishing the stick and quaking in my boots, I threatened, "Come and get yours, you lily-livered chickens. I'll even the odds." A branch snapped and my heart lurched. Another snagged my cap and I tussled with the tree to get it back. I crept forward.

I activated the light on my cap and caught a neon green reflection. In my haste to get to the vest, I almost stumbled over Maverick. He lay on his side, scraps of the vest yards from us. I dropped the stick and fell into the snow. My hands hovered over him, afraid to touch him, to hurt him. His eyes opened and he blinked. He licked his lips and raised his head to lap my face, then he collapsed back into the snow and swallowed hard.

I swung my head and gaped at the twigs, bits of fabric, animal tracks, and dark splotches dotting the snow. I ran the light the full length of my dog. Although I couldn't find a wound, something was wrong. "I have to turn you over, Mav." He swallowed hard. I couldn't swallow at all.

At sixty-five pounds, I didn't think I could lift him, but he wasn't willing or able to move. I dug a trench in the snow at his back. I plowed quickly. When the depression was deep enough, I removed my vest and lined the trough. I cradled his head in my left arm and slid my right under his belly. He licked his lips again as if to say, *Let's do this.* I rolled him over with a faint yelp. It could have been his yelp, or it could have been mine.

I sat back and panted. Blood seeped from three gouges on his flank. "Oh, Maverick."

I pulled out my phone. No charge.

I gathered the tattered strips from his vest and wound them around his backside, packing the injury with snow. I wrapped my vest around him and secured the makeshift bandage. I threaded the staff through the armholes and hauled Maverick until his nose hung over the stick. I caressed his face. "Good boy." We touched foreheads. "Here we go."

I hefted the limb and dragged my injured friend on the crude travois, trudging, one foot after another, to the welcoming door of the center.

I slumped against the entrance to catch my breath. Maverick wriggled. "Stay," I said and straightened. The keypad cover flopped open. I took off my mittens and entered the code. I turned the handle on the door and pulled. It didn't budge. I tried again. It still didn't work. I blew warm air on my fingers. Third time was a charm and we scooted into the hall.

I knew I wouldn't get an answer, but I had to ask, "Anyone here?"

I dragged the frame across the floor, screeching and squeaking until we reached Yvonne's office. I turned the knob. "We're in luck, Mav." Maverick's head came up and he examined the orderly office. Gone were the folders, boxes, tins, packing material, and tubs. A sheaf of pages describing Bruckner's pieces lined up with the edge of the table next to a neat stack of plexiglass display boxes. I stowed the red bag in the knee hole of the polished antique desk and reached for the phone.

The storm had taken its toll. The phone was dead.

I arranged my puffy coat on the floor in the corner near the heat vent. I slid my precious package next to it and unwrapped him, careful of his wounds. I used his favorite dog biscuit to lure him onto my coat. "Let's get comfortable, Maverick."

He slumped onto the soft, padded fabric. I searched for a phone charger, snacks, blankets, anything to make our stay more agreeable. The cone-shaped paper cups didn't hold much but I filled one from the water dispenser, took a sip, and carried the rest to Maverick. He lapped the water and slumped back onto his side.

The small first aid kit, mounted on the wall next to a fire extinguisher contained an antibiotic ointment, gauze, scissors, bandages, and tape. I peeled back the strips of neon and cringed at the wounds. "Oh, Maverick." I cleaned two scratches and what looked like a bite mark the best I could with water. I patted the area dry, applied the cream, and dressed the injury, mentally conjuring CJ and begging him to heal my dog.

I sat next to Maverick, brushed his fur, and repeated my new mantra, "We'll be okay," until his rhythmic breathing took him to the sleep zone. To tidy the office, I threw away the water cups and bloodied cloths, straightened the chair, and reattached the first aid kit. I picked up my vest, intending to wipe the inside, and something in the pocket clunked against the desk. I dug out the tape I'd pocketed the day Maverick found Wicheck.

My finger traced the metal rim, and I closed my eyes, imagining the beautiful music Miss Grace might have recorded. Sadly, she hadn't converted her analog recordings to digital, and players were hard to find, but what good was a museum if it didn't house some vintage machines.

With Maverick softly snoring, I tiptoed down the hall, softly singing *Hark the Herald Angels Sing* to cover the echo of my footsteps, and meandered through the exhibit, heading to the radio station room to check out the equipment.

When I reached the scene, the power cracked, and everything went dark.

CHAPTER FORTY-FOUR

My hand found the wall and I turned to make my retreat when I heard a whoosh and the lights popped back on, but dimmer and wavering, covering everything with a golden hue. I looked at the tape in my hand and then at the flickering yellow reflection on the disc jockey's glasses. As long as I was here …

The reel fit the grooves and locked in place. I followed the arrows and fed the tape through the machine into a slit on an empty reel and rotated it. I turned the power knob. At first, the lights pulsed in tandem with the gauges and needles undulating right and left. When the sleeping giant woke and the motor rumbled, I depressed rewind, mesmerized by the dazzling display of colorful flashes.

The brittle tape coiled for about a half inch, back to

the beginning, and the rewinding stopped. I rubbed my hands together, and whispered, "Let's go." I pushed play.

The recording quavered with an eerie woo-woo. It ran too slow, and the piano sounded like a percussionist playing timpani. Then it played too fast with a pinched, high-pitched plinking before the tape juddered and settled into identifiable musical tones.

Miss Grace was a master on the keyboard, a professional performer for over fifty years. A sigh slipped from my lips, and I leaned against the console, crossing my arms over my chest.

The familiar opus elicited a smile. Miss Grace had recorded her own version of the Christmas arrangement she'd assigned Ida to perform for the children.

My mind juddered like the tape. What if we'd misunderstood Miss Grace's will and she'd given Ida the task of playing this recording to get the inheritance. Stuck on what ifs, what if Wicheck had never come to town? What if Daniella didn't kill Phillip? What if Maverick is permanently injured?

The room felt like it took a breath as if a door opened and closed, altering the air pressure. I turned down the volume on the player.

"Is anyone there? Can you hear me?" I listened intently. When no one answered, I restarted the recording. With a shorter woo-woo time, the musical pastiche surrounded me and sounded even better than when Ida played it. As the melody weaved its intricate patterns, shadows danced in the throbbing lights. I shaded my eyes and a silhouette coalesced in the doorway.

I shoved off the console and heaved a sigh. "Am I ever glad to see you." The figure remained in the arch, backlit by the dim lights in the art area. "Are the roads clear?"

The figure stepped closer and flipped on a blinding flashlight.

"Yvonne?" I released a breath. "I skidded off the road near the turn off. My phone's dead and the power went out. Do you have a phone I can use?"

I turned the volume up a notch. "It's Miss Grace. Isn't it beautiful?" I heard a grunt. "Lloyd?" The light came closer. Alarm bells went off in my head. I shielded my eyes but couldn't see past the beam.

"Daniella?" I wondered about her explanation to Chief West. Was she after the artifacts?

"I came out for my encaustics. Have you seen them?"

I relaxed for a heartbeat. Paula wasn't looking for Bruckner's treasures. "Are you an artist too?"

"Not in the sense you mean. Plants are my medium." She shook her head slowly. "I'm required to produce the four encaustics by tomorrow, remember?"

I morphed my frown into a questioning grimace. I hoped I could channel Ida's acting ability. "I thought Anita did the encaustics."

Her eyes darkened. "She did them with Phillip. They belong to the institute."

An abrupt change to the recorded music startled me. Before Miss Grace had played the dramatic ending and the final note, she'd stopped. Her voice triggered goose bumps. "Let me get you a glass?" Footfalls creaked across her floor. The recording picked up the sound of a cupboard door and of chinking ice cubes in a glass, the glug of liquid pouring, more footfalls, and the whoosh of fluffy cushions flattening.

"I hoped you'd come." I missed Miss Grace's warm voice.

"You made it clear my attendance was compulsory."

The words were less distinct, the speaker farther from the microphone.

"I remember how proud you were of your garden." The visitor snorted and I couldn't make out the garbled words. "Didn't you take second place in the plant competition? Ida beat you." Miss Grace coughed. "Would you get me something to drink, please?""

Steps receded then ice clinked again, followed by a long slurp. "Thank you." An arpeggio in a minor key introduced Miss Grace's storytelling voice. "Why did you kill Phillip?"

I gasped. My eyes and ears were glued to the rotating reel.

"Ida killed Phillip."

"No." Miss Grace coughed again.

I snuck a glance at Paula. Her eyes gleamed.

"I loved growing unusual greenery," she said. "Phillip and I bought that janky old house so we could convert the garage into a greenhouse, but he decided he needed the space. That was our first of many fights." Her strident voice filled the cavernous space. "I had a lucrative market for my plants, but Phillip never took my vocation seriously. He wasn't even all that good as an artist, but he decided he needed to take over my greenhouse. He turned off the heat and my plants *accidentally* froze. Right! He promised that his creations would make headlines and would bring in enough money for me to open my own shop. Fat chance. I stayed for years too long."

The sounds on the tape returned. Miss Grace said, "Why now?"

The voice on the tape said, "Phillip cooked up a foolproof scheme and said he'd compensate me with a lump sum that would set me up for a good long time. I figured he was cutting me out again, so I visited him to discover the source of his windfall."

Miss Grace's labored breathing came back on the tape. "I'm not feeling well." Something banged onto the treble keys. "Paula?" Miss Grace gasped. "I need help."

Doors and drawers opened and closed accompanied by a long moan.

"I'll call for help if you tell me where the safe is."

The breaths came at slower and slower intervals and the tape caught sounds of movement in the music room, sliding, crunching, rattling, knocking. A short silence preceded the squeak of a door against a cold frame, and finally Ida's voice calling, "Grace?"

The end of the tape flapped again bringing me back to the moment we found Miss Grace draped over her piano. We'd missed Paula by seconds.

Paula sneered. "I overheard Phillip tell Jericho that he'd done his job. It wasn't his fault Daniella failed to follow his directions to win the bid on one of the items on which he had embedded the combination. Phillip never remembered anything, so she'd have to retrieve the code herself. After she left, I confronted him. He was a cheapskate and a liar, and I deserved more. If he had enough to share with her, he had more to share with me. He laughed and told me to be happy with our arrangement. I fixed him his favorite drink, a toast to his genius. It was an accident. I only intended to scare him.

"Now, about those encaustics I have to produce tomorrow. Where are they?"

"I don't know."

"That's too bad."

I stared down the barrel of a small handgun.

Mary Seifert

Paula used the gun like a pointer and prodded me away from the vignette. After she ripped the tape from the machine, she herded me toward the art room.

"They know I'm here," I said, taking deep breaths.

"It won't matter. No one knows *I'm* here. It's too bad you got lost out in the cold and froze to death."

"Don't do this." I tripped.

"I'll collect the encaustics and fill the coffers of the institute which I'll shut down considering the tragic death of its founder. Move."

What would happen to Dad? And Ida? Acid rose in my throat. I wouldn't be there to watch the budding relationship between Jane and Drew. I had to think of something.

"I don't have all day. I've got to locate those paintings. Possession is nine-tenths of the law, you know."

"How did you get in?"

Paula smirked. "One of the many jobs I held to support Phillip's *passion* was taking tickets here. They never used the loading dock, and the lock code hasn't been changed in a century. I always came in that way." She waved the end of the gun down the hall. "I've tried all the storage areas. Let's check Yvonne's office."

My chest tightened. What would happen when she found Maverick. "I didn't notice the art in the office, and I searched it looking for a phone charger. Maybe they're hanging in the exhibit."

She poked me. "Hurry up. I'm tired of looking. I tried Mackey's house for the *Titanic* goodies. I need this over with. I want the money now."

We parted the curtains into the art exhibit, and my heart sank. My good intention to keep him safe would go for nothing. Maverick eyed me from a position between two statues. I put my finger to my lips. He blinked. Black against black, he'd be difficult to see. Paula's eyes roved, checking the art on the walls, and she overlooked him. If he stayed, someone would know that we'd been here, and maybe Paula would be held accountable for her nefarious actions.

We stepped abreast of the statues. "Some of the local artists aren't half bad," she said, dripping with sarcasm. "You can see the individual hairs on that ugly mutt."

She reached out to touch Maverick. He growled. Her creepy smile faded, but before she could register what she'd heard, he charged and wrapped his fangs around her gun hand. A shot rang out. They tussled. I searched for a weapon and stumbled against the nearest statue. It overturned and crashed to the ground. I grabbed one of the smaller pieces and threw it at Paula.

I missed the first time but connected on the second throw. When the ceramic met its mark, her sneer turned menacing. Imbued with evil energy, she cuffed Maverick. He collapsed next to her. She swiped the blood dripping from the slice on her cheek and looked at it, disbelieving.

I gritted my teeth. No one hurts my dog. I screamed and my wobbly legs propelled me forward three steps before I fell. Good thing. A bullet whizzed by my ear. I rolled, drawing attention from Maverick, and grabbed the fringe on her Mukluks. The recoil knocked her off balance and her leg buckled. Another shot rang out, but Maverick and I were running out of luck.

With a fanatical gleam in her eye, she turned and limped in Maverick's direction. She groaned, not finding him there, and I scrabbled deeper into the historical center, gauging the level of concealment each of the representations afforded, praying Maverick would stay out of her way.

Paula's asymmetric gait forewarned me. She dragged her leg and occasionally grunted. I crawled onto the drag sled next to the dusty hides, staring down the buffalo in the mural. After Charles died, my grief could have destroyed me. But I put all my energy into Dad's recovery and in so doing managed my own. Charles made me promise I'd live the best life I could. I had Dad and Ida, my students, my friends, and the love of a good dog. Paula would have to work hard to take that away from me.

Her footsteps increased in volume. "Katie," she sang. "No one's coming. Make this easy on yourself."

With a loud clunk, the lights came on full force. Distant voices and running feet reverberated through the hall from the *Titanic* exhibit.

Jane yelled, "Katie!"

Afraid to draw anyone else into the showdown, I strained to pick out any sound from Paula. I peeked through the skins, looking around me. Billows of dust rose, and I sneezed.

CHAPTER FORTY-FIVE

K atie?"
      "Watch out, Jane," I screamed as I crawled in front of the hunter, beneath the buffalo gun, into an empty room.

Jane's laugh preceded her around the corner. "Where are you?"

Drew, Pete, and Susie sauntered in without a care in the world. I rose from the pallet. They stopped as if haunted by an apparition.

"You look terrible, girlfriend. What happened?"

"We have to find Maverick. He's hurt. But watch out for Paula McCall. She has a gun."

The look that passed between Susie and Pete made me blush. "I'm not crazy and I don't have time to explain."

"Paula who?" Drew said, putting on his cop face and drawing his firearm.

As I peered into each panorama, I said over my shoulder, "Paula killed Phillip and I lost Maverick."

Pete tilted his head. "That can't be right."

"Ida took first place in the gardening competition. Do you remember who took second?" I asked.

Susie nodded her head. "Paula. She raised all those outlandish plants in horticulture class."

Pete slowed. "And failed the course because they were all poisonous."

Drew said, "We'll cover more territory if we spread out. Be careful."

They marched in different directions, and my heart raced. I had to find Maverick.

I approached the closed door to Yvonne's office and tentatively reached out to the knob. It didn't open. I wiggled the knob. I kicked the door expecting it to splinter as it would in any action film. Instead, I crumpled into a hurting heap, sobbing.

A hand touched my shoulder. "Katie, here he is. He was on the bridge, sprawled across a stack of encaustics." Pete carried Maverick, squirming for release. He knelt and held my dog close enough for him to lick the tears streaming down my face. He heaved the oversized dog into my lap.

I made cooing noises, smoothed his fur, and checked the makeshift dressing covering his injuries. "You saved my life again."

"CJ will fix him up just fine," Pete said, flicking imaginary dust from my shoulder.

Drew joined us.

"I brought Bruckner's artifacts out here and put them

under the desk in the office." I pointed to the closed door.

Drews eyebrows rose. "Exigent circumstances. We need to ascertain safety for all concerned." He had to kick twice, but the door fell open and he turned on the light. "No one here."

I made a beeline to the desk and peeked underneath. The bag was gone. "She's got it, but she can't have gone far. Wait. How'd you get out here?"

Pete and Drew exchanged strange looks and Drew said, "Snowmobiles. But it stopped snowing and they'll be able to clear the roads soon."

"What about Paula? She didn't get the encaustics and they're worth a quarter of a million to her. She is frantic and vengeful. What will she do?"

Sirens screamed from outside. We answered the pounding on the door and found an ominous shape, backlit by the headlights from a snowplow and three flashing police cars. Chief West glided into the history center, admiring the eclectic collection. "What happened here?"

I repeated what I'd heard from the tape and what Paula had told me. "But she took the tape and the articles we found in Miss Grace's safe yesterday."

Chief West might not have believed me, but Drew pointed out two bullet holes where the shots missed Maverick and me. "Where would she go?" she asked.

"She wants it all. We should warn Ida."

Drew punched in her number. A shrill voice answered, and Drew said, soothingly, "Katie's fine. She's right in front of me. She wants you to be careful. Paula McCall may have killed Phillip." I heard a rant, and he finished the call with, "I'm sure."

"Paula's desperate. She might believe Anita has the

encaustics." Pete pulled out his phone, punched in her number but Anita didn't pick up. The look on his face sent chills up my back.

"Go. Go," Drew said. "I'll get Maverick home for you." He herded us toward the exit.

I grabbed my coat from the floor and chased Pete out the door. He stood next to a rumbling sled, securing the strap at his chin. By the time I pulled on the other helmet, our conversation had digressed into sign language.

I straddled the machine behind Pete and at first didn't know where to put my hands. He caught one and yanked it in front of him. The engine started and my other hand flew across his chest as the snowmobile roared to life. He zipped cross country and didn't let up on the throttle until he stopped in Anita's yard.

I pounded on the door. "Anita. Ricky." No one answered.

"Maybe they're not here," Pete said without much conviction.

"Pete, look." A second-floor window slid up and Ricky's head popped out. His startled eyes glowed like dual full moons. I tore off my helmet so he'd recognize me, and his face lit up but only for an instant before his forehead creased. He crawled onto the incline of the roof.

Pete removed his helmet, dropped it in the snow, and stood under the eave, catching Ricky in his outstretched arms. "You've used that escape hatch before," he said as he settled Ricky on the ground. The knitted cap slid from his head. Pete picked it up and handed it back to Ricky who pulled it down over his ears. The sheepish look was answer enough. "And you're walking. Good job."

"Where's your mom?"

He shivered and the worry returned. "That lady said they had to go to the institute and as long as she went peaceably, I'd be fine." Pete made a call. Ricky retrieved a key from under the railing and slid it into the lock.

"What happened, Ricky?"

He rubbed the raw lines encircling his wrists. "She taped my hands together." He looked a little sneaky. "I did what Carlee taught me and broke the tape." Before he turned the knob, he asked, "Is my mom going to be okay?"

"I hope so, Ricky. She's lucky to have you."

"I'm going to the institute." Pete jumped on the sled, and he thundered down the street.

When the ringing in my ears stopped, Ricky and I went into the house. Tucker whined from his crate in the kitchen. Ricky lifted the latch and the puppy barreled into him. He secured the puppy in a football carry and scratched behind his ears.

"How are you" I asked. Ricky shrugged. "Are you tired or hungry?" He shook his head. "You're doing great. Can I get you something to drink?"

"I want my mom." His blue eyes misted.

I wanted him to think of something else. "Should we sing some carols? Or watch TV? Or read a book?"

Ricky looked at me with a bit of hope. "Carlee gave me a Christmas present. I know it's early, but I think it's books. Could I open it now? I promise I'll wrap it up again."

"Let's do that. I'm sure she wouldn't mind."

Ricky sorted the packages beneath the tree, drawing an elaborately cloth-covered gift from the pile. He pulled a cord and the wrapping fell away, revealing three pop-up books: *Twelve Days of Christmas*, *'Twas the Night Before Christmas*, and *Jingle Bear*. He plopped down on the floor and patted the carpet next to him. Tucker nestled on one side and as I sat, he opened the first page and started reading. He reverently touched the five rings encircling reindeer antlers.

When he turned the page on ten leaping lords, Tucker's ears perked up. Wide-eyed, Ricky froze, then whispered, "They're back."

I grabbed the books and the fabric and the three of us scrambled up the stairs as the back door opened.

"I told you the completed encaustics are still out at the history center." Something thumped to the floor.

After an exasperated sigh, Paula replied as if talking to a child, "That's why we picked up supplies. You'll just have to finish these here. And you'd better get started. You have less than twenty-four hours."

The voices sounded hollow after traveling through the duct work. "Let me check on Ricky."

"That'll be your reward after the first one is done."

We could hear Anita's infuriated voice. "There isn't time to do four."

"Make time."

The doorbell rang. Tucker squirmed but settled when Ricky quietly opened the top drawer of the nightstand and retrieved a package of treats. He broke off tiny pieces and Tucker sat patiently, waiting for more. I loved food motivated canines.

The bell rang again. A few seconds later, Paula hissed, "You know what will happen if you don't get rid of her."

The door made an awful noise. "Hi," Anita said.

"I'm so glad to see you, Anita. Is everything all right? You didn't answer your phone." Ricky gave Tucker another treat. and we strained to hear.

"It's just been a long day. What can I do for you, Mrs. Clemashevski?"

"Drew called to warn me and—" Ida's voice stopped. "Paula. What a pleasure."

"What was the warning?"

"You know, another storm is brewing."

"Come in, Ida."

"I really need to get back."

"I insist."

The door closed. "Over there, next to Anita. You said you taught that idiot husband of mine everything, so now it'll go twice as fast. Plug in … whatever that is."

Ida's measured voice explained every step of her production—warming the hot plate, melting the wax, mixing the colors, building up the medium, even describing the angle of the brush to create different effects. She'd ask an occasional question about the four-part composition and Ricky would stretch to hear his mother's voice. "Paula, if you want these paintings to coordinate, why not let me do the base work and Anita can put the finishing touches on them. That way they'll look more uniform. She's much better than I am. Everyone was gaga over the piece she contributed to the gala."

"You don't know anything." Paula's angry voice climbed.

"I know that Phillip stole artifacts from the *Titanic* exhibit and planned to fence them to support the lifestyle he always wanted. But I also know, he never could have created the movement and color in the auction piece. These are too good to pass off as Phillip's work."

"No one will notice. I just have to get them to the law office and collect my money."

Ida continued as if Paula hadn't spoken. "I helped Robert Bruckner curate his artifacts. All but one are reproductions and they don't have as much value as the boxes they were stored in."

"You're lying." Paula's voice rose.

"Why would I lie? The only authentic piece is a jade and diamond necklace found on the ocean floor at the site of the *Titanic*, and that was returned to the history center. It's worth almost four hundred thousand dollars. Just ask Daniella." Ida paused. "Goodness. Is she in on it too?"

"She and Phillip cut a deal, but now I'll be able to ransom the entire lot. That twit Yvonne will pay for the trinkets if she wants to keep her job. And then I'll figure out how to get Daniella blamed for Phillip's death."

"Yvonne won't have the money until after she's able to inventory the collection."

"Stop talking and hurry up with your picture. What are you doing?" I heard a slap.

Anita let out a cry. "Why did you do that?"

"Let's see if Ricky can help us."

"No," Anita said hurriedly. "He doesn't know how. Let him sleep."

"Then you'd better put your heart into it and get cracking."

Ricky looked ready to bust out of our hideaway. I cupped my hand around his ear to muffle my voice. He nodded and nestled into his chair.

"Ready?" I whispered.

CHAPTER FORTY-SIX

Ricky held his hands behind his back and screamed as loud and blood curdling as I'd ever heard. And he kept on screaming. We hadn't planned on a Tucker duet. Ricky raised one finger in front of his mouth and Tucker stopped yelping. He pointed to the foot of the bed and Tucker took his place on the dog cushion.

Anita cried out, "Ricky!"

Paula yelled, "Shut up." I heard a grunt and footsteps pounded up the stairs. Paula shoved Anita through the doorway. Anita knelt next to Ricky, caressing his cheeks. "I'm here."

"Stop it, or I'll shoot your mama."

Ricky quieted at once. His chin quivered. It looked real to me. Paula tossed the silver duct tape to Anita and said,

"He won't do that again. Tape his mouth."

"Leave him alone. He'll do what he's told." Anita sniffed. Tucker's head came up and he yipped.

"How did you get loose?" Paula aimed the gun at the puppy. I wound up and swung the bag of books at the back of her head. She stumbled and the gun flew from her hand. Although her movements were slowed, she was closer and she reached the weapon first and stood, ready to fire. I stopped short.

"You!" she said through clenched teeth.

Not that again. "I have a name."

She tilted her head, thoughtful, then gave that up and sighted down the firearm. Anita gasped. Ricky rose from the wheelchair, steadied himself, and kicked at the back of Paula's knee. She fell forward and this time I reached the gun first.

Anita hugged Ricky, kissing the top of his head. "Ah, Mom," he said.

Not to miss out on the fun, Tucker pounced on Paula, his four paws splayed across her back, and barked.

"Get it off of me," Paula cried.

Anita nudged Paula's left arm with her foot and said, "Hands." Paula quickly snatched Anita's ankle. Tucker growled and Paula opened her fingers. "Hands," Anita repeated. She taped Paula's hands together and, with Ricky's tips, made sure no one would be getting loose on her watch.

The harmony created by Ricky's light giggle and Anita's warm chuckle was music to my ears.

"What's going on here?"

Ida startled me and I nearly dropped the gun. Sighing, I put my arm around her as she teetered in the doorway, rubbing a bump on her forehead. "We're good. You?"

The doorbell rang. Someone knocked and banged. Then Pete yelled, "Katie. Ricky."

Ida rolled her eyes. "I'll get it."

Anita, Ricky, and Tucker made their way downstairs behind Ida. My hand shook as I stared down the barrel into Paula's leering face. It seemed like time stopped until a warm strong hand covered mine. "It's over."

Pete pried the gun from my scrunched fingers. Officer Christianson and Officer Rodgers lifted Paula and they seemed to move in slow motion. They replaced the tape with handcuffs and recited familiar words of warning as they dragged her from the room. Pete put his hands on my shoulders. My head dropped to his chest ... for just a moment. I looked up into his warm brown eyes. "Why did you come back?"

He searched my face. His eyes twinkled and he said merrily, "I needed my helmet."

Loud noises rose through the vent. Pete and I raced down the stairs into chaos. Ronnie held on as Paula wriggled back and forth, trying to get loose from the handcuffs. Anita sobbed into Ida's shoulder. Tucker yapped and slid back and forth over the gifts, tearing the colorful wrapping paper to shreds, and pawing the sparkling baubles dangling out of reach. Officer Rodgers held Ricky back with one arm and braced the Christmas tree with his other arm, trying to keep it from toppling. Chief West guarded the doorway, interrogating someone hidden behind a pile of presents. My heart thudded in my chest.

Anita looked up and when she understood what was happening, she ignored the uniforms, skirted the obstacles, and embraced the man behind Chief West in a bear hug. "Welcome home, Zac," she said through laughing tears.

CHAPTER FORTY-SEVEN

In her office, Dorene's eyes circled the shrunken pool of heirs. "With her role uncovered, Daniella Jericho sang like a well-dressed bird. She blamed McCall. The robbery was his idea. He talked her into using her expansive list of connections to fence the artifacts from the *Titanic* exhibit. Some people would pay well to own a piece of history. However, McCall didn't entirely trust Daniella.

"He recently visited Miss Grace and urged her to open her trinket vault, for old times' sake, and he stashed the goods for safe keeping. He was notorious for having a poor memory, so he embedded the combination on a few auction items and got rid of the copy linking him to the theft. Jericho failed to win the items at the gala because she didn't have the funds available, so she planned to steal the information she needed to retrieve the goods. Grace had given Jericho the necklace to return to Yvonne after the fundraiser, but when she stole Jane's wreath and pulled it apart looking for the combination, the pendant got mixed up with the costume jewelry and she tossed it too. She sabotaged the geocache to deter visitors from the history center so she could search without being disturbed.

"She'll answer for her crimes, but she didn't kill McCall," said Dorene. "Wicheck apologized for impersonating Jordan and is on his way home. He said he just wanted to meet the marvelous Grace Loehr. And Paula will spend the rest of her life behind bars Which brings us here." Carlee squeezed Ana's hand. I sat on one side of Ida and Dad sat on the other. Yvonne shuffled the papers on the table in front of her and then dangled the jade necklace from her clenched fist, shaking her head, unable to contain her excitement. Rachel stood guard behind Zac and Ricky, who whispered back and forth. Anita drummed her fingertips on the top of a wooden crate, lost, looking out the window.

"If I hadn't let my ego get in the way and swapped out Phillip's ill-conceived encaustic, he might not have died." A tear trickled down her cheek. Zac leaned over, took her hand, and kissed her fingers.

"Paula wanted it all and would have killed him anyway," said Ida. "I think she's wanted to test her poisonous plants since high school."

"Any words before we begin?" said Dorene.

The girls told us how wonderful Miss Grace had been after they were torn from the only home they'd ever known. Dad and I said she'd be missed. Ida told of her tumultuous and extended friendship with Miss Grace. Yvonne expounded on Miss Grace's support of the history center. Anita echoed that sentiment with her endless gifts to the

arts. Ricky smiled and waved, and we waved in return. Zac
stood, twisting his hands, and said, "I've been deployed for
the last thirteen months, and I never met Grace Loehr, but
I wish I had."

Dorene extracted a deed for Carlee and Ana to co-sign
with their parents. "And you get to keep the piano."

She produced four more checks. Yvonne grinned and
took the pledge dollars and the money she secured for the
history center by cataloging the remaining objects for the
Titanic exhibit. Ida had stretched the truth when she told
Paula they were worthless.

Anita blinked rapidly at the paper in her hand,
staunching her tears.

"Would you please show us the encaustics?" Dorene
said gently. Anita hesitated. "Grace wanted the art for the
hospital. Ida says yours are the best."

Zac and Rachel pried the top off the box and dug
into the crate for handholds. They lifted the deep blue and
vibrant gold swirling compositions. When arranged in a
square, raised ridges met and formed a heart.

"These are amazing, truly," said Dorene. "They would
make a nice addition to any collection, but the hospital will
provide a showcase for your brilliant work." Anita's jaw
dropped when Dorene handed over the check.

Then they pulled out the fabulous piece Anita had
completed for Ida. Ida's fingers hovered over her mementos
and her green eyes glistened. Anita beamed.

I think Ida would rather have had her friend and she
wore the incredible loss on her face. She didn't need music,
books, or archaic recording equipment, and she never
looked at her check. She seemed ambivalent about the
inheritance but more than thrilled with her encaustic.

When she finally glanced at the paper in her hand, she let out a hearty whoop and leaned over to show Dad. He chuckled with her.

"Party at the Clemashevski house. Seven o'clock, sharp. Be there!"

CHAPTER FORTY-EIGHT

"We haven't really celebrated the holidays the last two years, Katie." Dad watched me carefully. "What do you want for Christmas?"

Christmas Eve was a day away. CJ had checked out Maverick and my dog sat up tall, bandages and all, with his tongue hanging out. His tail stopped sweeping the floor and he cocked his head as if he too awaited my answer.

I glanced at Ida, fretting about the specific shade of green found in her linen tablecloth. Jane patiently stood beneath the mistletoe waiting for a break as Pete and Drew argued a sports call, shaking chicken wings at each other. Carlee and Galen performed magic tricks, and Ricky pleaded for them to reveal the secrets. Tucker snoozed in Anita's lap while she and Zac reveled in watching Ricky.

Rachel cornered Susie next to Ida's baked brie, regaling her with stories of her encounters with Daniella and Paula. Renegade behaved perfectly, of course, sitting next to CJ but leaning into Chief West's deep scratches.

"I have it all right here."

Dad beamed and hugged me. Then he yawned. "I need my beauty sleep." Rachel talked him into playing Santa for the children in the hospital. She also introduced him to three local day care centers, eager to provide their little ones with an opportunity to expend some of the excess energy brought on by bombardment of advertisements for toys in every shape and size and heightened by a December sugar boost. Dad would have his work cut out for him.

"Thank you, Katie." Ida squeezed an oomph from me. "You know, Christmas might be a good day to open the envelope from England." She squeezed again and wished me a good night. Her exit precipitated an avalanche of farewells.

When only Jane and the chief remained, Jane said, "Chief, do you think Grace knew?"

Chief West looked thoughtful. "We'll never know for sure, but she knew she needed to talk to Paula. Her time here was limited and she figured she had nothing to lose. Dr. Erickson feels she may have set herself up as bait, not realizing how far Paula would go. I wish I could have met her."

"Would you like to stay for a cup of hot cocoa and the best sugar cookies this side of anywhere?" I asked.

"I'd like that. The reports can wait until morning. I'm happy everything turned out for Mrs. Clem-a-shev-ski."

Jane laughed. "It's easier if you just call her Ida. Her surname's a mouthful."

"And you can call me Amanda."

"Whatever brought you to Columbia? Ida calls it ..."

"The cultural Siberia of Midwest Minnesota." Amanda finished my sentence. "And that is a very long story. How about you? What brought you two here?"

Jane and I looked at each other and laughed.

Jane said, "I'll get the wine."

WHITE CHOCOLATE MARTINI

1 oz vanilla vodka
½ oz white crème de cocoa
1 oz white chocolate liqueur
½ oz cream (half-and-half or whole)
Mix in a shaker. Garnish with a Luxardo or Fabri (dark) cherry.

Thank you for taking the time to read *Santa, Snowflakes, & Strychnine*. If you enjoyed it please tell your friends, and I would be so grateful if you would consider posting a review. Word of mouth is an author's best friend, and very much appreciated.

Thank you,

Mary Seifert

* * *

What's next for Katie and Maverick?

Minnesota winters are magical: sipping hot chocolate, cuddled in fluffy blankets, and warmed by crackling fireplaces, pristine snow blanketing the old world, seeming to swaddle life—until it isn't. Winters are also brutal: freezing rain, strong winds, and bitter temperatures. Katie is horrified when she learns of the plight of the homeless in Columbia who brave the elements, and she's further shocked when she finds one of them dead, having fallen through the ice on Lake Monongalia. When it's determined to be murder, Katie is stunned to learn that the number one suspect is Dr. Pete Erickson. She learns she can't completely trust the system, and she and Maverick become caught up in finding the real killer.

Watch for Book 5 in this acclaimed series, coming soon!

* * *

About the Author

Mary Seifert has always loved a good mystery, a brain teaser, or a challenge. As a former mathematics teacher, she ties numbers and logic to the mayhem game. The Katie & Maverick Mysteries allow her to share those stories, as well as puzzles, riddles, and a few taste-tested recipes.

When she's not writing, she's making wonderful memories with family, exchanging thoughtful ideas with friends, walking her dog whose only speed is faster, dabbling in needlecrafts, and pretending to cook. You can also find her sneaking bites of chocolate and sipping wine, both of which sometimes occur while writing. Mary is a member of Mysteries Writers of America, Sisters in Crime, American Cryptogram Association, Dog Writers of America, and PEO.

Get a collection of free recipes from Mary—visit her website to find out how!

Visit Mary's website: MarySeifertAuthor.com/
Facebook: facebook.com/MarySeifertAuthor
Twitter: twitter.com/mary_seifert
Instagram: instagram.com/maryseifert/
Follow Mary on BookBub and Goodreads too!

Made in the USA
Monee, IL
29 September 2022

14898553R00184